An Embarrassment of Corpses

Alan Beechey

ST. MARTIN'S PRESS
New York

A THOMAS DUNNE BOOK.
An imprint of St. Martin's Press.

AN EMBARRASSMENT OF CORPSES. Copyright © 1997 by Alan Beechey.
All rights reserved. Printed in the United States of America. No part
of this book may be used or reproduced in any manner whatsoever
without written permission except in the case of brief quotations em-
bodied in critical articles or reviews. For information, address St. Martin's Press, 175 Fifth Avenue, New York, N.Y. 10010.

Design by mierre

Library of Congress Cataloging-in-Publication Data

Beechey, Alan.
    An embarrassment of corpses / Alan Beechey—1st ed.
        p.   cm.
    "A Thomas Dunne book."
    ISBN 0-312-16936-1
    I. Title.
PR6052.E3155E63   1997
823'.914—dc21   97-17819
                                                 CIP

First Edition: December 1997

10 9 8 7 6 5 4 3 2 1

to Eileen Wolkstein

One

If Sir Hargreaves Random had been a character in one of his own adventure yarns—aptly named, for they were inclined to be woolly, drawn out, and clumsily wound up—he would surely have written a more glorious death for himself.

Not that death ever struck down the plucky heroes of Sir Harry's stirring stories for boys. And although the hero's best friend was occasionally required to hurl himself into the path of a flying *kris*, a rearing cobra, or a chillingly accurate Luger, Sandy (or Corky or Dusty) always managed to recover from his flesh wound in time for the next term's adventure.

But when an older and therefore more dispensable character was forced to sell himself dear for King or Queen and Country, Sir Harry made sure he was dispatched worthily: the Prof picked off by a Boer sniper as he tried to escape from the besieged fort, or the Doc stabbed with a treacherous alpenstock in the Kloster Pass, wielded by that tall, blond guide (who'd claimed to be Swiss). Sir Harry would never have written an embarrassing end like his own. A Random character simply wouldn't be seen dead in a Trafalgar Square fountain on an August bank holiday morning, floating face-down with a look of mild irritation on his face, mortified in all senses of the word.

It's also unlikely that the young man who had just run unsteadily into the deserted square could have featured in one of Sir Harry's books. His fine, hay-colored hair was too straight and floppy for a Harry Random hero, his chin was insufficiently square and firm, his front teeth were too prominent, and his blue eyes were rather docile behind wire-framed spectacles. The tuxedo he was wearing had clearly seen better days, most of them upon a former owner.

The young man trotted across the empty street to Nelson's Column, and with a nervous glance around, clambered unsteadily onto one of the plinths that supported Landseer's sentinel lions.

"Snark!" he shouted halfheartedly. He paused, hoping to hear an answering cry over the gush of the fountains and the flapping wings of petulant pigeons. When none came, he stepped gingerly onto the lion's paw and dragged himself onto the beast's neck.

"Snark!" he called again, holding onto the statue's mane as he scanned the square for any other sign of human life. His voice echoed from the porticoed front of the National Gallery, but there was no other reply.

Far above him, the rising sun was gilding the pigeon guano on Nelson's hat. The young man sank down on the lion and studied his cheap wristwatch: 6:13 A.M. "Nearly quarter past six," he translated. Feeling no time check was complete without an adverb, he detested the digital watch

2

face. Oliver Swithin believed the purpose of a timepiece was not to tell you what time it is, but what time it isn't.

From the other end of Whitehall, Big Ben tetchily confirmed the inaccuracy of its Japanese cousin. Swithin listened to the chimes, clear on the morning air, and yawned loudly into cupped hands, recoiling slightly from his recycled breath. He closed his eyes and gently massaged them with his fingertips. As he opened them again, he found himself staring at something black and shapeless, floating in one of the nearby fountains like an inflated rubbish bag. He frowned, aware that a terrible suspicion was penetrating his claret-fueled headache. Then he slithered awkwardly to the ground, and ran across the square.

Sir Harry Random's corpse was bobbing gently on the choppy water, the arms floating on either side. As Swithin stared, an eddy dribbled it into a jet of water spouted by one of the fountain's bronze Tritons, and it swirled away again like an adolescent losing his nerve at his first dance.

"Oh my fur and whiskers!" Swithin muttered. "It's a Boojum!"

There was nobody in sight. With a haste that would have pleased his tailor—if such a person had ever existed—he wrenched off his jacket and suede shoes and plunged into the cold water, splashing across to the corpse. He tried to turn it over, but Sir Harry's waterlogged dinner jacket kept slipping from his grasp. So Swithin grabbed the body by one outstretched hand and hauled it across to the edge of the basin, as if he were towing a boat.

Police Constable Urchin longed for the day when he could say he'd seen everything, but so far he'd seen nothing. In his first week on the beat, he'd dutifully spent each night patrolling the streets around the British Museum, but to his disappointment, he and P.C. Grunwick, his more experienced companion, had made no arrests. Grunwick's conversation was also taking its toll, as it consisted almost entirely of pointing out some hapless passerby and whispering: "I bet chummy there's got something to 'ide. I can spot a villain a mile off." When Urchin asked how, Grunwick would merely tap the side of his extensive nose and say "Ah, you have to be in the force as long as I 'ave, son," which only deepened the new policeman's discouragement.

But now Urchin, still in uniform as he made his way home through Trafalgar Square, was finally witnessing an incident. Two men were taking an early morning dip in one of the fountains. In black tie. The policeman locked his hands behind his back and strolled over.

"Bit early to see in the New Year, isn't it, sir?" he asked insouciantly, as he watched the younger man attempt to carry the older one over the fountain's rim. "Or is this perhaps some early morning baptismal rite?" Good, he thought, the right hint of erudition. More of the coiled steel than "Having a spot of trouble, sir?" and a considerable improvement on "You're bleedin' nicked, mate," which he suspected would be Grunwick's choice of phrase.

The young man, up to his hips in the cool water, stared at the policeman for a moment through glasses that were beginning to mist up. His lank, fair hair was dripping.

"So there is one around when I need one," he said calmly. "Here, take an elbow." Momentarily lost for a witty response, Urchin found himself obeying mutely, and between them, they maneuvered the body out of the fountain and onto the ground, where it lay in a spreading puddle of water. Swithin crouched quickly beside Sir Harry, grabbing him under the neck and sealing his lips over the older man's mouth.

"Here, I say, none of that, really, I don't care how drunk

4

you are," protested Urchin, with an anxious glance to see if they were being watched.

"I'm giving him artificial respiration, you donkey," Swithin snapped between gulps of air. "If you want to help, check his pulse."

Urchin felt for a pulse at Sir Harry's wrist. There was none. He started to reach into the buttoned-up jacket to feel for a heartbeat, but recoiled as his hand scraped across something sharp. Several needles with trailing threads were stuck in the wet lapel.

"Shall I do CPR?" he asked, sucking at his grazed skin. Swithin broke away abruptly.

"No," he replied. He wiped his mouth on his wet shirt-sleeve.

"Well, how long has he been in the water? We shouldn't give up this easily."

"It isn't the water," said Swithin. He took his hand from behind Sir Harry's neck and showed it to the policeman. It was smeared with thick blood. Pink rivulets began to run down his soaking wrists.

They sat the body up and stared at the shattered skull.

"I'd better call for an ambulance," Urchin said eventually. He turned reverently away and began speaking in a low voice into his radio.

"They'll be here in a minute," he said, looking back at the corpse, which was once again flat on its back. Swithin sat damply on the ground beside it, gathering his knees in the crook of each elbow. He had draped his jacket around his shoulders.

"Aren't you going to take a statement?" he asked quietly.

"The duty officer will do that, Mr. . . . . ?"

"Swithin. Oliver Swithin. And the recently departed is Sir Hargreaves Random. Harry to his friends."

5

"Is that *the* Harry Random? The writer of those old boys' stories? I didn't know he was still alive."

Swithin nodded sadly but inaccurately. "He was a good friend of mine. I've been with him for most of the night."

Urchin remembered from his recent training that in the presence of sudden grief, he should make a cup of tea for the bereaved. He scanned the terrain—plenty of water, but no kettle. "Then I offer my condolences, sir," he concluded lamely.

Swithin looked up at him. "I really think you should take a statement, you know."

"And why's that, if I may ask?"

"Because Sir Harry was murdered."

Urchin started and closed his eyes, as if flinching from a momentary attack of vertigo. A murder! Alas, poor Grunwick, where be your jibes now?

"You saw it happen?" he asked eventually, moving his tongue across suddenly dry lips.

"No. I found him floating here, just a moment before you came on the scene."

"Then how can you be sure it was murder?" Urchin asked, his mind racing. "Because of that bash on the head? Isn't it more likely that he stumbled into the fountain and hit his head on the bottom?"

Swithin hauled himself to his feet and located his shoes, which he began to tug over his soggy socks. "It takes a lot of force to do that much damage to a skull. If Harry had fallen accidentally into the fountain, the water would have cushioned him."

"Perhaps he fell into the fountain from a height?" said Urchin, gazing first at Nelson's Column and then more realistically at the main water jet, which sprouted from the middle of the fountain like a giant chalice. Swithin smiled.

"Harry Random was born on the twenty-ninth of February, so he claims he's only nineteen, but he's actually in his late seventies. He hasn't scaled a national monument since VE-night." He looked tenderly at the body sprawled by his feet. Urchin, notebook in hand, noticed the emotion.

"I *will* take that statement, Mr. Swithin," he said, with sudden decisiveness. Grunwick! thou shouldst be living at this hour. "When did you last see Sir Harry alive? In your own words, please."

"A couple of hours ago."

"I assume from your dress that this is a late night rather than an early morning."

"Yes. We'd been taking part in our club's annual Snark Hunt."

"Snark Hunt?"

"We play characters from Lewis Carroll's *The Hunting of the Snark*. You've heard of it?"

"Of course I've heard of it," snapped Urchin in an offended tone. "I went to Christ Church, Lewis Carroll's college, as a matter of fact, although I suppose *you* think it beneath the dignity of an Oxford man to be a police officer." He chose to ignore the fleeting slap from his superego for implying that he had, in fact, graduated.

"Not at all," Swithin answered quickly, detecting the distant metaphorical click of a can of worms meeting a tin opener. "I have the highest respect for the police force. My uncle, as it happens, is—"

"Well, never mind about that," Urchin interrupted, with a petulant wave of his notebook. O mute, inglorious Grunwick. "What's all this about Snark Hunts?"

"Sir Harry and I both belonged to a club for authors of children's books," Swithin said. "The Sanders, on Pall Mall." He pointed west. "It's just a few hundred yards that way."

"Why's it called that?"

"The club operates under the name of Sanders. Not a

7

Carrollian reference. We have to balance the enthusiasms of the members—the Pooh contingent can get quite militant."

"So you're a writer yourself?" Urchin asked, after taking down Swithin's exact words in longhand.

"I've written several books for young children."

Urchin looked up with interest. "What are they, perhaps I've heard of them? I've got two little nieces and I often read to them." He blushed. "They call me Uncle Plod," he added shyly.

Swithin was equally abashed. "Well, I write a series of books about a family of field mice who live on a British Rail train. They're called—"

"The Railway Mice!" exclaimed Urchin, with a slight hop from one foot to another. "I've read them! But I thought those books were written by O. C. Blithely?"

"A pen name, invented to spare me this kind of embarrassment."

"Oh, but you shouldn't be embarrassed," said Urchin sincerely. "My nieces love your books, especially since you introduced Finsbury the Ferret. But it's funny, I always pictured you as a woman. Oh well, back to business." The smile rapidly faded from his face, and he officiously licked the end of his pencil, only to discover with a grimace that it was a pen. "Go on about this Snark Hunt."

"Every year, the club organizes a Snark Hunt, in which ten members impersonate the fabled hunting party. You know, the Bellman, the Boots, the Beaver, the Banker, the Billiard-marker, etc. Sir Harry was the Bonnet-maker. Hence the needles and thread in his lapel—we all had a few props to identify ourselves. Well, all the other members who turn up become Snarks, and disperse themselves around St. James. We give them a few minutes' head start and then come after them. When they're all caught, we can 'softly and suddenly vanish away'—usually back to the club bar. That's where most of the Snarks hide in the first place, anyway."

"And what time did the Snark Hunt start last night?" asked Urchin.

"Midnight."

"So you and Sir Harry had both been wandering the streets for six hours?"

"Good heavens, no, Constable! Harry and I very quickly gave up and went back to the club. We've been playing poker most of the night. I'm afraid I dozed off about four o'clock, and when I awoke a little while ago, Harry was gone. The club porter told me he'd left ten minutes earlier, heading towards Trafalgar Square. I followed, and that's how I found him."

Oliver Swithin shuddered, as much from the memory as from his clammy clothes. Sunlight was trickling down the column above them like peach-colored paint, but the square was still cool in the shade.

"Okay, how about this?" said Urchin suddenly. "Sir Harry gets to the square and wonders if any of your Snarks could still be hiding. There are plenty of statues and bollards and parapets to conceal themselves behind. He notices that the water in the fountains is off and the basin is empty, and so he takes a look inside. In fact, he climbs in and looks around." The policeman started walking around the perimeter of the fountain until he drew level with a statue on an island a few feet from the rim. It was a half-man, half-fish figure holding sea creatures in his hand. Water gushed loudly from their mouths into the basin.

"He gets in front of this statue," he shouted, "just at the very second the water gets turned on. The force of it, flowing out of this dolphin's mouth, knocks him off his feet and onto the bottom of the fountain, stoving in the back of his skull. By the time you get here, ten minutes later, the fountain's filled up."

The harsh notes of an ambulance siren, like a crudely synthesized cuckoo, could now be heard above the steady rush of the water. Swithin, crouching over Sir Harry's body, looked up.

"Rather a convenient coincidence," he remarked.

"All right," said Urchin huffily, "the CID will need to check to see what time the water came on, but as a theory, it's no worse than yours, which posits the existence of a murderer for whom we have no evidence. The principle of Occam's Razor would say mine's the more likely explanation."

"Really," replied Swithin casually. "Then how do you explain this?" He unbuttoned Sir Harry's sodden jacket and flung it open. On the starched front of the dead man's dress shirt were a series of blue lines—a straight line drawn vertically, crossed twice by two semicircles, like a double-ended trident. "That wasn't there the last time I saw him."

The ambulance swerved into sight, slowed to mount the curb, and coasted toward them, scattering the slow-witted pigeons. A moment later, a crowded police car also made the turn from the Strand.

"You realize what you're saying," said Urchin hastily, as several men in belted raincoats clambered out of the car. "You're saying that a murder has been committed and you are the only person known to have been in the vicinity at the time of death."

"Well, yes, I suppose so."

Urchin tucked his notebook into the breast pocket of his tunic and placed his hand grandly on Swithin's shoulder.

"In that case, Oliver Swithin, alias O. C. Blithely, I arrest you for the murder of Sir Hargreaves Random. By the way," he added quickly, as the ambulance team descended on the body, "can I have your autograph? It's for my nieces, you understand."

Unlike Police Constable Urchin, Detective Superintendent Timothy Mallard *had* seen it all during his thirty-five years with the Metropolitan police force, and the deep creases etched into his forehead showed how much of it had challenged his dogged belief in the basic decency of the human animal. Otherwise, he appeared younger than his age, which was closer to sixty than fifty. His milk-white hair, which showed no signs of thinning, always looked a fortnight overdue for the attentions of a barber, and his handsome features were decorated with plain spectacles and a slightly rakish moustache. Tim Mallard's slim frame, military posture, and remarkable vigor continued to win him decent roles with his local amateur dramatic company, the Theydon Bois Thespians, and also discouraged his superiors at New Scotland Yard from starting conversations that might involve the word "retirement." (Through a clerical oversight, which had muddled Mallard's personnel file with the criminal record of a video bootlegger from Streatham, the system had so far failed to pension him off.)

The superintendent was currently rehearsing the role of Banquo for the Theydon Bois Thespians' autumn production of *Macbeth,* and, although resentful that this wouldn't involve any swordplay, he was comforted that the character's early death would allow him to play a "blood-baltered" ghost in the third act and a ghastly apparition in the fourth and still get to the local pub before closing time, if he didn't wait around for the curtain call. (The audience rarely did.) He was pleased to get such a large part; it was a standing joke in the company, which was exclusively Shakespearian, to give Mallard roles that slyly reflected his profession, such as the Constable of France, Snout, Pinch, or Paroles. (Alas, not

11

Dogberry yet.) For the current production of *Macbeth*, he had narrowly avoided being cast as the Bleeding Sergeant.

On this scorching bank holiday Monday morning, Mallard would much rather have been sitting under a tree learning his lines, in his North London garden, than standing in a cell in Bow Street police station staring at the alleged murderer of Sir Hargreaves Random.

Oliver Swithin, feeling Mallard's eyes upon him, stirred and turned over awkwardly on the narrow bed. The single blanket fell onto the floor.

"Hello," he said huskily to the frowning policeman. He ran his tongue over his lips and scowled. Mallard closed the door behind him and leaned against it.

"Ollie, I wish you'd accept it that alcohol is not one of the major food groups," he said. Oliver lifted his head from the grubby pillow.

"I didn't know this was your manor, Uncle Tim," he said, registering pain as he sat up.

"It isn't. Your friend Geoffrey Angelwine called me in a panic and said you'd been arrested. I thought I'd better come and bail you out. I was expecting a 'drunk and disorderly,' but you certainly don't do things by halves. Murder of a Knight of the Realm—I wonder if that means you can be hanged by a silken rope. Or is that reserved for peers? Perhaps they'll attach a tassel, anyway."

Oliver slowly dropped his feet to the cold floor of the cell. Without replying to his uncle, he reached for the trousers of his dinner suit, dragged them over his damp underpants, and stood up, clutching the waistband. (His braces and shoelaces had been removed to prevent any self-administered justice before the Crown could make its case.) Still half a head shorter than Mallard, Oliver yawned and pushed the fair fringe off his forehead with his free hand.

"God, you look awful," said Mallard distastefully. "And

would you mind staying downwind of me until you've brushed your teeth. Preferably your tongue and tonsils, too. I brought you a toothbrush. And a sweater. And you'll need these."

He reached into his breast pocket and handed Oliver his glasses.

"What are the charges?" the young man asked.

"No charges. Not a stain on your character, which is more than can be said for that suit."

"Not even resisting arrest?" Oliver persisted.

Mallard smiled for the first time. "Oh, they were considering it. But not after the statement you gave that young constable—what was his name?—Urchin. How did it go? Something like 'It's a fair cop, guv. Gorblimey, I reckon you busies 'as got me bang to rights, so 'elp me, I should cocoa.' "

Oliver grinned as he pulled his laceless suede shoes onto his bare feet. He slipped the damp socks into a jacket pocket.

"Urchin took it all down," Mallard continued, knowing better than to upbraid his nephew for wearing Hush Puppies with a tuxedo. "And I can just see the magistrate's face. So the locals have decided not to press charges, providing you turn up at the inquest and say all the right things."

"Thanks, Uncle."

"Oh, don't thank me. Believe me, I had little enough to do with it. I'm as welcome here as a fart in a spacesuit. The last thing any local shop wants on a bank holiday Monday is a visit from the Yard."

"Not even when Sir Harry Random has been murdered?" asked Oliver quietly, without looking up.

"Now don't start that again," snapped Mallard. "I've heard about that story you were trying to spin earlier, and I put it down in equal parts to the alcohol and your diseased imagination."

" 'Judgment of beauty can err, what with the wine and

the dark,' " Oliver quoted. "Ovid," he added smugly. Mallard stared at him.

"Maybe they should keep you here, after all," he murmured.

Still clutching his trousers, Oliver followed his uncle out of the cell, and after a brief visit to the washroom, joined him in the main public room of the police station. Mallard was deep in conversation with one of the detectives who had responded to Urchin's call earlier that morning, and who, despite the warm weather, was still wearing his belted Burberry.

"Mr. Swithin, sir?" A stout, shirtsleeved policeman behind a counter was waving a mustard-colored envelope at Oliver. "Your belongings, sir, if you'd just sign for them." He smiled in a macabre manner, showing too many teeth, and Oliver found himself thinking inexplicably of the lyrics to "Mack the Knife." (Although for some reason, he was hearing them to the tune of "Clementine.")

The policeman tipped the contents of the envelope onto the counter and checked them off on a clipboard. "Handkerchief, still rather soggy, I'm afraid, sir." He smiled again, and Oliver shivered. In the local pubs, P.C. Axelrod was very successful at selling raffle tickets for police benefits. "One pair of braces, pink; one pair of shoelaces; one digital watch; one bunch of keys on an ornamental keyring."

He lifted it to his face, with a frown of feigned concentration. "Ah, I see. The young lady's bathing costume sort of trickles off when you hold it up the right way."

"It was a present," said Oliver weakly.

"What'll they think of next, that's what I say, sir," said Axelrod with another smile and returned to the list. Oliver took off his jacket and pulled on the sweater that Mallard had brought him.

"One diary—rather spoilt by its illegal dip in a municipal waterway; one similarly sodden membership card to what seems to be the Sanders Club; one jelly baby; one small plastic telescope; one red plastic clown's nose; one tuning fork; and several slips of paper in different colors that appear to me to be counterfeit banknotes."

"Monopoly money, actually."

"Some of us just live for pleasure, don't we, sir?" Axelrod swiveled his clipboard. "Right, sign here."

Stuffing his belongings into the pockets of his dinner jacket, Oliver rejoined his uncle. They stepped out into the blazing midday sunshine of Bow Street and walked toward Covent Garden.

A nation's character is the child of its climate, which probably explains why conversing in the open air has never been an English habit. Unlike the squares and marketplaces of Europe, public spaces in England are designed as places to go past rather than places to go to. When reluctant Londoners got their first Italianate piazza, in the seventeenth century, the empty space made them so nervous that they quickly filled it with fruit and vegetable stands and called it Covent Garden, convincing generations of tourists that the English speak better than they spell. Now the original Inigo Jones houses that first framed the piazza have all gone, and its main attraction is the renovated Victorian market building that was eventually built in the middle. Covent Garden's architectural history always reminded Oliver of the ingenious American company that sells blobs of batter as the holes from long-departed doughnuts.

A handful of tourists, with Nikes and Nikons, were straggled in a loose, sweating crescent around a young man who was trying to juggle meat cleavers under the portico of Jones's barnlike church.

"Are you hungry?" Mallard asked Oliver as they stopped to watch.

"Not really." A cleaver clanged onto the cobbled pavement and skidded into the sunlight. The tourists moved away, to seek the shade of the shops and stalls in the old market building.

"Good," Mallard continued unpleasantly. "Because I have strict instructions from your Aunt Phoebe to bring you back for Sunday lunch, and I don't want to. You're her favorite nephew, although I can't think why. Personally, it's part of my daily routine to thank the Almighty that I'm only related to you by marriage. By the way, Oliver, I'm sorry about Harry."

Oliver smiled, and not just because he had made eye contact with a big-haired American teenager, who had blushed and cracked her chewing gum. He knew he was the favorite nephew of both members of the Mallard partnership.

"Thank you. And you'll get to the bottom of his murder, I know."

Mallard sighed. "Before I got you released," he said quietly, "I had a long talk with the CID officer who's in charge of the case. Harry's death is easily explained as an accident, there's nothing to indicate foul play, and you said yourself that you didn't see anyone around."

"But, Uncle . . ."

"But since you seem determined to but me buts and uncle me uncles, I'll give you five minutes of my professional ear."

"Fine," said Oliver irritably. "Let's revisit the scene of the crime."

A few minutes later, the two men were scooting through the ring of slow-moving sightseeing buses that by this time were besieging Trafalgar Square. Several hundred tourists had already slipped through these defenses and were commemorating England's greatest dead naval hero by feeding the pigeons that besmirched his statue. There was no trace left of the more recent death.

Oliver and Mallard stood beside the fountain where Sir Harry had been found, watching water gush from the mouth of a dolphin, held tightly by an ornamental merman. The water level was high, and occasional wavelets spilled over the stone rim. Spray from the huge central element of the fountain blew in their faces. For Mallard, the spritzing was a welcome relief from the midday heat; Oliver, still wearing damp clothes next to his skin, hardly noticed.

"There's a Sherlock Holmes story in which Holmes sarcastically asks Inspector Lestrade if he's dragged the Trafalgar Square fountains in his hunt for a missing woman," Oliver mused.

"Are you keeping me from lunch just to tell me that?"

"No, but I'll tell you something I didn't tell Urchin. Harry had some kind of meeting arranged for this morning. We were going to have a late night anyway, so he decided to stay up."

"When, where, and with whom was this alleged meeting?"

"You're not in court now, Uncle. In order, obviously some time early this morning, I don't know, and I don't know. Harry was deliberately mysterious, the silly old buffer."

"Any corroborative evidence?"

"He was waving around a piece of paper—a letter or note. I didn't see what was written on it. I don't think he showed it to anyone else at the Sanders Club, but the porter may have seen him with it just before he went out."

"The police didn't find any letter on him," Mallard commented tersely. "Just the usual personal items, some needles and thread, a thimble, and the remains of a small bar of carbolic soap."

"He had the needles and thread because of his role in the Snark hunt. He was the Bonnet-maker."

"Which explains the thimble, too?"

"No, several of us had thimbles. It's from the verse in the poem:

> *They sought it with thimbles, they sought it with care:*
> *They pursued it with forks and hope;*
> *They threatened its life with a railway share;*
> *They charmed it with smiles and soap.*

"I'm amazed you can remember all that," said Mallard, as Oliver began to fumble through the pockets of his clammy dinner jacket, "but totally forget your aunt's birthday year after year."

Oliver produced two items: a bluish metal tuning fork and a tiny red plastic telescope. "I had a fork, just as in the verse. And my character carried a telescope in one of Holiday's original illustrations for the poem."

"Uh-huh. So far, we only have a mysterious note that can't be found. You'll have to do better than that if you want to make a case for murder."

Oliver thrust the objects back into his pocket. "Harry left the Sanders Club at about ten to six, or so the porter told me," he continued. "I'd fallen asleep in the card room at about four, and woke up at six. I went out to look for him."

"Why?" Mallard asked.

"I was concerned. The streets are very quiet at that time, especially on a bank holiday. Who knows what could have happened to him? And I was curious about where he was going. The porter said he'd headed in this direction along Pall Mall. I came into the square at a quarter past six—I heard Big Ben strike. And I saw him floating here."

"Did you see anyone else?"

18

"No. But there are plenty of places where the killer could have hidden, even if he was still around."

"So Harry was seen alive by your porter at ten to six," speculated Mallard, "and it would take him at least five minutes to get here. He was dead before you found him at quarter past. Then the accident—or assault—must have happened between 5:55 and 6:10 A.M. What time do these fountains come on, I wonder?"

"Why do you ask?"

"Because I think Harry got here, saw the empty fountain, and climbed into it for no other reason than he'd never been in an empty fountain before. And I think he either slipped and hit his head on the edge or the floor—and the evidence of that would have been washed away—or the fountain came on while he was still frisking around. Look at the force of those jets. He could have been knocked right off his feet."

Mallard indicated the spouting sea creature, but Oliver was shaking his head.

"That's what P.C. Urchin said, but it's not like Harry to behave that way. He was terrified of new experiences. He was a craven poltroon when it came to anything like travel, for example, because he hated to speak any language other than English. And he once told me he took cabs everywhere in London because he had no idea how to pay for a ticket on a bus and didn't want to look a fool the first time he tried. Harry got all his background information for his stories from guidebooks and articles. He liked a quiet life, and the last thing he'd do is clamber into a fountain for the hell of it, especially at his age."

"Well he didn't *fall* in from this side," said Mallard. He rested his palms on the waist-high parapet. "He must have been standing up on the rim or actually in the fountain to end up where he did."

"That's one reason why I say he was hit first and then dumped into the water. And then there are the marks on his shirt. Did you see them?"

It was Mallard's turn to shake his head.

"On the starched front of his dress shirt," Oliver continued, "there was an odd sign, a series of crossing lines. It wasn't there when I was playing poker with him in the club."

He felt in his pockets again, but realizing he had no pen, he dipped his hand in the water, bent down, and traced the symbol on the pavement. A straight vertical line, crossed near each end by a semicircle, like a squat, two-ended trident.

"Seen that before?" Oliver asked. His uncle shrugged.

"All right, that's an oddity. But he could have done it himself after you'd fallen asleep."

"Why?"

Mallard didn't answer, but turned and surveyed the square, with its monuments and bollards arrayed like condiments on a banquet table. A troop of pigeons strutted past, changing direction together, like a game of Simon Says played by clairvoyants. Eventually, Mallard spoke again.

"Sorry, Oliver, it won't do. There are several unanswered questions here, certainly, but not enough for the Murder Squad to push their noses in where they're neither wanted nor invited."

"Occam's Razor."

"What about it?"

"Urchin brought it up just before he arrested me."

"Really? What is the Met coming to? Most of my lads would assume that Occam's Razor is exhibit A in a G.B.H. trial." Mallard grinned. "Well, if I understand that principle correctly, it means we first try to solve a problem using the evidence we already have. Now I'm going to check what time these fountains came on this morning, but I've got a

20

feeling it was six o'clock on the dot, exactly the time that Sir Harry was here, unseen by you. A plain, unfortunate coincidence, which doesn't involve notes that nobody can find and invisible murderers given to scribbling cabalistic symbols on their victims."

"So how does that account for the symbol?"

Mallard glanced down at the diagram Oliver had drawn, but the water had evaporated. He scraped the crude outline again with his toe cap.

"Try this," he said. "Harry decides at six o'clock in the morning to get a breath of fresh air and have a few more minutes of Snark hunting. With Carroll's verse rolling around in his befuddled mind, he elects to prepare himself a little better for the fray. He remembers that the hunters pursued their quarry with 'forks and hope.' So on his way out of the club, he picks up a pen and idly draws a fork on his shirt front. A toasting fork, or a pitchfork—something with three tines. But he catches sight of himself in a mirror and realizes that he's made a mistake. He drew the fork looking down at his chest, so it's upside down to anyone who sees him, like a nurse's watch. To correct the mistake, he draws a couple of tines at the other end. And there you are."

"A refrigerator light," Oliver muttered.

"What?"

"How would Occam's Razor account for a refrigerator light? I mean, you see the light on, and you close the door. Then you open it again, and the light's still on. So isn't the simplest explanation that the light is on all the time, even when the door is closed?"

"I know someone whose light isn't on all the time, and I happen to be his uncle, God help me." Mallard paused and wiped his forehead. "Ollie, you've just lost someone very dear to you, and you had the misfortune to be the person who found him. One moment Harry was a fun-loving playfellow,

21

the next he was gone. It's natural on these occasions to look for some meaning, some explanation beyond the absurdity of the word 'accident.' But please don't let that seduce you into believing something for which there's no evidence."

Oliver sniffed the air. A sea gull landed on the merman's head.

"I'll have to go and see Lorina, I suppose," he conceded at last. Mallard seemed pleased.

"See her tomorrow," he said gently. "You can't bring her much comfort today."

"Okay." Oliver looked over the scene one last time, and started to walk away. "Let's consider Mr. Occam shaved."

Two

IT WAS A BEAUTIFUL spring day at Thistledown Halt. Mr. Bat-fowler, the engineer, had decided to stop the train for a few minutes to enjoy a cup of tea and a muffin with his old friend Mrs. Witherspoon, the emancipated station master.

Billy Field Mouse, the tiniest member of the family of mice who lived on the sleepy, branch-line train, jumped down onto the warm wooden sleepers and scampered along the track until he was underneath the guard's van. He knew by now that he had to run quickly, because if the train started up, he would be left behind, and there would be lots of strange adventures before he was back with Dolores Field Mouse, his mummy, and Henghis Field Mouse, his daddy, and Reginald, his big brother, and their three sisters, Anastasia, Tiffani-Amber, and Tracy. Goodness knows it had happened before.

The guard's van was where his friend, Finsbury the Ferret, lived. Billy was pleased to see the big white ferret, swinging gently in a hammock hung beneath the train.

"Hello, Finsbury," the little fellow cried gaily. "Isn't it a lovely spring morning? The pussy willows are bursting on the branch, the coltsfoot is in the meadow, the daffodils are splashing the embankments with their bobbing yellow heads, and the leaping woolly lambkins will soon be off to the abattoir. Aren't you glad to be alive on such a beautiful day, Finsbury?"

The ferret turned his bleary pink eyes on the tiny mouse. Were they even pinker than usual?

"Piss off, Billy, you annoying little wanker, or I'll devour you," Finsbury drawled in his bored patrician tones. "Stanford the Stoat slipped some 'ludes into my Stoli last night and next thing I knew I was . . . I was . . . trying to . . . What? Come on, Ollie, something suitably lubricious. And do you mean 'patrician'? You know you always have to look that one up."

Oliver grumpily erased the last paragraph, got up from his desk, and stumbled over to the shelf where he kept the Thesaurus. It was ten o'clock on Tuesday morning, the day after he had found his old friend, Sir Hargreaves Random, taking his final early morning dip, and Oliver was back in the small suite of offices off the Cromwell Road, occupying his role as general assistant and sole employee of the firm of Woodcock and Oakhampton, Ltd. Or rather, because neither Mr. Woodcock nor Mr. Oakhampton ever gave him any work to do, he was back in the persona of O.C. Blithely, using the firm's word processor to write the next novel about The Railway Mice, and wondering what foul deeds Finsbury would be up to in this story. Last time, the vicious creature had introduced little Billy to glue-sniffing, got young Tracy Field

Mouse drunk on hazelnut gin, and attempted to open a brothel for badgers in the station waiting room. And once again, the Mouse family had thwarted him and made him see the error of his ways. So what now? Depravity never came easily to Oliver. He often wished he had never created Finsbury the Ferret.

Finsbury's birth had been an accident. Oliver had made up a few picaresque tales about a family of mice who lived on a train to entertain his young godson, and at Sir Harry's urging, he had submitted them to a children's book publisher, who bought them and wanted more. It was easy enough— only a few thousand words and a ready-made denouement: Get Billy Field Mouse safely back on the train before it left. With an old Bradshaw's guide and his *AA Book of the British Countryside* for technical reference (Oliver rarely ventured outside London, to his rural parents' relief), he was able to keep Tadpole Tomes for Tiny Tots supplied with a fresh story every couple of months. The income just about paid his gas bill and gave him an excuse for not thinking about a career.

But then came the Day of the Ferret.

Frustrated with yet another tale of Billy, who this time was trying to help some Boy Scout voles deliver mushrooms to old Mrs. Quackenbush, the motherly Aylesbury duck, and reeling from a bagful of snooty letters informing him that bluebells are not to be found in March, as he had stated in *The Railway Mice and the Tenderhearted Tortoise*, Oliver had let fly. He typed a few paragraphs about a foulmouthed, chain-smoking, ex-public-schoolboy ferret called Finsbury. For ten inspired minutes, Oliver indulged his alter ego, giving the beast all the vices he had never possessed, and one or two he couldn't even spell. Finsbury sang the praises of Oliver North, coconut-flavored chewing tobacco, video-nasties, Japanese whisky, the piano-accordion, and brown polyester safari suits; then he bit Mrs. Quackenbush and slipped a magic mushroom into Billy's basket. And then Oliver deleted him. Or so he thought.

Unfortunately, Oliver's ignorance of Woodcock and Oakhampton's cheap word processor caused the words to disappear from the glowing screen but not from the document. Finsbury was alive and well on the page when Oliver hurriedly printed out the story and sent it, without a glance, to his hungry publisher. His editor, trusting Oliver's formula, handed the manuscript unseen to a clueless sub-editor, who massaged Finsbury's transition in and out of the story without a raised eyebrow. And so the ferret survived, through typesetters, proofreaders, and layout artists. Because the usual illustrator of the Railway Mice series was drying out in hospital, the task of giving Finsbury an appearance went to an arrogant art student on half pay, who felt that any consultation with editor or author was irrelevant to the creative process.

The first Oliver knew that his creation had survived was when copies of the new book arrived in the mail, smelling of fresh ink. In two minutes, he was on the telephone to his editor, who was also his current girlfriend. For three days, they had gone into hiding, sharing the expense of the hotel room. And then, shortly after the current girlfriend transformed herself into the embittered ex-girlfriend, the reviews appeared.

"Ms. Blithely has succeeded where Milton failed," trumpeted *The Times Literary Supplement*. "She has created an evil character with no perverse appeal whatsoever."

"The sins of Finsbury the Ferret have no vicarious attraction," cried *The Spectator*. "Destined to become a classic."

"Just the thing for the Christmas stocking," hailed *Woman's Realm*. "It's *Lord of the Flies* with rodents."

Finsbury was acclaimed as the perfect tool for exposing

the children of Britain to evil and immorality without making them want to try it. Every publication raved about the ferret's "refreshing honesty and realism," a phrase that occurred verbatim in seven reviews. (Only *Animal Rights Now!* dissented, noting yet another misrepresentation of a mammal that was affectionate and essentially harmless, once would-be handlers had learned the simple pinch that would cause it to release body parts from its relentless bite.) And after Oliver had finished grumbling about the reviewer's assumption that he was a woman (and about some of the criticism that had been voiced in the hotel room about his intelligence, creative talents, and personal hygiene), he realized he was on to a winner.

Since then, in successive best-sellers, Finsbury had exposed the infants of England to the evils of alcohol, drugs, pornography, promiscuity, soccer hooliganism, smoking, and country and western music (an unpublished moment of self-indulgence by the author). But this morning, the iniquity wasn't flowing. All Oliver could think of was the death of his friend and mentor, Sir Harry Random. The symbol scrawled in blue on the dead man's shirtfront—where had he seen it before?

"How are my woodland chums today?" asked the ever-gleeful Mr. Woodcock, hovering near Oliver's cubbyhole as the young man gloomily closed the thesaurus. "That waggish Billy Field Mouse . . . ah, how I love his antics!"

Oliver's employer was a stout man in his late seventies, with as much gray facial hair as it was possible to sprout without actually having a beard and moustache. It was always Mr. Woodcock who represented the firm to Oliver, usually encouraging him to spend all his time writing children's novels. His partner, Mr. Oakhampton, rarely put in an appearance at the office, and on the one day a month when he did materialize, he would hurry past Oliver's desk with the merest nod and duck into his own sanctum, where he would remain behind closed doors all day.

"I'm not really in the mood for writing about Finsbury today, Mr. Woodcock," Oliver said. "Is there anything I can do for you? Some filing perhaps?"

A look of horror crossed the old man's face.

"Goodness gracious me, no!" he cried emphatically. "My dear Oliver—I may call you Oliver?—I trust I haven't indicated that I might want 'filing' to be undertaken when there is that young scamp Finsbury to be evinced. And this, *this* is tamping your fecundity? Culpability! I name the guilty man, and it is Woodcock!"

Oliver assured his distressed employer that he was not to blame for the lack of enthusiasm and told him about the events of the previous morning.

"Yes, I read Sir Harry's obituary in this morning's *Times*," Mr. Woodcock's sherry-cherished voice confirmed. "Such a full life. But I had no idea you reposed in the Random bosom, as 'twere."

"Harry and I have known each other for several years, since I became romantically involved with his daughter, Lorina," Oliver confided. "It was Harry who encouraged me to write *The Railway Mice* and recommended me to my publisher."

"Romantically involved," the old man echoed awefully. "You make it sound both wonderful and clinical in the same breath—ah, the talents of the true wordsmith! But I trust you have commiserated with this sweetheart?"

"*Former* sweetheart. I was planning to go round after work today."

Mr. Woodcock flung his arms into the air, as if trying to capture a high-flying beach ball, and addressed the ceiling.

"Oh, Woodcock, Woodcock, you are once again keeping

this fine young man from his manifest destiny," he exclaimed to the chandelier. "No, no, my dear Mr. Swithin, Oliver, you must not put the affairs of this establishment before your desires—nay, your *duty*—as a friend. Eschew the trivial round, the common task! The maiden must be comforted! You must leave immediately!"

"But it's only ten o'clock in the morning."

"And the sun is over the yard-arm in Mandalay. Leave these fripperies, I say." Mr. Woodcock's chubby hands fluttered over Oliver's cubbyhole like pink bats. Oliver shrugged, thanked his employer, and flicked off the word processor without saving the morning's work. Only as he left the building five minutes later and headed for the tube station did he remember that he still hadn't heard from his uncle.

Superintendent Mallard had remembered his promise to tell Oliver what time the Trafalgar Square fountains were turned on, but other events had intervened. When Oliver left the premises of Woodcock and Oakhampton, Mallard was only a quarter of a mile away, at Sloane Square Underground station, and he was not pleased, for two reasons. First, the previous evening's rehearsal of *Macbeth* had not gone well. And second, he was staring at a dead body that had bled profusely on the westbound platform of the District and Circle Lines.

There was an odd connection between the sources of Mallard's irritation. The Theydon Bois Thespians were trying out a new director, who had clearly seen too many Hammer films in his youth. As Humfrey had revealed last night, his "concept" of "the Scottish play" (he insisted on maintaining the precious superstition of not uttering the title) was to set it in Transylvania at the end of the nineteenth century, with the witches portrayed as sexy succubi, and Macbeth's retreat into paranoia and solitude interpreted as the vampire's fear of the daylight. The giggling Thespians were already referring to the production among themselves as "Drac-beth."

But what had driven the last tooth into Mallard's jugular was the director's insistence that every character who died should immediately become undead, wandering aimlessly through the production—and sometimes the audience—until the final curtain. This, and the amount of fake blood Humfrey had promised ("Darlings, I want your *teeth* to bleed!"), suggested to Mallard that his dreams of an early escape to the pub stood as much chance of survival as Bela Lugosi on a tanning bed.

Staring at real blood seldom affected him. If anything, he was more nauseated by the color of the station's walls, a hue known as "avocado" when used for bathroom fittings. But his habituation to the horrors of real death never stopped his offering a brief prayer for the deceased before the professional in him took over.

In defiance of its name, the Underground railway was open to the sky as it passed through Sloane Square station, although a long, curving roof covered each platform. The police had erected a low barricade of orange plastic around the body, a woman in her late middle age. Despite the blistering weather, she was wearing a head scarf and woollen coat, which indicated to Mallard that she had risen early and possessed the natural meteorological pessimism of the British working class. She lay on her back, dead from a single, massive blow to the forehead that distorted her features and had clearly shattered her skull.

Behind him, an eastbound train trundled slowly through the station without stopping. Westbound trains had been halted on both the Circle and District Lines.

"Why am I here?" Mallard muttered to himself. Getting no answer, he decided to ask his sergeant, who was talking to the scene-of-crime officer a few yards away. "Strongitharm!"

Detective Sergeant Strongitharm, Mallard's assistant for the last eighteen months, hurried over to the superintendent, taking the low makeshift fence in a single stride. This action caused several other police officers to catch their breath, not so much because of the quality of Strongitharm's legs—although the policemen were unstinting in their silent admiration—but because of the abruptness of their revelation. A second later, and Effie Strongitharm's pleated skirt had returned to her knees. Most of her colleagues knew better than to make any audible comment, and the one detective constable who let slip an involuntary grunt was immediately treated to a glare from Effie's large, light-blue eyes. For some reason, he found himself remembering the impulse he'd had as an eight year old to be a missionary to the Congo, and wondering if he'd forgotten his parents' wedding anniversary again.

"Why are we here, Sergeant?" Mallard asked again.

"Because I read your note about Sir Harry Random."

"Ah, good. Did you find out about the Trafalgar Square fountains?"

"Of course, first thing. They'd been on all night."

"Rather wasteful of the earth's resources," Mallard commented ruefully. "So it seems as if Ollie may have a point. How could Sir Harry have struck his head so severely if the fountain was already full of water? We'd better have another look at the evidence."

"That evidence is why we're here, Chief," said Effie. "You mentioned the symbol drawn on Sir Harry's shirtfront. When the report of this new murder came in an hour ago, it said something about a sign or symbol found near the body. I thought you'd like to take a look. The scene-of-crime officer is D.S. Welkin."

"Good work, Sergeant."

Effie beamed and checked the resilience of her hair ribbon, readjusting a couple of sizeable hairpins. Her hair, which varied in color between gold and mouse, was long and excessively curly. Although she started every day by brushing it vehemently and tying it back with a ribbon, its springiness would inevitably triumph, and by lunchtime her head took on the silhouette of a truncated Christmas tree.

Most people noticed Effie's hair first. When they moved on to her round, soft-featured face, they might also notice that she was exceedingly pretty. And yet from Effie's first appearance in the male-dominated culture of a Scotland Yard incident room, there had been no wolf whistles, no loud sexist remarks or dirty jokes, no semi-accidental groping or squeezing. Neither her easily burlesqued name nor her easily caricatured outline had ever appeared as graffiti in the toilets, and no older detective had ever brushed against her breasts under the pretense of adjusting her seat belt.

This was all imputed to the Strongitharm "Look." Effie had developed a way of turning a gaze on you—not long-suffering, but placid and quizzical—that could nevertheless reduce you to the mentality of salad dressing. It was a "would you do this if your mother was watching?" expression that had made several lapsed Catholics think wistfully of confession. One detective, who had chanced to use the word "floozy" in Effie's presence, described a sudden feeling of abject shame, as if he'd pinched a woman's bottom in a crowd, only to discover his target was his little sister.

The Look wasn't natural, Effie's colleagues had concluded. It was clearly a form of the old religion. That, as much as Mallard's proud patronage of his talented and loyal sergeant, must account for her success. (Mallard, of course, was so far from doing anything to deserve a disapproving stare that he was unaware of the legend; he just thought, and said frequently, that Effie was a "bloody good copper.")

"Could you spare us a moment or two, Sergeant Welkin?" asked Mallard affably as he approached the scene-of-crime officer, who had just signaled the mortuary attendants to move in with their stretcher.

"Of course, Superintendent," Welkin chirped, in an unnecessarily thick Cockney accent. He was an overweight man in his thirties, with a black moustache and a harsh boxer's face, who invariably reminded people of someone else they knew. He bred Burmese cats.

"Do we have any idea what happened?" Mallard asked.

"Well, sir, it seems the lady—whom we've yet to identify—was bashed with a blunt instrument, a length of lead pipe, which was dropped immediately. There don't seem to be any fingerprints on it. It happened just as a train was in the station, and there was some confusion, as you might expect, what with people getting on and off. So by the time anybody realized she'd been clobbered, the train had left, and the murderer could easily have jumped on before the doors closed. The station manager called us in time to have the train held up at South Kensington—the next station— but the doors were already open, so chummy could easily have got away. Or he could have mingled with the people who got off the train here. The station staff did a good job of keeping potential witnesses here until we arrived, but as I said, there was confusion."

"The first report said something about a sign or a symbol."

"Yes, sir, but it doesn't seem to mean much. Actually it was attached to the pipe with a rubber band. Here, I'll let you have a butcher's."

He opened an aluminum case and took out two plastic bags. The larger contained a nondescript piece of lead pipe, about eighteen inches long and an inch and a half in diameter. The smaller held a plain white card with a hole punched in the corner, through which a rubber band had been looped. Mallard took this bag and pulled the plastic tight to read what was on the card. One side was blank, apart from a faint smear of blood. On the other side, in dark blue ink, was a pair of parallel zigzag lines.

"Don't suppose it means nothing," offered Welkin.

"Maybe not," Mallard said cautiously, as he handed the bag back. He took out a notebook and sketched the lines.

"Hello, Tim, who rattled your cage?" boomed a voice behind him. Mallard turned to face Chief Inspector Oliphant, a substantially built CID officer who was presumably in charge of the investigation. Oliphant's tone was friendly, but he was clearly suspicious of the Murder Squad's early appearance.

"Good morning, Desmond. Sergeant Strongitharm and I were just in the neighborhood. Quite a mess."

"Yes, well, I sure it'll come your way if we can't handle it," said Oliphant distractedly. "But right now, I've got about thirty witnesses upstairs impatient to be interviewed. They all seem to be called Camilla and they're all threatening me with a daddy who knows the Home Secretary personally. So I'd appreciate it if you could let me finish up here, and then we can start the trains running again."

"Certainly, Desmond, we were just leaving. Come along, Sergeant Strongitharm."

Mallard pocketed his notebook and led the way along the platform, past a small man in an even smaller suit who was hovering nervously near the stairs to the street. Effie paused and with a gentle pat on Mallard's arm, turned back to the man.

"You must be the station manager," she predicted, assuming no other member of the public would be allowed onto the platform. The small man gazed up at her with admiration.

"I am indeed," he replied with a self-satisfied purr, if any sound passing principally through the nostrils can be described as a "purr." "My name's Noss. Like Moss, only with an en."

"An em? Moss already has an em."

"No, not an em, an en. For November."

"Oh, *Noss.*"

"That's right, Noss."

"Quite a day you're having, Mr. Noss," she said, with a winning smile. Noss straightened his shoulders, causing lozenges of off-white shirtfront to appear between the buttons of his jacket.

"Oh, we can handle it," he said with a modest glance at his shoes. "This is my fourth murder, you know. I've had several attempteds, too. I've even had babies twice. But you know, Miss . . . "

Effie ignored the invitation. "Yes?" she said, feigning delight. Noss leaned forward.

"I've never had an accident."

"I'm so pleased to hear it," Effie gushed. She unconsciously untied her ribbon, and her ample curly hair sprung into its pyramidal shape. Noss, expecting an effect that showed more regard for the law of gravity, opened his eyes another notch.

"Well, you must be commended for the way you're handling this, Mr. Noss," Effie continued. "I was only saying to Mr. Mallard—oh, this is Superintendent Mallard of Scotland Yard's Murder Squad—that your swift thinking has saved us all a lot of work."

Mallard stepped forward imperiously and grasped the overawed station master's hand.

"Mr. Noss, your actions prove to me that you are an intuitive and insightful man," he intoned, taking over smoothly from Effie. "But I see more. Something is on your mind, Mr. Noss. You know something about this business. And yet you hesitate, perhaps for fear of wasting our time with trivia." Mallard finally ended the handshake and placed his palm on Noss's dandruff-strewn shoulder. He winked. "But let me confide in you, my dear Noss, nothing is trivial in a murder investigation. You, and you alone could have the key—you who have been here from first to last."

Mallard stepped back and waited majestically. Effie's smile broadened, encouraging the little man. Noss cleared his throat.

"Well, I suppose there is one thing," he began tentatively.

"Yes," they both replied.

"I didn't think to mention it because it seems so silly."

"Go on," Effie said breathily.

"Perhaps it only interests me . . . "

"It will interest us all, Mr. Noss, be assured," claimed Mallard. "This is your moment. Your, er, once-in-a-lifetime."

"All right. All right, I'll tell you. You see that tube."

He pointed to a large gray duct that ran orthogonally through the station, almost directly above their heads.

"What about it?" asked Effie, looking up.

"Can you guess what's in it?"

She shrugged, conscious of a sinking feeling. "A walkway? Water mains?"

Noss laughed gleefully. "No, that's what most people think, if they think about it at all. But it's not that. It's a river."

"A river?"

"Yes, the River Westbourne. It runs out of the Serpentine and goes straight through here to meet the Thames at Chelsea. Of course, like the Fleet River, it runs mostly through the sewers now. But when they dug out the Underground, they had to provide a channel for it. So when you walk along this platform now, you can say you've walked *under* a river."

Mallard stared at Noss. Then he stared at Effie, rather more meaningfully.

"Mr. Noss," she said eventually, "you have provided an answer that lives up to our expectations of you."

"Yes, it's interesting, isn't it? A station manager's life is full of tidbits like that. Do you know in 1940—a bit before my time, of course—a bomb landed smack-bang on this station? Killed eighty people, but didn't make a dent in the river."

"Ah, Mr. Noss," Effie sighed, "if only there were enough hours in the day, how I would love to wander through your extraordinary brain." ("Having removed it from your cranium first," she added silently.)

Noss smirked and tugged at his sleeves. The action caused a cuff button to fly off and roll over the edge of the platform.

"Oh, only too happy to be of service, Miss . . . " he prompted again. But Effie and Mallard had vanished.

"Rivers!" exploded Mallard as they emerged into the bright sunshine of Sloane Square. It had taken a few minutes to squeeze through the crush of potential witnesses in the ticket hall. All the activity at the station had slowed the traffic around the square to a crawl, and the noise of horns and gunned engines was deafening.

"Sorry, Tim," mumbled Effie contritely. By mutual consent, they used first names only when they were unaccompanied.

"I bet that self-important little git was responsible for that appalling color scheme."

"How about the card?" Effie asked, after they had moved through the concentric rings of police cars, cordons, and bystanders, who stared at them rudely.

"I don't know. It's certainly a puzzle, but I'm not sure if there's any connection with Sir Harry Random's death. The symbol was entirely different, and I can make a case for Harry drawing his upon himself. In this instance, however, the murderer was clearly leaving some message. What did you make of those lines—a little like two lightning bolts?"

"Could it be a sales tag? Or a trademark?"

"What about those packs of cards that are used in telepathy experiments? Don't they have parallel lines?"

"I think those are wavy, not zigzag."

Mallard stopped in front of the Royal Court Theatre, pretending to study the black and white photographs of the current production.

"I promised I'd call Oliver," he said, after a momentary fantasy in which his own monochrome image as a blood-soaked Banquo stared back at him from the display cases. "Maybe he'll have some ideas."

Effie sniffed, and Mallard, watching her reflection in the glass, noted the passing expression with interest. Although Effie said nothing, she always had some physical reaction whenever Oliver's name came up. Mallard assumed there was an element of jealousy, because he often discussed their cases with his nephew-by-marriage. The Yard frequently turned to civilian experts for technical advice, and when Mallard had no idea what sort of expertise was needed, he found Oliver's vast store of useless information a useful starting point. But Effie, who had worked hard within the system to get where she was, clearly resented the treatment of the outsider Swithin as the superintendent's equal, taking it to be an example of literal nepotism.

"Stay on top of this murder, Effie," Mallard said as they parted. "I have a feeling it will come our way."

* * *

It was nearly twelve o'clock by the time Oliver reached Barnes, and he was taken by surprise when Lorina herself opened the front door of the substantial Random home.

"Are you alone?" he blurted out.

"Why, have you come to have your wicked way with me?" she said with a smile. "At long last, I might add."

"No, it's just that I thought you'd have someone here," Oliver explained quickly. "Because of your loss. Your father. I'm sorry. I mean, I'm sorry about Harry's . . . your father's . . . I'm sorry about what happened. Oh God, can I start again?"

"Let me help you," said Lorina firmly as he flushed crimson and trailed off. "Hello, Ollie. Thanks for coming. I appreciate your condolences. Are those for me?"

She pointed at a bunch of roses that he was clutching to his chest. He handed them over mutely.

"They're lovely. Why don't you come in?"

"I didn't do that very well, did I?" Oliver lamented, as the front door closed behind them.

"Sympathy's tricky." She laid the roses on a small table. "In answer to your first question, I'm quite alone. A surging sea of aunts came by yesterday, and they took the phone calls while I cried all day. I sent them away this morning. They didn't mind; people tire of death very quickly. It's all right to say 'death' to me, by the way. Rather a nice write-up about Daddy in the *Times* this morning, don't you think? Want some lunch? Sandwiches okay?"

Lorina Random was in her mid-twenties, the same age as Oliver. They had met at university when she had applied his makeup in a student-written rock musical based on the life of the Brontës, called "The Bell(e)s of Haworth." (The deconstructive parentheses drew attention to the triple pun in the title, but even this was less labored than the show's lyrics, which made several revisionist suggestions about Charlotte's

39

sexual propensities for the sake of a cheap and obvious rhyme.) Their romance lasted little more than a year, and, as Oliver remembered it, he had spent most of their time together studying the mane of straight brown hair that fell across her face while she addressed her latest radical political beliefs to the bottom of a coffee cup. But the relationship also introduced him to her father, and the friendship between the two men quickly flourished. Oliver and Lorina also remained friends, although since adopting the Sanders Club as a place to meet Sir Harry, he hadn't seen his former girlfriend for several months.

"Lorina, you look wonderful," Oliver said, with genuine admiration, as they stood together in the kitchen. She was cutting slices from a loaf of fresh granary bread.

"What a nice compliment for a grieving daughter," she replied graciously. But it was true. Since leaving university and joining the Ministry of Defence, Lorina had transformed herself. Gone was the uniform of student dissent—the determinedly unfashionable glasses, the peasant clothes, the bitten fingernails. Contact lenses were clearly in place, or she would have severed a well-manicured finger with the bread knife by now. Her long hair had been cut and given body. And her body . . . well, Oliver had never before seen her shape revealed so fetchingly outside her bedroom. Tight denim jeans and a dusty white tank top were unusual mourning clothes. Her feet were bare.

"In case you're wondering, yes, there's a reason why I'm dressed this way, and no, I wouldn't have opened the door if I hadn't known it was you." Lorina handed him a ham sandwich and an open bottle of beer. "Consume that quickly. I have a job for you."

While they ate, he told her briefly about finding the body the previous morning, omitting the more distressing details—including his murder theory. She took it well, pausing only once to bow her head and rub at her eyes. Then she put the plates onto the draining board—the sink was full of cellophane-wrapped chrysanthemums—and led him into Random's study.

Sir Harry's reluctance to travel had left him totally dependent on research for the background and color of his adventure stories. As well as a remarkable collection of reference and travel books, he also kept newspaper and magazine clippings and his own copious notes on every subject that appealed to him. Much of Random's credibility as a writer came from these files, which he used as an extension of his prodigious memory. He knew exactly where to find the single fact or observation that brought an unfamiliar setting to life, such as the way a smoldering mosquito coil in Trincomalee smelled like a mix of frangipanni and mineral oil (noted in a 1958 *National Geographic*), how the tintinnabulation of metalworkers provided a sonic backdrop to a chase through a Tunisian souk (a *Berlitz* pocket guide), or what poisons could be masked by the sickly taste of candied banana offered by a street vendor in Chiang Mai (*Good Housekeeping*).

Over the years, the material had grown until it filled several metal filing cabinets and well-stocked bookshelves, all crammed meticulously and neatly into the little study. But now all the drawers were open, and manila files windmilled from them at crazy angles, as if the cabinets were playing poker with oversized cards. Other files had been pulled out and lay on Harry's huge desk, on the chair, and on the floor.

"Burglars?" Oliver asked cautiously. Lorina's black cat, Satan, who had been sleeping in a makeshift nest of papers, peered at them suspiciously.

"Just me," Lorina replied. "I've been looking for Daddy's will."

"Well, you've nothing to worry about. He rewrote it last year, and I was a witness. Everything goes to you."

"Why did he rewrite it?" she asked with a frown, tickling Satan under the chin. The cat stood up, hoping that food was to follow.

"He cut your half-brother out, I'm afraid."

"That was mean of him. I suppose that makes Ambrose my financial responsibility."

"Have you heard from Ambrose?"

She shook her head. "But it wasn't really Daddy's will I needed," she explained, changing the subject pointedly. "I was looking to see if he'd left any instructions for a funeral service, and I assumed it would be with his will. You know what's in here better than I do—I never took much notice."

Too busy picketing American missile sites, thought Oliver, as he glared round the room helplessly. "Okay," he said aloud, "your father probably kept his private stuff and his story research separate. Do you know where the personal files are?"

Lorina shrugged, a move that showed off the chevron of her well-exercised deltoids. "There's a lot of papers about his own life in the desk."

Oliver pulled open the lower left-hand drawer of the large oak desk, which was stuffed with hanging files. Colored plastic tabs revealed the subjects. He flicked through the cardboard hammocks, his fingers moving like the legs of a demented heron. Satan, stretching front legs and back legs in turn, goose-stepped over to sniff at Oliver's shoes.

"Alphabetical order," Oliver commented, reading the hand-lettered tabs. "Identity cards, inoculations, international publishing rights, jewelry, jury duty, kitchen appliances, knighthood, laundry, legal actions, library membership, life insurance, loans, Lorina . . . Want to see what he kept about you? It's quite a thick file. Actually, it's several."

He hefted the files out of the drawer and piled them on top of the desk. Several odd-sized papers and documents avalanched across the shiny surface. Most had other sheets of notepaper stapled to them, covered in Sir Harry's spidery handwriting. More recent records were adorned with fluorescent yellow labels. Lorina picked up a booklet with a little cry.

"This is my school report, from when I was eight years old," she cried in amazement. "And here's my certificate of confirmation. And an article from the local newspaper about a ballet recital when I was twelve. God, I look awful in this picture. No, you don't," she added laughingly as Oliver tried to snatch the sallow clipping. Satan chose the moment to bite firmly into his ankle, but Oliver was used to the beast's habits and pushed him away.

"I think he always wanted to write his autobiography, which is why he made notes about everything that ever happened to him." Lorina chuckled. "Who'd believe the old fraud had never traveled further than a day trip to Boulogne?"

"There's no entry under *L* for 'Last will and testament,' " Oliver reported. "Shall I try *W* for 'Will' or *F* for 'Funeral arrangements'?"

The doorbell rang. Lorina looked startled.

"Can you get that?" she asked, looking down at her clothes. "I'll search in the meanwhile. Oh, and Ollie—try to be diplomatic."

Bristling at the last remark, Oliver headed for the hall and opened the front door without using the peephole. He was surprised to find himself staring into his uncle's necktie.

"So Harry's death was murder," he breathed, raising his eyes, in which glimmerings of triumph were appearing.

43

"Actually, I'm here pay my respects to Lorina," Mallard replied scornfully. "And I sincerely hope you haven't been bothering her with your half-witted theories. Can I come in?"

"It's my Uncle Tim," Oliver called as he ushered Mallard across the threshold. Lorina hurried into the hall and hugged the detective. Satan rubbed his cheek against Mallard's trouser leg.

"Found it," she said to Oliver, waving a piece of paper. "O for 'Obsequies.' "

"Lorina, my dear," said Mallard, after he had recovered from his astonishment at her casual appearance, "I didn't know your father as well as I hoped. His passing has sadly taken away the pleasure of achieving that ambition."

"How nicely put!" she said with delight. "Oliver, you could learn a lot from your uncle. Now, you two make yourselves comfortable in the living room, I'm going to put the kettle on for tea. Give me a few minutes to change first, though."

She skipped away. The men stared at each other uncomfortably, then drifted into the large, paneled living room. Satan followed them, trying to make his destination look like a coincidence.

"Not much like a house of mourning," muttered Mallard eventually, as he inspected the lineup of Sir Harry Random's literary awards on the stone mantlepiece. Oliver perched on an unyielding recamier and patted his lap. The cat ignored him and began to wash himself in offensive places.

"It's her way of dealing with it," Oliver said. "She cares, I can tell."

"Strange to think she's now a rising star of the Civil Service, when she was neither civil nor serviceable in her student days," Mallard continued. "You do realize, dear nephew,

44

that if you want me to investigate Harry's death as a murder, Lorina becomes a suspect? It was well known they didn't see eye to eye."

Oliver didn't look at his uncle. "I thought you said it was a dead issue, excuse the pun."

"I don't think I should in the house of the deceased," Mallard replied huffily. "Anyway, I meant what I said before. Officially, Harry drowned accidentally unless the inquest says otherwise."

"So why are you here? You didn't know the family that well. A sympathetic greeting card would have sufficed."

"I called your office and Mr. Woodcock said you'd come here." Mallard fished in his jacket pocket and pulled out his notebook, turning to the page on which he'd copied the two zigzag lines. He thrust it under Oliver's nose.

"Mean anything?"

Oliver stared at the paper. "Some sort of trademark?" he ventured.

"That's what Effie Strongitharm said, but I don't think so," Mallard replied, noticing Oliver's unconscious flinch with curiosity. "Effie also found out, by the way, that the fountains in Trafalgar Square had been on all Sunday night, although I probably shouldn't tell you that since it ruins my theory of Harry's death."

"Good old Effie," muttered Oliver, trying to determine Mallard's mood. "So what's the story with the squiggly lines?"

"They're a clue to a *real* murder. Some poor woman, so far unidentified, who was clubbed to death at Sloane Square tube station this morning. This symbol was on a card, attached to the murder weapon. A rather prosaic length of lead piping."

"Sounds like a board game. You know, 'Colonel Mustard, in the Ballroom, with the lead pipe.' " Oliver grinned. "I take

45

it you thought this symbol might have some connection with the symbol drawn on Sir Harry Random's chest?" he ventured.

"Not officially," said Mallard guardedly.

"Then officially, I can't think of any connection."

"And unofficially?"

"Unofficially, I still can't think of any connection," Oliver conceded. "Although they do seem somewhat familiar. I'll think about it." He grinned again, for no apparent reason. The cat sneezed.

"Funny thing about Sloane Square station," Mallard continued in an airy tone, idly stroking his white moustache. His nephew's self-satisfaction was beginning to wear on him. "It's got a river running through it."

"Oh, yes, the Westbourne. Goes through in a big pipe, doesn't it? The station took a direct hit from a Nazi bomb in 1940, but the pipe didn't break. Ah, now there's a connection," Oliver exclaimed, unaware of his uncle's growing exasperation. "A bomb once went off in Trafalgar Square, too. Some time in the 1880s, planted by the Irish Nationalists. Nearly destroyed Nelson's Column."

"I asked you if you recognized a symbol, I didn't want a bloody history lesson," Mallard growled. He reflected for a moment. "I suppose Harry's views on Ireland weren't noticeably controversial?" he added, with insufficient nonchalance.

"He thought the Irish Question was rhetorical."

Mallard snapped his notebook shut. "Well, I doubt there's much connection between his death and a century-old Fenian outrage. Just as I truly doubt there's any connection between Harry and this morning's victim."

"Perhaps the two symbols will turn out to be the start of a coded message," Oliver persisted. "Like the 'dancing men' in the Sherlock Holmes story."

"Oh, enough with the Sherlock Holmes, already," Mallard protested.

"Sherlock Holmes?" echoed Lorina from the doorway. She had changed into a simple, dark dress—navy, not black, both men noticed—and was carrying a loaded tea tray. Mallard stepped over to take it from her. "Did you know that Oliver adores Sherlock Holmes?" she continued brightly, with a smile at her former boyfriend. "He likes anything to do with detection. You've been quite a role model for him, Uncle Tim."

The two men fell into an embarrassed silence, each pretending to have a deep fascination with the way Lorina was placidly stirring the tea, like closely packed riders in an elevator studying the floor numbers. Mallard had more reason to be distracted, because he was trying to decide if he should be complimented or insulted by Lorina's remark. Suddenly, Satan lifted his head and unspooled himself from his chair. A few seconds later, the doorbell rang and, with an apology, Lorina followed the cat out of the living room. They heard the front door open, and a strangely high-pitched voice declaimed a greeting.

"So, Squire Random's finally trodden the primrose way to the everlasting bonfire, eh Ina, old thing?"

The voice stopped abruptly. Half a minute later, Lorina put her head around the door of the living room and smiled awkwardly at them.

"Look, sorry about this, but Ambrose has turned up, and I think he may have been drinking."

Mallard got to his feet instantly. "I have to leave anyway, my dear," he said quickly. Thank you for the refreshments, and once again, my condolences on your loss, which I trust you'll extend to your brother. Come, Oliver, I'll give you a lift home."

He brushed his lips against Lorina's cheek and swept into the hallway, which was visibly empty of Ambrose, although a well-stuffed backpack had been dropped on the parquet.

"Will you be okay?" Oliver asked her anxiously as they stood at the front door. She nodded.

"I can handle Ambrose, whatever mood he's in. He's scared of me."

She hugged him closely and watched him until he reached Mallard's Rover. Then, with a sigh, she closed the door.

Three

"YES, SIR, THEY CERTAINLY were innocent times," said Dworkin wistfully. "Take the literary works of Arthur Ransome, for instance. Boys and girls—barely adolescent—camping together, bathing together, living as free as nature intended. Did they hide their shame behind scraps of clothing, the swaddling bands of civilization?"

"I seem to recall some mention of bathing drawers," muttered Oliver to the porter's shoes.

"Ah, but there was nothing about scurrying behind bushes to change, was there, sir? Swallows, Amazons—these are names from nature, from myth. Bold and free, as nature intended. I certainly picture them all naked. That island in the lake was a return to Eden for them. Where else could a young girl be proleptically called 'Titty' without the vile sniggerings of censorious society?"

"Where indeed?" grunted Oliver, finding himself wondering where Dworkin, the day porter at the Sanders Club, had picked up the word "proleptically." Must have been reading Anthony Burgess again.

Dworkin's obsessions with Adamitic innocence were notorious at the club, and most members avoided eye contact with the dapper ex-sapper. It had been noted that, since Dworkin had arrived a couple of years earlier, the club's copy of Hans Christian Andersen's collected tales always seemed to fall open at the picture of the Little Mermaid, and all the illustrated editions of *The Water Babies* had disappeared. Unfortunately, Dworkin was the only other occupant of the club lobby, and because the porter had initially applied for the job after serving on a jury with Sir Harry Random, Oliver felt obliged to put up with him for his late friend's sake.

Oliver was at the club that Wednesday afternoon because of a brain wave that had struck him earlier in the day. On the night Sir Harry died, Oliver recalled, he had been waving a piece of paper that was in some way connected with his supposed assignation at six o'clock on Monday morning. This paper was in Harry's possession while the two men were playing poker in the club's card room; but it was gone by the time the police searched the body that he and Urchin had dragged from the fountain. Oliver knew that Harry never disposed of any paper carelessly—the state of his study suggested that Harry seldom disposed of any letters or notes at all. So where had the paper gone? If Harry had dropped it outside the club, Oliver knew there was no chance of recovering it. But the fastidious old man was much more likely to have tossed it into one of the club's rarely emptied wastepaper baskets. So at five o'clock, Oliver had hurriedly left the sleepy premises of Woodcock and Oakhampton and splashed out on a taxi to the Sanders Club.

The basket in the card room had yielded nothing, so

Oliver had moved on to the lobby. Under the curious eye of the dreaded Dworkin, he had scattered the contents of the metal rubbish bin across the lobby floor and was on his hands and knees, examining every piece of paper. If this failed, he would be forced to investigate the noisome rubbish pail in the gentlemen's toilet. But even this had its appeal, if it meant escaping the porter's flapping tongue.

"And then there's Enid Blyton," droned Dworkin, idly watching Oliver. *Five Have an Adventure.* I bet they did, with no adult chaperons. Ah, good morning, Mr. Scroop!"

These last words were addressed to a tall and well-dressed member—the author of a several short novels about a boy whose football turns out to be an entire alien world—who had hurried in from the sunshine and, like most members, was not prepared to break his stride until he was well past Dworkin. But catching sight of Oliver, crouched at the porter's feet, he paused.

"Afternoon, Swithin."

"Hello, Mr. Scroop," said Oliver, hardly looking up. He disliked the author, who used a constant veneer of flippancy to mask his shallowness.

"Any particular reason why you're treating the lobby like a garbage tip? Still hunting your precious Snark? Or is this the remains of some attempt on the world origami record?"

Scroop laughed, too loud and long for the weakness of the joke, and Dworkin—who had just realized he would have to clean up after Oliver—switched sides quickly and joined in the mockery. Oliver smiled.

"Actually, Mr. Scroop, I've lost my ferret."

"Your ferret?" Scroop repeated nervously.

"Well, my books have been so successful since I introduced a ferret that I thought I'd buy a real one as a mascot. He just got away. Can you help me look for him?"

"You brought a ferret into the club?" Scroop said aghast.

51

"Yes, I wanted to show it to Mr. Dworkin. But I suppose it will turn up. Somewhere."

"You're mad!" spluttered Scroop. "Ferrets! Why, they're like long rats. They *bite!* Oh, my God! The committee shall hear about this."

As he scurried away, his elegant boot caught a screwed-up piece of paper, sending it across the marble floor and under the porter's desk. Oliver made a dive and fished the paper out again. He flattened it carefully and read it. Then he calmly folded it and slipped it into his pocket.

Under the cloudless sapphire sky, the Royal Botanical Gardens at Kew were basking in the warm coral and amber light of the early evening. Although still an hour from setting, the sun was hovering low above the broad, tree-lined horizon, almost dim enough to look at directly. Long, mauve shadows stretched across the elegant lawns. Inside the Temperate House, the massive Victorian greenhouse designed by Decimus Burton, the white girders and mullions were overlaid with a competing web of soft-edged shadow, which climbed slowly as the sun descended, creating new moirés and traceries with every minute. Former Colour-Sergeant Derwent Prussia, now a park attendant at the Gardens, observed the delicate effect from a walkway and hated it.

Prussia glanced at his watch. Nearly time to throw out the last remaining visitors, gawping at the tall palms and other plants that thrived in the hot, humid conditions. Which is more than could be said for him. He hated heat, hated summer, and only ventured into the Temperate House for the pleasure of shouting "This building is now closed!" at the end of the day. He liked that. It reminded him of his days in the army. His new boss had thought so, too.

"You sound like a sergeant-major," Mr. Birdwich had

once murmured, overhearing the park attendant at closing time. Prussia had been flattered. A sergeant-major! That was more than he'd ever dreamed.

"Have you ever considered asking them to leave politely?" Birdwich had continued, with a smile that disturbed only one side of his moon-shaped face.

"We'd never get the place emptied, sir. They'd take their time, pausing for one more read of the labels, one more sniff of the flowering shrubs."

"Well, we can't have people enjoying themselves in a public park, can we," said Birdwich reflectively as he drifted away.

Prussia, immune to irony, smiled at the memory. Good head on that one, despite his youth, he thought. He looked at his watch again and braced himself against the handrail.

"This building is now closed!" he shouted at the top of his lungs. "Visiting hours are over!"

Prussia was poised on a catwalk that girdled the interior of the vast, rectangular greenhouse, about halfway up its sloping side, giving a view of the Kew pagoda across the treetops. He liked to deliver the message from an elevated position; it awakened some atavistic sense of authority within him. Perhaps he should try it in more than one language, what with all these foreign tourists—they were the hardest to get rid of. For some reason, German struck him as an appropriate alternative.

Fifty feet below, after several startled glances in his direction, the few visitors began to wander along the gravel paths toward the main doors of the building, the central pavilion in a string of greenhouses. Good. Obedience was good. He would be home early at this rate. But wait a moment! What about those two down there? Two men—were they men? The one staggering toward the spiral staircase in the opposite corner of the building certainly was. And he was climbing it!

"Oi! You're going the wrong way!" Prussia shouted. The man paused, staring over the curving banister at the attendant above him. Then he ran on.

"Right!" thought Prussia, who habitually addressed himself in the same tones he used for members of the public. He marched swiftly along the catwalk, hoping to intercept the man, who was still climbing upward in an awkward helical path. But the man reached the top of the staircase first, and headed around the walkway in the opposite direction. There was nothing else for it. Prussia was forced to run.

"Just you stop there!" he shouted as he made the turn. The man was wearing a lightweight business suit and seemed to be in his early forties. He looked back, grinned, and stumbled, striking his head on a girder. But he stayed on his feet and kept trotting away. The perspiring Prussia was starting to regret his vow never to remove his uniform jacket under any circumstances.

They reached the next turn, and again, Prussia's quarry slipped, falling heavily onto his hands and knees on the metal balcony. He scrambled up and scuttled on for half the width of the building, stopping at the bottom of a long flight of metal steps. These steps, which were suspended under the sloping glass roof, climbed even higher to a small inspection platform, slung from an iron crossbeam. A padlocked gate sealed them from the public. Prussia reached the man as he stood staring fixedly at the steps, apparently wondering how to ascend.

"Just where do you think you're going?" Prussia gasped. The man smiled foolishly and pointed.

"Gotta go up," he said in a slurred voice. He appeared to be drunk, yet Prussia couldn't detect any alcohol on his breath.

"Can't go up there," panted Prussia. "Official business only. Members of the public not allowed. I can go up there, if I want, but you can't."

"Gotta go up," the man said again, falling against Prussia. "Treasure's hidden up there."

"There's no treasure," replied the attendant, steadying the man with a firm hand on each lapel. "Now come on, or there'll be consequences."

"Awright. Sorry. Nice park keeper," mumbled the man contritely, idly brushing Prussia's sleeves. Then he struck out, catching Prussia on the cheek and making him fall back. Prussia toppled against the handrail, skidding on something oily that had been spilled onto the catwalk. Recovering, he watched in horror as the man swung the gate open and began to climb.

"That's supposed to be locked!" Prussia shouted helplessly. But the other man continued to drag himself up the long iron staircase, his feet sliding on every tread, and slithered onto the inspection platform. Prussia tried to follow, but his shoes wouldn't grip on the steps. There was more oil.

"Now for the treasure!" shouted the man, spinning around above Prussia. "Not here! Gotta go further!"

He stepped off the platform onto another narrow catwalk high in the roof, singing wildly.

" 'Sixteen men on a dead man's chest,' " he caroled, leaning out over the dizzying void. " 'Yo ho ho and a rottle of bum.' Look at me, I'm walking the plank! Wheee!"

His balance became precarious. Prussia made another attempt to scale the steps, but fell, catching his chin. Some blood dripped onto the white paint, but he didn't notice. His eyes were on the interloper.

The man was swaying wildly, laughing all the time and waving his hands in a last attempt to stay upright. Then he was gone. Prussia almost expected him to hover there, a hundred feet above the foliage, like a cartoon character granted a temporary deferment of the law of gravity. But the man plunged instantly to the floor of the greenhouse, far below. The falling body slapped the overhanging leaves of a towering Chilean wine palm and landed in the planted beds with less noise than Prussia had anticipated. The man moved his arm once, then didn't move at all.

Prussia stood up and walked cautiously back along the catwalk, hoping he would wake up from the dream in a minute or two. But the sudden pain from his bleeding chin convinced him this was real. He hurried on, keeping the body in sight and praying that it would move again. Nobody else was left in the building—Prussia had been the only witness to the stranger's brief flight.

He paused at the top of the spiral staircase, scraping his oily shoes on the edge of the catwalk and trying to clear his misty vision before attempting the corkscrew descent. His concentration taken up with the need to stay upright, he wasn't sure if he really saw the figure dart into the building, lay something on the body, and slip out again.

"More than my job's worth," Prussia wheezed as he reached the bottom and passed out on the *Pavonia Spinifex*.

Oliver let himself into the Edwardes Square house that he shared with three of his friends, clutching a take-out meal from a nearby Indian restaurant. He had tried to telephone his uncle from the Sanders Club, but Mallard was unavailable. So Oliver had walked home, enjoying the early evening sunshine and thinking again about Sir Harry Random's death.

"Hello, Ollie," said Geoffrey Angelwine, looking up from his saucepan as Oliver drifted into their shared kitchen. "Hey listen, I have a great idea for a Railway Mice story."

Oliver had known Geoffrey for years, long before he became a junior executive with the public relations firm of Hoo, Watt & Eidenau, which was also the firm hired by Oliver's publisher to market Finsbury the Ferret. Geoffrey was considerably shorter than Oliver, with nut-brown hair, a razor-bill nose, and small, piercing eyes that always looked amused. He resembled a puffin who'd just heard the one about another puffin's mother-in-law. He also had the irritating habit of finishing other people's sentences, unfortunately with little accuracy. Oliver adored him.

A muffled, rhythmic groaning was coming from the upper floors of the building, which were used by their friend Ben Motley as a photographic studio. There was also a faint squeaking of bedsprings.

"I hear Ben's on the job again," Oliver commented, tipping his curried chicken onto a plate and mixing rice sadly into the indeterminate curry sauce. As an excellent practitioner of Indian cookery, he found the mere existence of anything as vague as curry powder depressing. The groaning above them rose to a deafening scream and then stopped abruptly.

"I hope he's not weakening the joists," Geoffrey murmured. "My bedroom's directly underneath."

"Those clients keep the rent down."

"Yes, but can the floor take it? I don't want some gorgeous starlet and half a ton of plaster to land on my bed some night. I can do without the plaster, anyway."

"Who is it this time?" asked Oliver.

"Just some businessman's wife. Oh, your uncle telephoned. He wants you to get back to him as soon as you get a chance."

"I'll call him after I've finished—"

"—listening to my idea for Finsbury," Geoffrey cut in.

Oliver was going to say "eating my dinner," but he let it go. It was noted that Geoffrey often used his conversational tic to his own advantage.

The arrival of Finsbury the Ferret had caused the Railway Mice books to shoot to the top of the best-seller lists, snapped up by the kind of parents who make their kids call them by their first names and take showers with the bathroom door open. Almost overnight, the albino beast had ironically become the leading bête noire for the pre-teen set—and a cultural folk hero for many childless adults—and so Tadpole Tomes for Tiny Tot decided they needed a public relations company to develop a marketing campaign for the character. Geoffrey persuaded Oliver to suggest his employer as a candidate, and Hoo, Watt & Eidenau went on to win "the Blithely Account" as it was known, based on Oliver's pseudonym. Geoffrey's reward was to be co-opted as the most junior member of the HW&E team, and in hopes of career advancement, he had been firing off suggestions for Finsbury ever since.

"So this is my idea," Geoffrey said enthusiastically, bringing his soup over to the large pine table and sitting beside Oliver. "You've seen television soap operas, right?"

"Never."

"Well, you've heard about them. And you know how soap operas use 'evil twins.' It gives an actor a chance to play two roles, one good, one bad. Lots of fun with trick photography and mistaken identities. Quite an old convention, I believe."

"Goes back at least to P—"

"Peyton Place?"

"I was going to say Plautus. What's your idea?"

Geoffrey smirked. "Let's give Finsbury an evil twin."

Oliver, whose mind had been partly on his discovery at

the Sanders Club, eyed his friend with sudden suspicion. "What for?" he asked cautiously.

"Everything's relative. If Finsbury has an evil twin, he'll look good by comparison. Improve his chances in the soft toy market."

Oliver dropped his chapati and stared at his friend. "Geoff," he began, "Finsbury is already just about the most debauched and dissipated animal in the history of children's literature. He has introduced perversions that psychiatry has yet to find names for, he has personally discovered that there are, in fact, forty-three deadly sins, and he has a criminal record as long as a damp Sunday in Carlisle. Furthermore, he chews gum with his mouth open. Now can you think of any-thing—*anything*—that an evil twin could do that would make Finsbury seem virtuous by comparison?"

Geoffrey was silent for a moment. Then he brightened. "Okay, then let's give him a *good* twin. A paragon of ani-mals, as it were. Someone for the kiddies to identify with."

"And what would this good twin do?"

"Oh, I don't know. Wear a sailor suit and ringlets. Eat kale. Floss. Recycle. End global warming. Buy the Cratchits a goose for Christmas. Be polite about the French. That sort of thing." He trailed off, frowning into his soup. "Now that I think about it, I'd rather identify with Finsbury," he mum-bled ruefully.

Oliver patted his friend on the shoulder. "So would the readers, Geoffrey. But keep trying."

They heard footsteps on the stairs and through the half-open door to the hall, they caught a glimpse of a passing fur coat, followed by the permanently bejeaned form of Ben Motley. The front door opened.

"I hope he doesn't have any more appointments tonight," sighed Geoffrey, as the noise of a car door slamming drifted in from the street. "I need to get to bed early. By the way, Ollie, where does that phrase 'paragon of animals' come from? Is it George Orwell?"

"Sounds more like Oscar Wilde to me," said Ben, wandering into the kitchen. Oliver raised his eyes to the cracked ceiling.

"It's *Hamlet,*" he groaned. "Didn't you chaps learn anything at Oxford?"

Ben and Geoffrey looked at each other with puzzled expressions. "Were we supposed to?" Ben asked tentatively. He peered cautiously at the remaining soup in his friend's saucepan and then reached for the kettle.

"Business still booming?" Geoffrey asked.

"That last one was easy, anyway," Ben replied. "She brought her own Walkman. I'm really getting bored with orgasmic women, Geoff. I want to do some religious work."

"Some might say you were," Geoffrey giggled. "So what do you mean, religious work?"

"Well, I was in the National Gallery yesterday and I had this amazing idea. You've seen those wonderful late gothic and early Renaissance altarpieces—you know, Adoration of the Magi, Virgin—"

". . . on the ridiculous," interrupted Geoffrey. Ben grimaced.

"No, Virgin and Child," he said firmly. "I want to recreate those images in modern *tableaux vivants*, and then photograph them with a large-format Polaroid camera. We could get our friends to play various parts. Can you see Susie Beamish as a Virgin?" He referred to the fourth member of the quartet of friends who shared the house.

"Frankly, no, but then I've only known her since she was twelve. The whole thing sounds a bit postmodern to me. What do you think, Ollie?" But Oliver, who had been brooding over his empty plate, seemed not to hear. "Ollie, you have to call your uncle, remember?" Geoffrey reminded him.

Oliver stood up suddenly, sending his chair crashing to the floor. "Virgin!" he shouted.

Geoffrey looked embarrassed. "There's no need to be personal," he said in a hurt voice. "I've had my moments."

"What?" said Oliver, frowning at his friend. "Oh, sorry, Geoff, I wasn't listening. But thanks, you've given me a great idea."

"About virgins?"

"No, about twins. Ben supplied the virgins. I have to call my uncle."

He ran from the room, and they heard him pick up the telephone in the hall.

"Did I miss something?" Geoffrey asked.

"Is the Pope Jewish?" said Ben laconically.

"After a year of ferrets, he gets to twin virgins and he doesn't stop to tell us about it," Geoffrey grumbled. "And he didn't put his plate in the dishwasher."

Oliver rushed in again. "I have to go out," he cried breathlessly. "To Kew Gardens. Can someone lend me the taxi fare until I get to the bank tomorrow?"

"I'll drive you," said Ben.

"Great, just give me five minutes to check something."

"Can I come?" asked Geoffrey.

"It's only a two-seater, sorry," shouted Ben, as he and Oliver hurried from the kitchen. Geoffrey sighed and picked up the dirty china.

Tall, dark, muscular, and square-jawed, Ben Motley attracted women like a sale in a shoe shop (and mainly the kind of women who like a sale in shoe shop), but his professional success had been entirely on the operating side of the cam-

61

era. A keen photographer while still a student, Ben had tried to explore every possible photographic style. His one attempt at pornography had been an experimental roll of his university girlfriend while in the heat of passion, but being an instinctive gentleman, he took the pictures from the neck up only. Finding the contact sheet unflattering—and blurry—he promptly forgot about it and moved on to still lifes of parsnips. The girl later married a film producer and became a well-known and celebrated movie actress in America, and so, when Ben came across the pictures one day, he felt it diplomatic to send her the contact sheet and the negatives in a plain envelope. The husband intercepted the package, but far from being horrified, he sold the photographs to a leading pictorial magazine.

"The image of woman," the magazine had rhapsodized in its captions. "She is unaccommodated. She is feral. She is beautiful. It is the power and the passion of creation—the Promethean scream that steals the fire-seed from Man and creates her own world within. Touch her. Touch her not. . . ." And so on, for several pages of twenty-four–point copy.

The edition sold out in three days. Suddenly, every fashionable woman wanted to be photographed at the height of sexual abandon by the handsome young photographer, who had learned a lot about controlling camera shake since his college days. Ben's appointment book rapidly filled with the names of actresses, singers, dancers, wives of the leaders of industry, and socialites (a word whose very existence made Oliver shudder), all of whom wanted a crisp, black and white eight-by-ten for the drawing room Broadwood, plus a few wallet-size prints for their husband to show his colleagues. And it had to be a Motley—no other photographer had the cachet. Several men wanted to be pictured, too, but Ben had refused point blank. "So call me a sexist," he had spluttered to Oliver one evening, after putting the phone down on a bishop.

Ben had rapidly needed a larger studio, and with his first month's income, he had made a down payment on the Edwardes Square townhouse, using the top floors as combined living and working space, and letting the lower floors to three of his old friends from university. Oliver Swithin, Geoffrey Angelwine, and Susie Beamish were now used to the parade of well-known ladies who trooped up the stairs alone, spent an hour or two in Ben's company, and came downstairs freshly showered with private smiles on their faces. The three tenants had long given up speculating on Ben's methods, but they knew he always kept his jeans on and needed two hands to operate his Hasselblad.

Ben was also the only one in the house who could afford a car, and he ungrudgingly offered his services to his friends as part-time chauffeur in times of emergency. In Oliver's case, however, his good nature was mixed with a dash of opportunism. Ben knew that if Mallard ever summoned his nephew at short notice, there was always a chance that the young photographer could find himself at a crime scene in advance of his Fleet Street colleagues. So he was delighted, on reaching the Kew Bridge entrance to the Royal Botanical Gardens as darkness fell, to find himself and Oliver waved onto a winding route that had been marked with red flares. He followed them past the dim, phantasmal outline of the Palm House and then piloted the black Lamborghini slowly along the gravel paths toward the other Victorian hothouse, until their way was blocked by a fleet of official vehicles. The carnival of the cars' revolving red, white, and blue lights swept across the hothouse's skeletal facade, causing it to flicker patriotically in the darkness. The bright temporary lighting among the plants was like a fire in the building's rib cage.

A uniformed policeman carried the message to Mallard that a Mr. Swithin had arrived, and few minutes later, Oliver, with Ben following cautiously, was ushered beyond the rope barrier, to the annoyance of the reporters and photographers kept behind. Inside the greenhouse, the floodlights caught Mallard's untidy white hair and lined face. He seemed tired. Effie Strongitharm, noticing Oliver's entrance, busied herself with her notes.

Mallard greeted Ben distractedly and drew Oliver over to a huddled lump on the dirt, covered with a black plastic sheet. The other detectives around the dead man withdrew to a discreet distance. At Mallard's signal, a uniformed policeman pulled back the sheet to reveal the broken body, which had bled a little from the ears and nose. Oliver, who had seen corpses before—including one only a couple of days earlier—did not flinch.

"His name's Mark Sandys-Penza," said Mallard. "He's an estate agent. We learned that much from his wallet."

"Where did he come from?"

Mallard pointed vertically. "Up there, most recently. Before that, Richmond. Not too far away."

Oliver looked up at the catwalk, picked out starkly by a spotlight, high up under the ethereal metal vault. Despite the stifling humidity, he shivered and looked down again. The plants gave him the odd sensation of still being in the open air, as if the enormous glass and wrought-iron structure were a wire net, suddenly dropped over the jungle by a giant botanist.

"Pushed, jumped, or fell?" he asked.

"Fell, but as good as pushed. Park attendant by the name of Prussia says Sandys-Penza seemed drunk and kept talking about some treasure hunt. There's a set of stairs to the highest catwalk, normally locked, but someone had picked the padlock. And whoever opened up the gate to the stairs also smeared the steps with motor lubricant. Get that stuff on your shoes and you're sure to fall over sooner or later. Up there, blind drunk, and skidding like shit off a shiny shovel, Mr. Sandys-Penza was bound to come a cropper as fast as you can say *Brunfelsia Abbottii.*" Mallard looked smug. "That's the name of this plant that our late friend here smashed into twigs on his descent."

"Yes, I can read the little labels, too," Oliver remarked caustically. "Any witnesses?"

"Only this said Prussia. He adds that he may have seen someone with the deceased before he started his climb and he may have seen someone run over to the body after it landed, but in neither case is he sure of height, weight, race, or even gender." Mallard nodded to the policeman, who covered the dead estate agent again.

"Poor Prussia took a tumble and knocked himself out. It was half an hour after the death before anyone found him and the police were called."

"That explains why you're here," Oliver commented. "Why am I here?"

The superintendent beckoned to Effie, who came over with her usual purposeful stride, aware that she would have to acknowledge Oliver's presence.

"Good evening, Mr. Swithin," she said coldly. "I've just had the pleasure of meeting Mr. Motley. What a charming gentleman. And something of a celebrity."

"Hello, Effie . . . sorry . . . Sergeant Effie," mumbled Oliver, studying the corpse's protruding brogues. Her presence always made him nervous. "Some of my friends are quite presentable, you know."

"I understand he's also your landlord," Effie replied acidly. Mallard rescued his nephew.

"Let's see those papers, Sergeant," he said. She took two clear plastic envelopes from her shoulder bag and passed them across.

"We found both of these on the dead man," Mallard continued, passing an envelope to Oliver. It contained a white, unlined index card with a single figure drawn in blue ink—an odd symbol like a cursive upper case *T* with a loop attached to the vertical. It might have been a child's attempt at a treble clef or a quaver.

"This was placed on his chest after he fell, so the killer was here for some time. I think there's little doubt that this card connects the death tonight with yesterday's murder at Sloane Square. But that doesn't mean I'm suggesting a link to Sir Harry Random's death."

Oliver nodded, handed the card back, and took the other, larger envelope. It held a sheet of regular A4 typing paper, with crease marks to indicate that it had been folded in three. A few lines were printed in Helvetica type:

Further to yesterday's phone conversation, please meet me in the Tropical House in Kew Gardens this evening at 6:30 P.M. I hope to have more good news for you.

"Found in his pocket," Mallard said.

"From a laser printer, I suppose," Oliver speculated, returning the exhibit.

"As far as I can tell. Now, what have you got for me?"

"Me?"

Mallard sighed. It had already been a long day. "Oliver, you first telephoned me at the Yard at half past five this afternoon, long before I called you about this murder—before it took place, in fact. You wouldn't call me at work unless it was urgent. And relevant."

Oliver blinked inscrutably at his uncle from behind his

cheap eyeglasses. Then he reached into the pocket of his blazer and pulled out two pieces of stationery.

The first was a card with a symbol drawn on it—an odd symbol like a cursive upper case *T* with a loop attached to the vertical.

The second was a dirty, crumpled sheet of A4 typing paper, on which a few lines had been printed in Helvetica type:

> Further to yesterday's phone conversation, please meet me in Trafalgar Square tomorrow morning at 6:00 A.M. I'm sorry it's so early, but I think the good news will make it worth your while.

"Lord love a duck and the horse he came in on!" bellowed Mallard, gazing at the papers in amazement. The other policemen in the hothouse paused in their duties, staring at the two men. "Ye Gods and little tiddlers, Ollie," Mallard said more quietly, "if this was the seventeenth century, I could have you burned at the stake." He passed the paper to Effie, who raised one eyebrow.

"Arrest him," she suggested dryly.

"He's been arrested once," Mallard told her.

"I found the letter in the wastepaper basket in the Sanders Club," Oliver explained. "It must be the same letter I saw in Sir Harry Random's possession on Monday morning—too much of a coincidence otherwise."

"And the symbol on the card?"

"That was a lucky guess that I took before coming out. You see, Ben, Geoffrey, and I were talking about virgins in the kitchen."

Here he was unable to resist a glance at Effie, whose expression hardened further, making him blush in turn.

"Nice conversations you boys have," she muttered. "Did you find any?"

"No, no, these were religious virgins," Oliver said hastily.

"Nuns?" speculated Mallard.

"Blessed Virgin Marys, actually."

"But there was only one B.V.M. And what was she doing in your kitchen? Has young Angelwine had a visitation?"

"Oliver means paintings," said Ben, who had wandered over, impatiently fingering his thirty-five-millimeter camera. "Paintings of the Virgin Mary and other religious subjects. We're a very devout household."

"Thank you, Ben," said Oliver, rather more firmly than he had intended. "Anyway, Geoffrey had also been talking about a twin for Finsbury and it all came together."

"What came together?" asked Mallard, who was beginning to show some irritation. "The Finsbury twins? Sounds like a music hall act."

"What's that got to do with virgins?" Effie asked icily.

"Everything. Twins and virgins. Now do you get it?"

There was a pause. "No," the other three said simultaneously.

"Gemini and Virgo. The signs of the zodiac." Oliver snatched the index card from Mallard's fingers and wafted it enthusiastically under their faces. "These drawings you're finding are the symbols used by astrologers for the signs of the zodiac. And it *does* connect Sir Harry Random's death with the others. That symbol drawn on his shirtfront represents Pisces, only we were looking at it sideways—it was in the correct orientation for someone standing or crouching beside a corpse to write it on his chest. The squiggly lines you found yesterday at Sloane Square are Aquarius." He held the index card steadily in front of Mallard's spectacles. "This is Capricorn. It's the next in the series. I took a chance and copied it out." He stopped, aware that the others needed to absorb the new information. Then Mallard

68

staggered back a few paces and opened his arms to the iron vault around him.

"Oh, my stars!" he groaned, with unconscious relevance. "You know what this means? We've got a bloody serial killer!"

Four

THE CONVERSATION IN KEW Gardens had halted when the mortuary attendants, who had come to collect the body of Mark Sandys-Penza, lifted the plastic sheet, causing Ben Motley to drop his Canon and faint on the spot. So after quickly listening to Oliver's story, Superintendent Mallard had told his nephew to come over to New Scotland Yard the next morning—Thursday—at about eleven o'clock. Oliver, aware that Mallard's team was resentful of outsiders (particularly overeducated, underemployed nephews), had spent the night with visions of himself cowering in the corner of a cramped, smoke-filled room, while twenty shirtsleeved Murder Squad detectives with truncheons and attitudes glared at him. Geoffrey Angelwine, who spent his working day leaping from meeting to meeting, like an inoffensive frog crossing a lily pond, had coached him over breakfast. "The way to

70

control any meeting is to hop up to the flip chart, get hold of the big felt-tip pen, and hang on to it at all costs," he had advised.

Oliver was a little relieved, therefore, when Mallard met him at the reception desk and diplomatically suggested a walk, accompanied by Sergeant Strongitharm, in St. James's Park, coinciding with their morning break. But Effie's presence alone was enough to intimidate him.

Oliver had first met Effie Strongitharm shortly after she began assisting Mallard, nearly eighteen months earlier, and he had thought of her every day since. But although she was otherwise available, Oliver believed strongly that Effie's professional relationship with his uncle placed her firmly off limits, almost as if she were married, and he had so far kept his captivation a secret. (He had no idea that Mallard had often told his wife, Oliver's Aunt Phoebe, that he thought their vague nephew and his overworked Sergeant would have been good for each other.)

This presented Oliver with a considerable conflict, because from the little he saw of Effie and the more he heard of her and thought about her, the more he became convinced that she could be the next (and first and last) Mrs. Oliver Swithin. And the fact that, even in that espoused condition, she'd undoubtedly insist on being called Ms. Effie Strongitharm (what *was* "Effie" short for?) only made him like her more.

Not that Oliver had his sights on a wife. For him, wooing was a strictly sequential process, and pair-bonding for life came only after several earlier fences had been jumped in more or less the right order. It was more that, so far, despite trying hard, Oliver had yet to find any compelling reason why Effie and he *couldn't* spend their lives together, and it intrigued him. Attraction, admiration, respect, hope, desire—they were all there, even though he admitted a slim acquaintance with the slim woman. But this didn't fully explain why it was her face and her voice that echoed in his mind on so many mornings, when he tried fruitlessly to seize the quicksilver memory of a dream, rather than just the memory of a memory; or why the distant possibility of Effie had not been dislodged by the warm reality of the one or two girls he had dated since meeting her, including that editor at Tadpole Tomes for Tiny Tots (and just who was the "Bill" tattooed on *her* creamy thigh, anyway?).

What it came down to, he lamely concluded, was not what Effie was, but who she was. Oliver wanted the exceptional woman who was Effie Strongitharm, and it defied analysis. It wasn't love. Not yet. Oliver knew that, for him, love was a place where two people arrived, not where one person started from. One mile at a time on that journey, and it would start when Effie was somehow a legitimate target, and he would ask her if they could ever be more than friends. He had done so innumerable times in his imagination, inventing replies that ranged from a snorted "With *you?*" to a breathless "At last—take me now, my shy young hero among men." But to be more than friends, they had to become friends in the first place.

"I hope you got Mr. Motley home safely," she said stiffly, when Mallard had dropped behind for a moment to observe a widgeon on the St. James's Park lake.

Asking about Ben? Bad start. That is entertainment my bosom likes not. "He was fine after a cup of tea and a lie down," Oliver admitted.

"It's so refreshing to meet a man who doesn't need to disguise his sensitivity. He offered to photograph me, you know."

"I'll bet he did," muttered Oliver. "He hasn't had a policewoman up to his studio."

"I think I'll take him up on the offer. It might amuse my friends and family."

Oliver stopped, aghast. "Oh, Effie . . . I mean, excuse me, Sergeant. Are you sure you want to do that?"

"It sounds a most interesting project," Effie remarked, the way Queen Victoria might have commented on high-definition television. She kept walking, smiling privately at the hint of jealousy she had detected.

"But to be seen that way . . ." spluttered Oliver, trotting after her. He tried to picture it. Then he tried to not picture it. "By everybody. I just . . . I don't think it's right for you."

Effie looked indignant. "It's the highest compliment Mr. Motley could pay me, I would have thought, although I am not myself a Catholic."

"What about your reputation?"

It was Effie's turn to stop. "Mr. Swithin," she said primly, switching on the Strongitharm Look. She'd spared him during his monologue on virgins the previous evening because she knew Mallard wanted to hear his explanation of the symbols, but really. . . . "If you think that appearing as the Virgin Mary in one of Mr. Motley's *tableaux vivants* can damage my reputation, then you must have a very unflattering opinion of me."

"The Virgin Mary," Oliver echoed with relief, remembering the new project that Ben had mentioned the previous evening. "Oh, that's all right. I'm sorry, I was thinking of you having sex!" he continued with a beatific smile. Effie stared at him without speaking, turned her Look up three hundred per cent, and stalked off toward an empty, shaded bench beside the lake. Oliver followed, still smiling contentedly.

When Mallard took his place between them a minute later, it was with a wry comment about the generous amount of space they had left him.

"Let's understand one thing immediately," he continued. "I am the Law around these parts, and in that capacity, I choose to use Oliver as a consultant for the next thirty minutes."

"Great, do I get a badge?"

"You'll get a thick ear if you don't tell us all about the stars."

Oliver opened the time-worn, leather school satchel in which he habitually carried a book and a folding umbrella and very little else. He took out a sheet of lined paper, covered in symbols, and spread it on his lap.

"I copied this from the dictionary. Each of the signs of the zodiac has a symbol, which is used in casting horoscopes. There are signs for the sun, moon, and planets too. The three symbols we've seen so far were Pisces on Monday, Aquarius on Tuesday, and Capricorn yesterday."

"Now, you said these were in sequence, which enabled you to guess at Capricorn."

"Yes. But this is weird. Aries is traditionally regarded as the first sign of the astrological year, even though it covers the months of March and April these days. Pisces, our first murder, is actually the last sign. And the sequence—Pisces, Aquarius, Capricorn—is going *backwards* through the year."

"What's the next sign?"

Oliver consulted his paper. "In reverse order, Sagittarius."

"Anything else you've spotted?"

"That's it."

Mallard stretched self-indulgently. "I've been reading up about serial killers. One thing they have in common—as well as being intelligent, solitary, and principally male, so with due deference to Effie, I'm going to refer to the killer as a 'him'—is that there's a link between their victims that often points to their motivation. A man who feels sexually inadequate may target prostitutes. The man who believes he was held back in life because of his social class may choose middle-class college girls. And it's not unusual for him to send letters, or notes, or signs—usually to the police—crowing about his success. But serial killers are generally caught by getting a lead on an individual crime rather than by trying to fathom these crazy messages or by anticipating their patterns. That's why I have a team of a dozen detectives back at the Yard going over the little evidence we have and making all the necessary inquiries, and I need to get back to them fairly soon. Now, if you're right, Oliver, and if we have a serial killer who plans to keep to the same schedule, somebody is going to die today and have a Sagittarius sign attached to him. Unfortunately, that's all we can conclude."

"You mentioned a link between a serial killer's victims," said Oliver. "Clearly, the three victims we've encountered aren't all prostitutes or college girls. But is there anything else?"

"That's what I was hoping we might find out." Mallard turned to his sergeant. "What do we know, Effie? Effie?"

Effie, at the far northeast end of the bench, had been staring distractedly at Buckingham Palace across the lake. She was worried. For the first time since she had perfected the Look at age sixteen, after a long-haired classmate had single-handedly unclipped her brassiere through her school blouse at a carol concert (he had entered a seminary shortly afterwards), her defense mechanism seemed to have failed. Oliver hadn't cringed. In fact, his inane grin had only broadened since their unfortunate conversation. Hearing Mallard call her name, she started and swiftly pulled several lime-green cardboard folders from her capacious shoulder bag.

"The lady at Sloane Square was called Nettie Clapper," she reported quickly, reading from one of the files. "She lived in Harold Wood in Essex. She was sixty-two years old, a part-time home help, married, with five grown children, none of them residing with her. I spoke to her husband yesterday evening—he's a retired bricklayer. He says she got a telephone call on Monday evening telling her that a distant relative had died and left her a large sum of money. What sounded like a man's voice said she had to go to a solicitor's office in the Sloane Square area the next morning. Nettie was very enthusiastic, Mr. Clapper said, because they'd just moved to Harold Wood from Brentford, and they could use the money for decorating their new home."

"Our man knows how to push the right buttons," Mallard remarked sadly.

"Later that night," Effie continued, "this note was pushed through their door."

She passed over a photocopy of a sheet of A4 typing paper, on which a few lines had been printed in Helvetica type:

Further to this evening's phone conversation, please meet me tomorrow at Sloane Square Underground Station at 9:15 A.M. I'll show you the way to our offices. I'll recognize you.

"Nettie didn't take the note with her, and because she was being met at the station, she didn't get the address of the supposed offices, either. Mr. Clapper doesn't remember the name of the person who called, or even if he gave a name."

"I suppose the husband's clean?"

"Oh yes. The CID started a thorough investigation, because we thought it was a one-off murder. Mr. Clapper had a confirmed alibi, and Mrs. Clapper didn't have an enemy in the world."

"All right, what do we know about last night's Tropical House high-diver?"

Effie changed files. "Mark Sandys-Penza, aged forty-two,

married with two young children. His second marriage. Had his own estate agency in Richmond. Detective Sergeant Moldwarp's done some checking and he gets a few suggestions of shady property dealings and the suspicion of a mistress."

"Hardly a likely reason for murder," said Mallard. "Go on."

"He apparently got a phone call at home on Tuesday night, asking him to meet a potential new client, who wanted to be anonymous for a while. The letter we found on him, which confirmed the appointment, was delivered at his office yesterday morning."

"Anybody remember who delivered it?"

She shook her head. Mallard turned to Oliver, who had been wondering how far he could run his fingers through Effie's hair before they became hopelessly entangled in her curls. "Want to tell us about Sir Harry Random?" he asked.

Oliver cleared his throat and attempted to concentrate. "Well-known writer, seventy-eight years old, widowed twice with two grown-up children, a son and a daughter, one from each marriage. The daughter still lived with him in Barnes. I would imagine that the killer knew about our Snark Hunt on Sunday night. How else would he expect Sir Harry to be up so early in the morning? I have no idea when Harry got that letter I found, nor what he was expecting from the meeting. Lorina didn't mention it either."

"Lorina?" Effie queried. Why was Oliver still articulate? By now, he should be remembering the time his godmother spotted him scanning a naturist magazine at a station bookstall.

"Harry's daughter," Mallard told her. "An old flame of Oliver's," he added mischievously, watching his nephew shudder. Effie chose not to react.

"So we have an eminent writer, a home help, and an estate agent," Mallard continued. "Not much in common there."

"Maybe their residence has something to do with it," Effie speculated. "Until the Clappers moved recently, all the victims lived in west London—the Pisces in Barnes, the Aquarius in Brentford, and the Capricorn in Richmond."

"Probably just a coincidence," said Mallard, yawning. "But put it all in the computer, Effie, and see what comes up."

They paused while a uniformed nanny pushed an enormous perambulator along the path in front of them. A large head in an oversize baby's bonnet poked up momentarily, and then ducked again. Oliver rubbed his eyes, trying to convince himself that he had not seen a thick ginger moustache above the pacifier jammed into the baby's mouth. Mallard and Effie had not noticed.

"What if there's a connection, but not between the victims?" asked Oliver suddenly.

"Come again."

"What if the connection in each case is actually with the killer's signature? Effie—Sergeant, I mean—you just referred to the victims as the Pisces, the Aquarius, and the Capricorn. Could those actually be their birth signs?"

Mallard absorbed the idea. Then, without a word, he turned to Effie and nodded to her to consult her files again.

"Nettie Clapper was born on the twentieth of January, 1932," she reported. "And Mark Sandys-Penza's birthday was Christmas Eve. We don't have a file on Sir Harry Random, because it was never a murder investigation. Do you know Sir Harry's birthday, Mr. Swithin?"

Oliver liked the way his name sounded on Effie's soft lips. "He was born on the twenty-ninth of February," he told them. "A leap-year baby."

"So what are their birth signs?" asked Mallard.

Oliver shrugged. "Search me, I never look at those things."

"Effie?"

"I refuse to follow the foolishness of horoscopes, Chief."

Mallard sighed with irritation. "Well, do you two skeptics know your own signs? Maybe one of the victims was born about the same time."

"My birthday's the first of March and I'm a Pisces," Effie said. "So that would make Sir Harry one, too."

"One match, at least. Oliver?"

"I was born in August, on the cusp between Leo and Virgo."

"Typically pretentious answer and no bloody help at all," Mallard complained.

"It's not my fault. Half the horoscopes put me at the tail end of Leo and half at the very beginning of Virgo."

"I thought you never looked at those things," Mallard sneered. "You must be one sign or the other. It depends on the year you were born. And when's my birthday, Oliver? Not that you've remembered any time during the last twenty-five years."

"I don't know, Uncle."

"Fifth of June and I'm a Gemini. So that's no good." Mallard thought for a second. "There's an old song called 'Jesus was a Capricorn.' So if Sandys-Penza was born on Christmas Eve, he's probably a Capricorn, too. Another potential match. And Nettie Clapper's birthday falls between the others, so I'll lay odds she's an Aquarius. It looks like you may be right again, Ollie. Excuse me for not leaping up and down and shouting 'Hallelujah!' but it still doesn't help us much."

"Thanks to Mr. Swithin, we know the next victim's birth-sign," Effie conceded. "That limits him or her to only a twelfth of the population."

"Maybe, but we can hardly put out a stop press horoscope: If you're a Sagittarius, avoid meetings with tall, dark strangers brandishing lead pipes."

They paused again while the large perambulator made its return journey past their bench. Mallard smiled politely at the nanny and turned to help Effie collect the files. So only Oliver saw the nanny grope in her handbag for the baby's bottle and thrust it under the pram's hood. Was it a trick of the sunlight, or did the liquid in the bottle seem amber in color? And was that an anchor tattooed on the nursemaid's somewhat hairy forearm?

"There *must* be another reason why the killer is choosing these particular victims," Mallard continued thoughtfully, as the oversized vehicle trundled away toward Buckingham Palace. "Could they have all worked together at some time, for example? Or could they have all been witnesses to the same event?"

"If the pattern persists, we're going to have one victim for each of the twelve signs of the zodiac," said Oliver. "I'm no mathematician, but I would think there's a pretty low probability that twelve co-workers or twelve witnesses—that is, twelve people taken at random, at least in terms of their birthdays—should each be born under a different sign of the zodiac."

"One in eighteen thousand, six hundred and fourteen," said Effie idly, fixing her gaze on a Canada goose that had settled on the bank of the lake opposite them. The two men stared at the policewoman and then at each other. Finally, Mallard cleared his throat.

"So you're saying the probability of any group of twelve people representing all twelve zodiac signs is so small that we can probably write off any other connection between the victims?"

"Not exactly," Effie replied. "It depends how big a group

you have to choose from. You can probably find a representative of each of the twelve signs quite easily in, say, a large company, or a church, or the same street. It gets harder as the original group gets smaller, hardest of all when you only have twelve to choose from in the first place, such as the twelve apostles or the Dirty Dozen. And maybe there aren't going to be twelve murders. Maybe the killer's already finished. The odds of any three specific people, such as the three of us sitting here, having adjacent zodiac signs is much smaller."

"What are they?"

"Only one in one hundred and forty-four. And they get even better if you choose your three from a bigger group." She smiled at them, and Oliver caught his breath. Wonderful nostrils, he decided. How do Aquarians match up to Leo-Virgo cusps?

"Well, I can't afford to assume the killer's finished," said Mallard blandly. "And I still can't help thinking that there's something else to these deaths. The murderer is going to a lot of trouble for what seems quite an easy pattern. Using the zodiac as the secret code—it's almost trite."

He stopped, and they sat in silence, watching the goose. She ambled reproachfully into the water and turned her back on them.

"Everyone's a critic," stated Mallard. "I have to go back to the Yard. Effie, why don't you and Oliver continue to ponder this through an early lunch.' "

"No, I'll come with you," she replied swiftly. "I can start getting this personal information into the computer." She stood up and hoisted the shoulder bag into place. Mallard gave a long and elaborate shrug behind her back. This annoyed Oliver, who felt quite capable of arranging his own social calendar.

"I have an errand to run for my employer, anyway," he claimed, although Mallard knew he was lying; in the two years Oliver had worked for Woodcock and Oakhampton, they had never asked him to perform any task except to greet visitors—who never came—and answer the telephone—which never rang for business purposes.

"Then give us an hour and a half and join us at the Yard."

But an hour and a half later, Detective Superintendent Tim Mallard and Detective Sergeant Effie Strongitharm were not to be found in New Scotland Yard's offices.

"Sagittarius?" Mallard asked, as he squeezed into the hastily erected tent.

"We haven't found any label or card yet," Effie replied, stepping back from the body. She had arrived ten minutes earlier, leaping up from her desk the moment the message flashed on her computer screen. "But the situation is unusual enough. Sagittarius is the sign of the Archer. It's not every day you find someone killed with a bow and arrow in the middle of Piccadilly Circus."

She hummed the opening fanfare from the old "Robin Hood" television series. The young pathologist looked up from the body and smiled in a way that irritated her. "Robin Hood used a longbow," he said suavely. "This is a crossbow bolt. Think William Tell, instead. A little Rossini, perhaps, Sergeant?"

"I heard that the definition of an intellectual is someone who can hear the *William Tell* Overture and *not* think of the Lone Ranger," Mallard remarked, to cover Effie's bewilderment. He knew her tastes ran more to techno-funk than opera seria. "Come, Sergeant Strongitharm, let's give the good doctor some room to practice his craft."

They took one more look at the victim—a stout man in his thirties, sprawled face down on the enclosed patch of pavement, the bolt protruding from the back of his neck—and stepped outside the hot and crowded tent.

"Mr. Swithin's notes said the symbol for Sagittarius is an arrow with a short line drawn across the shaft," Effie said.

"It'll turn up," muttered Mallard. "I can feel it."

The police had cleared the tear-shaped peninsula of pavement in front of Lillywhite's store, driving curious onlookers from the steps around the statue of Eros. The scores of aimless tourists and unemployed locals in Piccadilly Circus, many of the men bare-chested in the unremitting heat of early September, had crossed the street, where their view of the tent was partly blocked by stranded vehicles. Yellow and red carrier bags from Tower Records caught the sun, making the scene look like the daubs of a color-blind pointillist. Every window around the Circus—at least, those that weren't covered by the massive hoardings—had a figure leaning out, waiting for the tent to come down and for the corpse to make its reappearance.

Mallard, one of the few figures on the empty pavement, stared out at the thousands of expectant faces. "Since we have so great a cloud of witnesses . . ." he whispered.

"Actually, we have one very good witness," said Effie, who rather enjoyed the theatrical aspects of her job. "A man who was talking to the victim when he was shot. Hit. Stabbed. Bolted."

"Shot will do."

Effie led Mallard to the curbside, where several eyewitnesses to the murder were leaning against an unmarked police car. She gently pulled one man aside, out of earshot of the others, and introduced him as Edmund Tradescant.

"They say that if you stand in Piccadilly Circus long enough, you're bound to meet somebody you know," remarked Tradescant sadly. He was a well-dressed, clean-shaven man in his late forties. "But you don't expect him to be killed in front of you," he added.

"You're saying you knew the victim?" Mallard echoed.

"Oh, yes. He was a colleague of mine. We both work for the same pharmaceutical company. I was very surprised to see him here. Gordon's from our research division in Yorkshire, a bit of a recluse."

"Gordon . . . ?

"Sorry, Gordon Paper."

"And he lived in Yorkshire, you say?"

"Yes, just outside Richmond."

"He'd never lived in London?"

"Never, as far as I know."

"Not west London."

Tradescant shook his head. "He hated anything that wasn't Yorkshire. He had a complete laboratory in his home, which he'd converted from an old windmill. You couldn't get him out of it, so the firm let him work from home. You see, Superintendent, Gordon Paper suffered from acute travel sickness. Couldn't take a bus ride without losing his lunch. That's what he was working on—a cure for travel sickness, with himself as his guinea pig. A fruitless task, of course, but some of the by-products of his research are our best-sellers. In pure economic terms, he'll be a terrible loss to the company." He winced. "Sorry, that's an appalling way to look at it, of course."

"Tell us exactly what happened."

Tradescant collected his thoughts. "I had an appointment to meet someone here, and as I was waiting, I caught sight of Gordon, strolling along in front of the statue. I called to him and started to walk over. He turned, but as he did so there was a whizzing sound, a thud, and he plunged forward into my arms. I lost my balance and fell over backward. I'm afraid I just lay there until someone else lifted him off me."

"Very distressing for you, sir," said Mallard with sincerity. "So Mr. Paper didn't have the chance to tell you why he was here?"

"He didn't say a word. It was over so quickly."

The pathologist emerged from the unsteady wigwam behind them and signaled to Mallard that he was ready to talk. Mallard nodded.

"Thank you, Mr. Tradescant," he said to the other man. "You've been a great help."

Tradescant frowned. "Is that it? I'd like to help more, of course. Gordon was a good man. A little odd, in his way, but harmless. Certainly unworthy of this sort of end."

"That's all for now," Mallard continued. "Leave us a phone number."

"Don't you want to know if he had any enemies, or that sort of thing?"

"No, sir."

"Old scores to settle, long-standing feuds? Although I can't think of any, I may add."

"No, thank you, sir."

He stared from Mallard to Effie and back again.

"Don't you want to know *anything* more about him?" he whispered incredulously.

"Well, there is one thing . . ." Effie said.

"Yes?"

"What sign was he?"

"Sign?"

"Sign of the zodiac."

Tradescant's mouth dropped open. "I don't know," he stammered.

"Ah, modern police methods," said Mallard brightly to Effie as they moved away from the baffled witness. "Poor Mr. Tradescant probably thinks we read our tea leaves and rub a rabbit's foot before setting out on an investigation."

Effie chuckled. The pathologist thought this was a smile of greeting and gave her a casual salute, pivoting one finger beside his forehead. Effie contemplated turning on the Look, but a moment of self-doubt caused her to hesitate.

"Killed by the crossbow bolt, obviously, which ended up in the brain stem," the doctor reported, unaware of how readily he could have been made to remember an incident with a staff nurse and a bedpan. "Crossbows pack quite a punch, as I'm sure you know, but the bolt didn't penetrate very far. This leads me to conclude that it was fired from a distance, and so lost a lot of its momentum in flight."

"Estimates?"

"I need to consult a few files. We don't come across medieval weaponry too often in this game, Superintendent. But it could have been as far as four or five hundred feet. Judging from where the victim was standing, with his back to the street, the bolt may have been fired from any of the buildings on the far side of the Circus, probably with a slightly downward trajectory."

Mallard scanned the facades of the buildings around him, about three hundred feet away. To the left, the old Swan and Edgar building, its arched windows flaming with the red neon of Tower Records. Then, beyond the start of Regent Street's curving Quadrant, the County Fire Office building—several windows there. Another break for the angular arrival of Glasshouse Street, then more buildings designed in the typical London fricassee of Palladian and Beaux-Arts, which quickly and mercifully disappeared behind a mosaic of neon billboards, drab and dirty in the bright sunlight. A gap for Shaftesbury Avenue and finally one side of the triangular London Pavilion, with waxwork rock stars waving incongruously from the balconies of its classical frontage.

"Must have been a damn good shot to hit his man bang on target, allowing for the loss of power," he commented. "Could it have been nearer? From a bus, perhaps?"

"A bolt fired that close wouldn't have been stopped by the mere presence of a skull," replied the young doctor. "You're dealing with rather a splendid marksman, Superintendent. Someone I'd like to take shooting myself some time. Do you shoot?"

"Only nephews," Mallard said with a perfunctory smile. He had caught sight of Oliver attempting to talk his way past a policeman.

"When I got to the Yard, they said you were here," Oliver panted as Mallard waved him through. "I came as fast as I could. The traffic's at a standstill, so it was quicker to dallow my way through the Park to Piccadilly. Is it Sagittarius?"

"It could be. Shot with a crossbow, probably from the other side of the Circus, so there's some connection with the Archer. There's been no sign left, however, and we don't know yet where the killer was stationed."

"I may have an answer to that," said Oliver humbly. "Can I try something, Uncle?"

The superintendent shrugged. "Be my guest," he said blandly.

Oliver stalked over to the tent, which was now being dismantled by two uniformed constables, sweating in the heat. The body had already been spirited into an ambulance, but the noisy and nosy crowd showed no sign of thinning. Mallard watched his nephew scuttle around on the pavement, shifting position from side to side and looking all the time across the Circus. Then he bobbed up and down a few times on the same spot, and squinted harder into the distance, shielding his eyes with the flat of his hand.

"He's not from your side of the family, is he?" Effie asked quietly as Oliver scurried back to them.

"Do you have any officers searching those buildings?" he asked, pointing at the wall of pinstriped neon opposite. Mallard nodded. "Then ask them to look on the roof right where that dormer pops up," Oliver continued. "Above the sign advertising Foster's Lager."

Effie relayed the instructions to the scene-of-crime officer, who spoke quietly into his radio. The three waited in silence, observed still by the public from behind the barriers.

"I heard you people sometimes used psychics," remarked Edmund Tradescant. He had been watching Oliver's antics curiously, as if trying to relate them to the apparent police interest in astrology, and now wandered over to Effie. "Does he possess some kind of sixth sense?"

"No, Mr. Tradescant," Effie claimed, "Mr. Swithin has quite enough trouble with the basic five." She returned to monitoring the portable walkie-talkie.

"Some things do seem to be more than coincidence, though," Tradescant continued. "This is the second person I've known in a week who's been killed in a public place. Poor Gordon here in Piccadilly Circus, and last Monday there was Harry Random in Trafalgar Square."

"Oh, you knew Sir Harry Random," said Mallard, with interest, well aware by now that the two deaths were more than a coincidence.

"Only slightly. We once served together—"

"They found it," said Effie suddenly. "Bring it over," she shouted into the radio as Tradescant wandered away again. A figure on the rooftop opposite waved something once and then disappeared from view. Mallard made a mental note to see if any of the other victims had served in the military, and turned on his nephew.

"Okay, Oliver, talk," he commanded. Oliver indicated the statue.

"Sagittarius the archer," he said. "There's a very famous archer."

They followed his pointing finger. On a slim pedestal,

balanced delicately on one foot, the epicene and nearly naked figure of a boy was aiming a bow and arrow almost directly at them.

"Eros," breathed Mallard. "Of course."

"Actually, it's not really supposed to be Eros," said Oliver smugly. "It represents the Angel of Christian Charity, in honor of Lord Shaftesbury. Funny how a Christian image so quickly became distorted in popular imagination into a pagan god . . ." He trailed off, catching Mallard's long-suffering expression.

"So you think the killer was using the statue of Eros as his sign this time?" Effie asked.

"Not exactly. I think we'll still find the written sign, just like before. In this case, the killer couldn't tie it to the crossbow bolt—it would throw off the trajectory. No, I believe he wanted to make it look as if Eros himself killed the unfortunate Sagittarius. So I simply guessed he would take up a position more or less in a direct line with the statue's aim. Our killer has a sense of humor."

"They're the worst kind," mumbled Mallard.

Two policemen pushed their way briskly through the crowd and stepped into the arena. One of them carried a black plastic bag, containing something rigid and vaguely cruciform. He opened it slightly, showing Mallard the stock of a high-powered crossbow. Taped on the polished wood was a plain white index card with the Sagittarius symbol drawn in blue ink.

"You know, Oliver," said Mallard reflectively, leaning over the rim of the Trafalgar Square fountain and staring blankly into the rippling water, "I'm starting to feel like a child watching a conjuror."

They had needed somewhere more private than the roped-off crime scene in Piccadilly Circus, and Oliver had suggested the short walk to Trafalgar Square. The fountain where Sir Harry Random had died three days earlier was far enough from the road for their voices to be heard above the relentless fanfare of car horns.

"You bring out each of your predictions like a fluttering dove from a silk handkerchief," Mallard continued, "leaving Effie and me gaping in the audience and asking 'how did he do that?' I don't think this is a dignified feeling for a Scotland Yard detective. I have to remind myself constantly that I'm the professional, and you're a mere half-wit who writes about ferrets and field mice. So let's agree to tell your old uncle and that nice Sergeant Strongitharm everything you know about this case. Right now. Before I ask Effie to bite you in the limb of her choice."

"That won't be necessary," said Oliver with a grin, "although it's certainly a tempting offer."

Effie prepared her countenance for the Look, but paused. What if it failed again? And was that such a terrible thing to say, after all? It may have been meant as a compliment. Anyway, Mallard had started it.

"We know the victims are chosen because of their birthdays," Oliver was saying, "but we all had the feeling there was more to these murders than just birthdays. And yet as each murder takes place, the odds against finding any other link between the victims increase considerably."

"Twelvefold," murmured Effie.

"We've even lost the connection with west London," said Mallard. "The late Sagittarian lived in Yorkshire."

"Well, over lunch, I decided to forget about the victims, apart from their birth signs, and I started thinking more about the murders themselves," Oliver continued. "Why does the killer make these elaborate arrangements? It seemed like a rather ridiculous and macabre game of Consequences, with each player writing in an outlandish time or place or way of killing. Why otherwise did the meeting with Harry Random take place at six o'clock in the morning? Why did the murderer entice poor Mrs. Clapper all the way from Harold Wood to Sloane Square to kill her? And what was the significance of making Mr. Sandys-Penza jump from the roof of the greenhouse? Well, I think I've found *three* possible links, which explain these oddities, and the answer does lie in the stars. The zodiac doesn't just predict *who* is murdered. It decides *how* the victim is killed and *where* the murder takes place."

"Colonel Mustard with the lead pipe in the ballroom," mused Mallard, remembering an earlier conversation. "It *is* just like that board game."

"Only in this case, the who is the victim, not the murderer."

Mallard nodded slowly, chewing on his lower lip. "So today," he said, "we have a man whose birth sign is Sagittarius—that's *who*—shot with a bow and arrow—that's *how*—in front of the most famous statue of an archer in the city, perhaps in the world—and that's *where*."

"But does it work for the others, Oliver?" asked Effie excitedly. It was the first time she had used his first name. Oliver couldn't see her because of the fountain's spray on his glasses, but he hoped she was smiling encouragingly at him.

"I raised the question as to why poor Harry had his meeting at six o'clock in the morning," he said. "But if you want to push someone into the fountain in Trafalgar Square and get away with it, then the early hours of a bank holiday morning are surely the best time."

"Sir Harry was a Pisces," said Effie. "How does that connect to Trafalgar Square?"

"Fish," replied Oliver. He began to walk around the edge of the fountain.

"No fish in there," muttered Mallard as he followed his

nephew. Oliver stopped beside one of the gushing water-spouts near the fountain's perimeter, a brawny merman wielding two sea creatures. They had noticed it on Monday, when Mallard had wondered if it had been the accidental cause of Sir Harry Random's death.

"I found Harry floating in this part of the fountain. Look at the statue." Oliver pointed to the merman. "The water comes out of the fish that he's holding."

"That's where. What about how?"

"Isn't drowning rather closely related to fish?"

"Okay, the pattern works for Pisces, too," Mallard admitted. "But then what about the Aquarian, the sign of the water-bearer?" Effie slapped him mildly on the arm.

"Come on, Tim, it's obvious now," she said. "Nettie Clapper was clubbed with a lead pipe, which is used for plumbing. It's a water-bearer. And this happened almost underneath a large aqueduct that carries the River Westbourne. A perfect water-bearer. And you were so rude about that nice Mr. Noss, the station master," Effie added, with mock deprecation.

"As always, Effie, an ounce of your charm is never wasted," Mallard admitted gallantly. Oliver found himself wishing she would waste a little charm on him, too. About a lifetime's worth.

"So what about Capricorn the Goat, Oliver?" she was asking. His name again!

"Mark Sandys-Penza plunged to his death from a height when leaping around high places, just like a mountain goat," he explained. "As the killer's note reminds us, this happened in the Tropical House in Kew Gardens, which gets its name from the Tropic of Cancer and . . . the Tropic of *Capricorn*."

They fell silent. A passing Japanese tourist photographed them.

"Who and how and where," Mallard repeated contentedly. "And it's when, too, because he's kept to a daily routine so far."

"Is this more the level of complexity you were looking for, Chief?" Effie asked.

"It might give us a chance of predicting where tomorrow's murder will take place," he replied. "We just have to think like the murderer. What's the next sign on the list?"

"Scorpio," said Oliver and Effie together. "The sign of the Scorpion," Oliver added unnecessarily. Mallard sighed.

"Okay, Oliver, where do we find a scorpion in London?"

Five

EVER SINCE HE WAS four years old, when an attempt to feed a Mivvi to a grouchy donkey on the beach at Llandudno had led to fifteen stitches and a tetanus shot, Geoffrey Angelwine had been terrified of horses. The word *gymkhana* alone could bring him out in a sweat. So when Oliver arrived home that evening with his second take-away curry in twenty-four hours, he was intrigued to find his friend wearing knee-high riding boots and clutching a crop. At least, he assumed it was Geoffrey whose head was hidden in the cupboard under the kitchen sink, but not being skilled at recognizing him from his posterior (unlike Geoffrey's employers, Hoo, Watt & Eidenau, who used it frequently for metaphorical target practice), Oliver conceded that the kneeling figure could also have been a burglar disguised as a silent film director, taking a nefarious crack at the Harpic.

Oliver quietly placed his food on the kitchen table and waited. Geoffrey stayed frozen on his knees for another thirty seconds, and then lashed out suddenly with the riding crop. A baking dish flew out of the cupboard and scuttled across the kitchen floor like an overexcited tortoise.

"Damn," he exclaimed in a muffled voice.

"What are you doing?" Oliver asked brightly. There was a thump, such as may be made by a junior public relations executive lifting his head in a startled manner and forgetting about the sink's U-trap three inches above it.

"Damn," Geoffrey repeated, a little more poignantly, as he emerged from the cupboard and stood up groggily, rubbing his head. His hands were swaddled in mismatched oven mitts.

"Lost your horse?" Oliver inquired, taking his curry out of the carrier bag and sitting down.

"Very funny," mumbled Geoffrey crossly. He stared suddenly at the plastic bag on the table. "Did you check that?" he asked.

"What do you mean, check it? It's only had my dinner in it."

Geoffrey strode stiffly to the table, unable to bend his ankles in the unyielding boots, and swatted the empty bag several times with his riding crop. Then he peered gingerly inside.

"All clear," he said with relief.

"I realize the Taj Mahal Restaurant may not always specify the kind of meat they put in their curries," Oliver commented, "but you can usually assume the beast is dead."

Geoffrey pointed at him dramatically with the crop. "You may laugh at me," he said, although Oliver had never required permission before, "but that's just how scorpions can get in."

"Oh, scorpions," replied Oliver carelessly. Geoffrey must

have heard the radio broadcast. "I thought you were re-hearsing some extreme form of safe sex."

The broadcast had been Mallard's idea. He had smuggled Oliver into New Scotland Yard earlier that afternoon, secreting him in a small conference room with Effie and with instructions to find a scorpion somewhere in the capital. Then he had disappeared. So Oliver and Effie had stalked scorpions through every reference book on London in the Yard's library, but no arachnid had waved its venomous tail at them from the pages. "And the irritating thing," he had said several times, "is that I can remember seeing a statue or a bas-relief somewhere that had a scorpion in it. But I have no idea where, or even if it was in London."

Mallard's abrupt return two hours later, armed with a portable radio, caused Effie to take her feet off the table hurriedly and smooth her skirt, which peeved Oliver. He had been enjoying the growing spirit of informality that had led her to shed her shoes and prop her long legs on the conference table. (He had also enjoyed the legs themselves.) But he was even more peeved after hearing the news bulletin, which Mallard smugly professed to have written.

"Before the main points of the news," the announcer had articulated, using the same cadence for each sentence, "we have a special announcement from the Metropolitan Police. Listeners in the Greater London area are asked to look out for scorpions, which are poisonous insects found in many parts of the world, and which can be highly dangerous to humans. Several scorpions have been spotted in London recently, so exercise extreme caution, especially when opening parcels or food packaging. If you see a scorpion, please call 999 immediately."

Mallard's mistake had been to ask Oliver what he thought. The superintendent's pride of authorship give way to doubt when his astounded nephew painted a vivid picture of terrified Londoners in Wellington boots wielding cricket bats as they rooted through their larders and wardrobes, flooding police switchboards with reports of scorpions in the supermarkets, scorpions on the Underground, scorpions driving buses, and giant twelve-legged scorpions dancing the Watusi on the M25.

". . . and at least one lunatic will claim to have been forced to make love to a flying saucer full of large-breasted, green Venusian scorpions," Oliver spluttered in conclusion.

"Besides, scorpions aren't insects," Effie added serenely, returning to her reference book.

"We'll call off the warning tomorrow, of course," Mallard had muttered defensively. "We'll say it was a hoax." But Geoffrey's antics had confirmed Oliver's worst fears.

"You'll thank me when you wake up in the morning *not* all black and swollen and dead," Geoffrey was saying. "I've just spent an hour going through every kitchen cupboard, looking for signs of the ghastly creatures."

"Did you find any?"

"No, but I did find your missing cummerbund. I suppose it'll have to be dry cleaned. Now, you can check your room, and Ben can do the downstairs toilet, when he's finished his latest photo shoot."

Oliver had noticed the drumming of bed castors on floorboards, coming from Ben Motley's studio. He could now hear a faint whimpering, almost a giggling, wafting down the stairs and through the open kitchen door.

"Any idea who . . . ?" he ventured.

"I think we're honored by royalty again," said Geoffrey distractedly. He was glaring at the linoleum under his feet, as if the pattern might at any moment sprout claws and a stinger.

"Where did the riding boots come from?" Oliver asked.

"I found them in Susie's room. I don't think they're hers,

though, because they're too big, even for me. I had to stuff them with newspapers. Great protection against scorpions, eh?"

"Did you check inside before you put them on?" Oliver asked innocently. Geoffrey's beady eyes widened as far as the physical limitations of his eyelids would allow. Then, without a word, he dropped to the floor and began to tug frantically at his left boot, with little success.

"Oh dear Lord, I can feel them! I knew I should have worn two pairs of socks," he cried. Oliver decided the time had come to end his friend's anxiety.

"Look, about those scorpions . . ." he began, but was interrupted by the rattle of footsteps on the uncarpeted stairs. Next moment, Ben hurtled into the kitchen, consternation on his handsome face.

"You've seen one!" panted Geoffrey from the floor, his cheeks already flushed from his exertions. Ben ignored him.

"Quick, Ollie, tell me a joke!" he gasped.

"A joke?" echoed Oliver. "I can never remember jokes."

"You must remember at least one!"

"Well, there's this Englishman, Scotsman, and Irishman in the French Revolution . . ."

"Is that the one where the guillotine sticks?" Ben interrupted.

"Oh, you've heard it."

Ben was shaking his head. "No good. It's too long and I've already used it for foreplay. Come with me!"

"What about me?" wailed Geoffrey, rocking on his back as he tried to get a grip on the boot. "My toes are going to sleep. There must be a whole nest of them in there!"

But Ben grabbed Oliver's sleeve and hauled him out of the kitchen, sending a curry-laden fork spinning across the room. Oliver followed his friend up the stairs, aware this was not the time to ask Ben formally if he was a rival for Effie Strongitharm's affections.

"I have a rather important client," Ben whispered as he and Oliver reached the second floor landing. "But she has a peculiar quirk, and that's not a reference to her anatomy. She can only have an orgasm if she's laughing. So I want you to stand outside the door and shout all the jokes you know. We're up to the plateau phase, so I need some raucous belly laughs to finish the assignment. Get to work!"

"But I told you, I can never remember jokes!" Oliver protested, clutching Ben's arm. "The only stuff that comes to mind is that old music hall cross-talk act we learned for a laugh."

Ben paused. A faint chuckling came from the studio. "Then that'll have to do," he conceded. "But don't expect my timing to be perfect. I have f-stops to think of."

"So who is she?" Oliver asked slyly.

"I can't tell you that," whispered Ben as he opened the door. "But let's just say her great-great-great-grandmother-in-law would *not* have been amused."

Five minutes later, when Effie Strongitharm tentatively pushed open the kitchen door, it was to witness a small public relations officer apparently break dancing on the floor, while from upstairs came the noise of a shouted comedy routine being very enthusiastically received by an audience of one female.

"I say, I say, I say!" (Oliver's voice.)

"Yes?" (Ben's voice, a little fainter, after a pause to adjust his focus.)

(Deep exhalation by the woman.)

"Why does the Lord Mayor of London wear red, white, and blue braces?" (Oliver's voice.)

"I don't know, why does the Lord Mayor of London wear red, white, and blue braces?" (Ben's voice.)

(Anticipatory squeals of delight from the woman.)

"To keep his trousers up!" (Oliver's voice in triumph, followed by more raucous female laughter.)

Effie had found four possible reasons for Oliver's apparent immunity to her disapproving gaze: (a) he was too pure at heart to be bothered by it; (b) he was too depraved to care; (c) he was too stupid to notice; or (d) he was short-sighted. For some reason, which she couldn't fully explain to herself, she felt she needed to know the answer, and the only way was to find out more about the young man. So when Mallard muttered that he wanted to give Oliver some information but was too busy hunting scorpions to pick up the telephone, Effie had volunteered to stop by Edwardes Square on her way home to Richmond to pick up a change of clothes. Her immediate impression was that (b) was rapidly supplanting (c).

"I rang the bell but nobody heard me," she said to Geoffrey, who was looking up at her helplessly from the floor. "It's all right, I'm a police officer."

"Then do you know how to get a pair of riding boots off?" Geoffrey pleaded in desperation. "My feet are being eaten by scorpions."

Effie knew how to take control of a situation. She effortlessly picked Geoffrey up by his armpits and threw him into a chair.

"Put your leg out!" she commanded. Geoffrey cautiously extended a limb. Effie grabbed his foot and straddled his leg, keeping her back to him, as if mounting a small, thin Shetland pony.

"I say, I say, I say," wafted down the stairs, with an ostinato of more moans.

"Push against my bottom," Effie commanded, looking back over her shoulder. Geoffrey blushed.

"Why does the Lord Mayor of London wear red, white, and blue braces?"

"Not with your hands, you nitwit. With your other foot."

"To keep his trousers up?"

"Harder. Don't be a wimp."

"No, to stop them falling down!"

Effie shot forward, clutching the empty boot, accompanied by a high-pitched screech from upstairs that subsided into happy chortles. Geoffrey ripped off his sock and inspected his toes.

"Thank God, they're all there," he sighed.

"Of course they are," Effie replied briskly. "There aren't any scorpions. My name's Effie Strongitharm, by the way."

"Geoffrey Angelwine," replied the other, feeling that to shake the policewoman's hand now would only be a step backward in their acquaintanceship. "Oliver's told me about you. No scorpions?"

"Absolutely none. It's all a dodge made up by Tim Mallard. Didn't Oliver tell you?"

"No, he didn't," Geoffrey replied thoughtfully, eyeing the riding crop. They heard voices on the stairs and shortly afterward, the kitchen door swung open.

"So was it good for you?" sniggered Ben, as he and Oliver came in gleefully. They caught sight of Effie and froze.

"Effie!"

"Sergeant Strongitharm!"

She acknowledged their startled greetings with a slow nod of the head. "Good evening, Mr. Motley. How good of you and Oliver to provide some entertainment for poor Mr. Angelwine in his distress." She rested her hand on Geoffrey's shoulder.

"Oh, that, we were just . . ." Oliver attempted, trying to ignore Geoffrey's nauseating smirk. "You see it took two of us . . . I was helping Ben . . ."

"You clearly have hidden talents, Oliver," Effie remarked frostily. "I expect you took your wife to the West Indies for her holiday and your dog has no nose, am I correct?"

"You're looking every bit as charming as last night, Sergeant," cooed Ben, who had recovered more quickly than his friend. "Will you join us for some tea?"

Effie allowed a polite smile to dawn on her face. "It's very tempting, Mr. Motley, but I'm still on duty. I've called to give Oliver a message from Superintendent Mallard," she said, switching her attention to Oliver and her smile off. "Your uncle wanted me to let you know that Gordon Paper was born in July."

"I'm not sure I understand," said Oliver meekly.

"He *wasn't* a Sagittarius."

Oliver's blue eyes opened wide behind his cheap spectacles. "You mean it could have been a coincidence that the first three victims had the correct zodiac signs?" he asked incredulously. "What are the chances of that happening?"

"One in one thousand, seven hundred and twenty-eight," Effie said instantly. "No, Tim doesn't think that was a coincidence. But he's worried that the murderer's stopped being faithful to his pattern, which gave us our only chance of stopping him. After all, if the Sagittarius victim wasn't a Sagittarius, tomorrow's Scorpio victim may not be a Scorpio. And worse, the murder may have nothing to do with scorpions."

"That reminds me, Ollie," Geoffrey piped up. "Will you do something for me?"

"Of course."

"Can you help me get this other boot off?" Geoffrey asked, with a sly glint in his eye. "Effie's just shown me how to do it."

* * *

It was ten o'clock in the morning on the day of Scorpio—the Friday of a week that had begun with Sir Harry Random's death on Monday—and Oliver Swithin was looking quizzically at a scorpion. Maybe. He needed a closer look at the gnarled arabesque, picked out in stark relief by the sunlight strafing the Battenberg-cake brickwork. Oliver cursed his weak eyesight, not for the first time in his life, and leaned further over the stone balustrade.

"Found something?" asked Mallard, strolling down the curving ramp from the Natural History Museum's main entrance. He took a pair of powerful binoculars from the case around his neck.

"There, the stonework on that corbel," said Oliver, pointing to the stone tracery around a second-story window. Mallard trained the binoculars.

"It's not a corbel, it's a capital."

"Never mind the architectural lecture, is it a scorpion's telson?"

"No. Decidedly vegetable, not animal."

"Blast."

Mallard pushed the binoculars back into their case. "Ollie, the museum is crawling—almost literally, in the petrified sense—with carvings of flora and fauna, both inside and outside. I'm sure that somewhere, there's a scorpion. And, incidentally, full of scorpions is my mind, even though I'm an absentee Banquo, not Macbeth. But it doesn't matter—there's not an inch of this building that isn't under the eye of one of my men. Now come inside, it's cooler in there."

Oliver moodily followed his uncle through the basilica-like entrance to the museum and into the expansive, Byzantine space of its main hall. Light flooded in through windows high above them in the hall's barrel vault, giving a soft glow to the biscuit-colored stonework—more restrained than the polychrome exterior but still inclined to outbreaks of blue-gray bruising wherever it contorted into an archway or a groin. The massive space seemed like a cross between a cathedral and a railway station, husbanded by a crazed Victorian zoologist.

Mallard nodded to a group of men, who couldn't have looked more like policemen in plain clothes if they'd studied it at RADA. They were standing uncomfortably beside a Tyrannosaurus skeleton, which made them feel below the statutory height. Effie was not among them, Oliver noted, remembering with disappointment that she was coordinating the stakeout of the Zoo's Insect House, probably still muttering that a scorpion wasn't an insect. He'd rather be there, he decided, although he was feeling less than charitable toward the policewoman since she had found Geoffrey Angelwine's revenge so amusing. It was still painful to sit, but at least Geoffrey had already removed the first boot. Oliver guessed that Effie had been planning to add a few sardonic insults to his injury, but as he saw her to the front door, she had caught sight of the woman who wafted regally down the stairs, through the hallway, and into the waiting Rolls Royce with no license plates. It seemed to subdue her.

"Thanks for dropping by, Oliver," Mallard was saying.

"Well, the office is just around the corner, so I told Mr. Woodcock I was taking a long coffee break," Oliver replied. "He won't mind if I don't hurry back. Do you remember when you brought me here as a treat?"

"I remember," Mallard confirmed. "You were seven. I tried to leave you here as an exhibit, but they wouldn't take you. A small matter of your still being alive. I said I could fix that. I'd even pay for the taxidermist."

They headed for the Arachnid Gallery, which Mallard had already located. Oliver paused once to point out a likely bas-relief on an extrados above their heads, but Mallard scrutinized it carefully and pronounced it a stag beetle. Display cases were mounted on opposite walls of the low, white-washed gallery. Brief visual essays on the personal habits of the scorpion defiantly faced those of its cousin, the spider, like a particularly academic gross-out contest. Several small boys were studying the section on reproduction with great interest, watched gloomily by the burly Detective Sergeant Welkin, who had been scene-of-crime officer at Sloane Square three days earlier, and who was now assigned to Mallard's special zodiac task force. Other detectives were stationed by the museum's displays of scorpion flies and scorpion fish. Welkin saluted Mallard cautiously from the far end of the gallery.

"Gosh, and that's what's loose in London?" one schoolboy was saying.

"Yeah. Only they're bigger than that," replied his friend. "My mum said she didn't want me to come up 'cause I might get bitten."

"They don't bite, they sting. It says so here."

"That's just normal scorpions. The ones they can't find are a special breed. They're as big as sheepdogs."

"I heard they escaped from a mad scientist's laboratory and they're as big as horses."

"Well, I heard they were as big as elephants."

"If they're as big as elephants, the police would have found them by now."

"Not our police. My dad says the coppers today couldn't find a haystack in a haystack. Come on, let's find the ferrets. Maybe they'll have something on Finsbury."

The boys ran noisily out of the gallery, past the glowering Welkin, who for some reason found himself thinking fondly of King Herod. Mallard and Swithin passed at a more leisurely pace and returned to the main hall, which was beginning to fill up with visitors, thankfully escaping the heat outside. Mallard perched on a bench and watched the crowds around the dinosaurs. Many of the humans were wearing thick shoes, and one large woman rustled by in plastic bags secured around her calves with rubber bands.

"Everyone's heard about the scorpions," Oliver noted. He preferred to stand. "Won't the murderer figure out that we're on to him when he hears the radio announcements?"

"That's what I want," claimed Mallard. He took off his glasses and laid them carefully on his knees, lifting his face toward the sunlight. "A serial killer wants to tell the story of his pathetic life, and he does so in the language of death. Murder defines him—it's his art form, his game. Well, I want him to know we're in the game and we're closing on him. Maybe that'll provoke him into a dialogue. It's not unusual for serial killers to write directly to the police or to the media, taunting his chosen adversaries, crowing about his successes, his ingenuity. That would give us more to go on."

"What about those zodiac symbols? Aren't they his messages?"

"Yes. But they're not enough."

A group of lissome female students from Sweden thudded past, wearing loose T-shirts, tight shorts, and oversized green Wellington boots. They walked with their eyes anxiously scanning the smooth mosaic floor. Oliver found the effect strangely endearing. Mallard replaced his glasses.

"I read somewhere that a serial killer's prime goal is celebrity," Oliver said. He scented some post hoc self-justification in Mallard's explanation for the radio broadcast, and it irked him. "Isn't the scorpion scare giving him the publicity he wants?"

"No, because the newspapers don't know about the zodiac theme," Mallard replied, unsure if an appreciative comment about the Scandinavian ladies would get back to his wife via her favorite nephew. "The press know something's going on, but they've agreed to hold off on public speculation in return for the full story when we catch the killer."

"So what *does* the public think? That the deaths were unrelated?"

"Exactly. They think Sir Harry Random's death was an accident. That Nettie Clapper was viciously mugged at Sloane Square. That Mark Sandys-Penza's death in Kew was the result of drunken high spirits. And that Gordon Paper was an organized crime hit."

"Organized crime? With a crossbow?"

"Too many people witnessed that murder. We had to say Paper was the intended victim, or rumors will spread about mad arbalesters picking off people at random. And I have enough to worry about with scorpions. You said yesterday you thought you'd seen a scorpion statue somewhere. Have you remembered where yet?"

"No. Actually, it's more a bas-relief, and I vaguely recall that the main subject was another animal. But does it matter? Effie said that after yesterday's non-Sagittarian Sagittarius, you weren't necessarily counting on a scorpion-related murder today."

"I'm less certain, but it's still all we have to go on. And I'd rather be sitting here watching for scorpions than sitting at the Yard scratching my arse." Mallard stretched self-indulgently, rounding it off with a yawn. "What about tomorrow, though, assuming my lads haven't copped the bastard? Where would a Libra death take place?"

"That's easy," said Oliver. "Libra is the sign of the balance or the scales. And the most famous set of scales in London is in the left hand of the statue of Justice on top of the Central Criminal Court."

"The Old Bailey," said Mallard thoughtfully, giving the

court its more popular name. "Okay, I'll go with that for now. Can you join me there tomorrow, if necessary? It's a Saturday."

"Not until the afternoon. I have a book signing in the morning at a children's bookstore, organized by Geoffrey Angelwine. We're trying to extract the price of a Finsbury book from the kiddiewinks of Richmond. I think Geoffrey's role is to hold them up by the ankles and shake until the half-crowns drop out."

"Geoffrey's going with you?" Mallard asked with apprehension.

"Yes, his agency has finally entrusted him to help with, as they put it, 'flogging the Ferret.' Susie Beamish said it sounded like something Geoffrey should know a lot about."

"You're getting to be quite a celebrity, dear nephew. All right, back to business. What comes after Libra?"

"Virgo is the virgin or maiden. Perhaps that murder will take place in a church dedicated to the Virgin Mary."

"That's location. But how on earth do you kill someone with a virgin?"

"Next is Leo, the Lion."

"There's no shortage of lions in London, which is more than can be said for virgins. There are statues in Trafalgar Square, on the South Bank, on the York Water Gate, over the Royal Mews. There's Red Lion Square and Black Lion Gate. Then there are reliefs, pub signs, door knockers, symbols of livery company or guilds—and any place that flies the royal standard or displays the royal coat of arms."

"And the Zoo," said Oliver, thinking momentarily of Effie at the Regent's Park Insect House. "After Leo comes Cancer, the crab—I hope he doesn't get tasteless with that one. Gemini is the sign of the twins. Taurus is the bull. And finally, Aries . . ."

"The sign of the ram," Mallard concluded. "Then what? Does he go round again?" But Oliver had trailed off for some other reason.

"The bull," he repeated pensively. Then he stood up, staring ahead of him. "It was a bull!" he cried. Several museum-goers turned from the dinosaurs and stared at him.

"Says here it was a stegosaurus," whispered one puzzled child to his mother, who hurried him away from the two men.

"What are you bleating about?" asked Mallard crossly. He hated to wait for explanations. Oliver spun around.

"The sculpture, Uncle. Of the scorpion. I've just remembered what the other animal was. It was a bull. It was a Roman relief featuring a bull being sacrificed. And I think I know where I saw it. I must go." He picked up his battered satchel and headed for the door.

"Wait," called Mallard, "I can get someone to drive you."

"No need," Oliver shouted back. "I'll call you when I find it." His silhouette shimmered in front of the main door, and then was swallowed by the blazing sunlight.

It was only Constable Urchin's second week on the beat, but being an ambitious policeman, he was already baffled.

Last week, I arrested a murder suspect in Trafalgar Square, he would say woefully to himself, and where did it get me? Well, actually, it had got him out of Grunwick's company and off night duty, so it couldn't be all bad. But the fact that the suspect had turned out to be the nephew of a Murder Squad superintendent had been as welcome to his station sergeant as a flasher in a nunnery. When he tried to evaluate the incident, Urchin found the phrase "curate's egg" sprang to mind, and he took mild comfort in knowing the origin and meaning of the expression. Many of his colleagues, he speculated, would have trouble just defining a curate, and Grunwick couldn't even recognize an egg unless it was fried in bacon fat and doused in tomato ketchup.

So was his abrupt posting to Grosvenor Square a step up or another blot on the splattered Urchin escutcheon? (There actually was an Urchin family escutcheon, which had been pristine until he had been sent down from Christ Church after brawling with a militant atheist in Tom Quad on All Saints' Day. Urchin may have been pardoned this display of muscular Christianity, but when he dutifully told the Dean he had been "fighting a liar in the quad," the sensitive academic took it for the famous spoonerism and dismissed the student for cheek.) Urchin found the new beat refined, but still uneventful. Only the stretch that passed the American Embassy offered any relief. Here, in front of Saarinen's uncompromising building, with its golden statue of a bald eagle on the roof, he would occasionally stop for a brief conversation with one of the American guards. And he had spoken twice to a long-legged secretary from Omaha, Nebraska, who claimed she loved his accent. It hadn't yet occurred to him that, because she was in England rather than he in America, his accent was not exactly a competitive advantage.

Urchin was walking past the embassy now, noticing the sun glinting on the eagle's thirty-five-foot-wide wings. He muttered a polite "good morning" to a young woman who was also hovering on this side of the square, by the embassy entrance, as if waiting for someone. She wasn't bad-looking either, Urchin thought as he drifted away. Mid-twenties, blond, good figure, sun tan, thin white cotton sundress to show it off, Fendi handbag, sandals that suggested she had no fear of scorpions. Perhaps he could find some excuse to start a conversation?

He decided to retrace his steps instead of continuing his clockwise circuit of the square. Circling the statue of Eisenhower, he headed back toward the young woman, who was looking anxiously at the embassy's glass doors, although she made no move in their direction.

That's when it happened. A motorcycle that had been idling along the north side of the square abruptly accelerated and hurtled around the corner, heading straight for the woman. Urchin shouted a warning, but she looked the wrong way, staring at him rather than at the approaching vehicle. He pointed frantically behind her. She turned. At last, she started to react, darting toward the embassy for safety.

Urchin saw the motorcycle veer away, the rider's left arm held straight out to the side, holding an oddly shaped gun. As it drew level with the woman, the gloved hand pulled the trigger. But there was no report, even though she started to fall instantly. Urchin hesitated, not knowing whether to dive forward and try to catch her or throw himself into the path of the motorcycle. A second later, he was too late to do either. The rider sped past, out of his reach. A white card fell, fluttering in the sunlight. Then, the motorcycle was gone.

Urchin ran to the woman, who had dropped face down onto the embassy steps. An American guard rushed over.

"Why the hell didn't you shoot him?" he was shouting. "Ah jeez, you guys don't got guns, do you?"

"Did you see where that motorbike went?" Urchin asked calmly, turning the woman gently onto her side and feeling for her carotid artery.

"Nah. Maybe our cameras picked up something." The guard pointed to two security cameras, mounted on either side of the embassy's main entrance. "Hey, what's this?" he continued, as he reached out to a bulky feathered dart that protruded from the young woman's buttock. It had easily penetrated the thin barriers of her dress and underwear, spreading a small, round stain, starkly scarlet on the white fabric, like a poppy on a snowdrift.

111

"Don't touch it!" yelled Urchin, nursing the woman's head.

"Take it easy, man." The guard looked puzzled at the policeman's sudden vehemence. "I ain't gonna hurt her."

"You could hurt yourself. She's dead. And whatever may be leaking from that dart could kill you, too." Urchin laid the body down gently and rolled upright. He called in his report on his lapel radio, including the best description he could manage of the escaping motorcyclist, and then waited, still seated awkwardly and forlornly on the steps. People started to gather, forming a silent ring around the dead woman and the sitting policeman. As the sound of approaching sirens reached the group, Urchin heaved himself to his feet.

"All right, anybody who saw what happened, I want you to stay here," he said wearily. "The rest of you, move along."

The secretary from Omaha came out of the embassy, pushed through the crowd, and draped a blanket over the woman's body. "I was watching you through the window," she said softly to Urchin. "I saw what happened."

"So did I," said the guard. "And I saw the rider drop this. Think it means anything?"

He handed over the white index card that he had retrieved. It had a symbol drawn on it in blue ink—a cursive capital letter M, with an extra twist and an arrow at the bottom of the right-hand vertical. Like a scorpion's sting.

"Oh, yes," said Urchin. "It means something."

Six

THE RIDER DRIFTED INTO view, silently canting around the traffic island, a threatening, monochrome ghost. Slowly, the arm came out, straight and purposeful. The young woman in the white dress began to run, but as the motorcycle drew level with her, she fell, floating down onto the embassy steps. The point of view changed, snatching back two seconds of her life. She still fell, this time from right to left across the screen. Behind her now, the policeman jolted, as if the rider's gun had been a starter's pistol. The motorcycle slid into the frame again. Then they all slowed—policeman, rider, victim, moving only in brief, coordinated spurts, like mechanical figures on an ancient town clock. The gray shadows froze behind the glass.

"Run it again," Mallard ordered. A young detective constable pushed a button on the video player and the images retreated, Urchin backing out of the picture, the motorcyclist finding a mythical reverse gear, the young woman in white springing back into life twice. If only it were that simple, Mallard lamented privately.

They watched as the embassy's security cameras gave them their first glance of the killer, unidentifiable in a crash helmet, goggles, and loose track suit, coldly repeating the fifth zodiac murder in slow motion.

"Can't even tell if it's a man or a woman," said the detective constable, unhelpfully. "Again?"

Mallard shook his head. "Let's see if there's some way we can enhance it. Anything from forensic yet?" he asked, addressing his question generally to the dozen detectives gathered in the conference room in New Scotland Yard.

"The dart came from a tranquilizer gun, the kind used for sedating animals in zoos," said Effie. "The killer took the gun with him. We haven't identified the substance in the dart, but it must have been extremely toxic—perhaps acotine or some related compound. Respiratory arrest was virtually instant. The police constable said she was dead almost as soon as he got to her."

"Poor bugger," muttered Mallard. "Wasn't he the one who arrested my nephew?"

"Police Constable Urchin," confirmed Detective Sergeant Welkin. "He's new. Rather cut up about the murder happening under his nose."

"He couldn't have stopped it. Make sure his station knows that we know that. And where the hell is Oliver, anyway? I want him here. There's something wrong with this picture, and it's the complete absence of scorpions. Any lead on the motorbike?"

A glum-looking detective sergeant called Moldwarp checked his notes. "Stolen yesterday lunchtime on Frick Street," he reported. His voice was as morose as his face. "We don't know where the miscreant kept it in the meanwhile. After the killing, he nipped up past Oxford Street and dumped the motorcycle in Selfridges car park. Left the crash helmet and track suit in the lift, so he could've been wearing anything underneath. Nobody saw him. No prints on anything. Nothing in the bike's storage compartment apart from a small drinks cooler. Empty."

"An acotine solution would need to be kept cool, or it would lose its effectiveness," Effie murmured.

Mallard stood up and walked to the window, one hand toying with the longer hairs of his white moustache.

"I suppose there's no doubt this was the Scorpio death we were expecting?" he asked, staring across the rooftops to the towers of Parliament and the Abbey.

"The symbol on the index card was the Scorpio sign, sir," Effie admitted, almost apologetically. "And the victim had a letter in her handbag inviting her to a meeting. Same style as the others."

"But why the American Embassy? There's no connection with scorpions. Unless it's a xenophobic slur on our transatlantic cousins?"

"I got a theory, Chief," said Welkin, failing to subdue his thick Cockney accent.

Mallard turned around. "Let's hear it."

"If I understand about scorpions—and I spent all morning in that exhibit in the Natural History Museum—they got a stinger on their tails what makes them dangerous."

"That's correct. Factually, if not grammatically."

Welkin started to look uncomfortable. "Well, our victim was killed with a sharp dart up the arse . . . sorry, in the gluteus maximus." He corrected himself, catching Effie's frown out of the corner of his eye and fearing a full blast of the Look. The last time Welkin had failed to mind his language, she'd caused him to remember a particularly humiliating event at a birthday party when he was eight years old, which had been the reason for his lifelong bachelorhood.

"Anyway," he continued hastily, "a scorpion has a sting in the tail. And that's how the lady died—with a sting in her tail."

To Welkin's irritation, Mallard let the unkind laughter continue for about twenty seconds, and then he held up his hand.

"I think you're absolutely right, Sergeant," he said to the team's surprise, Welkin's included. "Unfortunately, that's only *how* she was killed. It doesn't explain *where* she was killed, and that's always been part of the pattern up to now. The only part, in fact, that gave us a sporting chance of being in the right place ahead of the right time. All right, anything else?"

"The lab reports came back on the Capricorn, Chief," offered another detective cautiously. Mallard waved him to continue.

"The pathologist found traces of an unusual chemical compound in his stomach, a synthetic narcotic related to mescalin, called tetra . . . tetraphen . . . tetraphenylflu . . . okay, it's known by its initials, TPFC, or by its street name 'squidgy.' Apparently, a few grams can induce an alcohol-like intoxication very quickly, without a hangover the next day. But it has an odd side effect, in that it can raise the user's suggestibility."

"So if this drug was slipped somehow to Mark Sandys-Penza, and he was told there was treasure at the top of the Tropical House, then he would probably lurch up there in a drunken stupor to find out."

"Yes, sir. Sandys-Penza's stomach also contained traces of sugar and peppermint. This suggests to the lab boys that the TPFC was given to him hidden in a breath mint."

"How easy is it to get this stuff?" Mallard asked.

"The squidgy or the breath mint?" asked the detective with a grin. Then he caught sight of Mallard's expression and hurried on. "It's new, but it's fairly easy to score on the street. A couple of our lads are checking with known suppliers."

"All the zodiac symbols were written in the same indelible blue marker on the same white index cards, available at any branch of Ryman's," said another detective. "We don't know about the writing on Sir Harry Random's shirt, but the ink must have been waterproof, because it survived a dunking in the fountain."

"Why can't we find out?" Mallard asked.

"Random's clothes were sent back to his home on Tuesday, before we were treating his death as a murder. His daughter threw the shirt away."

"Tidy girl," commented Effie. "She'd make someone a wonderful wife."

"Did we pull any prints off the letters?" Mallard asked her gruffly, ignoring the comment. Effie hastily consulted her files.

"The letter sent to the Capricorn, the Richmond estate agent, has his prints and those of his office receptionist, who opened the envelope."

"Attractive woman, incidentally," said Moldwarp sadly, who had interviewed the family and business associates of Mark Sandys-Penza.

"The letter sent to the Aquarius, Nettie Clapper, had only her prints and her husband's," Effie continued. "And the letter sent to Sir Harry Random has his prints and Oliver's."

"Obviously, because Oliver found the letter at his club. But how did you know they were his prints?"

"Bow Street took his fingerprints when he was arrested on Monday morning. I had them sent over."

"Good. You never know when you'll need them. Did we find any letter sent to Gordon Paper?"

"Not yet," said a detective who hadn't spoken, "although the Yorkshire police are still going through his windmill. He hadn't been there for a week, though."

"Did he have a hotel room in London?"

"We haven't found it yet."

"What about the lead piping that killed Nettie Clapper?" asked Mallard.

"Untraceable," lamented Moldwarp. "And no fingerprints."

"The crossbow that killed Gordon Paper?"

"German model," Welkin reported. "Not a top-of-the-line weapon, used more for entertainment or hunting than high-accuracy target shooting. The stock had been wiped clean of prints and the serial number was partly removed, but the manufacturer thinks it was part of a shipment that went to an Austrian retail outlet, about five years ago. Interpol are making a few inquiries for us, but we don't have high hopes. The killer needn't have been the purchaser, after all—it could have been stolen. The bolt had some fingerprints, but they all belonged to bystanders in Piccadilly Circus who tried to help Paper. We're also checking the membership lists of archery clubs, seeing the murderer was such a good shot. But we need some other clue before we can cross-reference the names."

"Well, we know he can ride a motorbike and he can score 'squidgy' on the street," said Effie.

There was a knock on the door, and a policeman let a breathless Oliver into the room. He recoiled momentarily on seeing the size of his potential audience, but his excitement overcame his stage fright.

"Here you are! Good afternoon, gentlemen . . . and lady.

118

Effie, I mean. Not that you're not a lady, of course, but I thought . . ."

Mallard rescued him, addressing the room. "In case you haven't met him before, this is my nephew, Oliver, who's been giving us some technical assistance on this case."

The men grumbled a curt greeting at the mere civilian. "You may want to take a seat, Oliver," Mallard suggested firmly.

"Oh, but this can't wait!" Oliver cried with enthusiasm, sadly oblivious to the differences between Mallard the indulgent uncle and Mallard the senior policeman. "You see, I've found the London scorpion. I was convinced I'd seen a carving of a scorpion somewhere, but I couldn't remember where. And then this morning, it clicked! When the Roman Temple of Mithras was excavated on Cannon Street, the archaeologists found a relief depicting a Mithraic legend, Mithras slaying a bull. On the edge of the image—in fact, snipping at his balls, sorry Effie, the bull's, I mean, not Mithras's, testicles I should say, sorry Effie—is a small scorpion. Of course, I hotfooted it to Cannon Street, but the sculptures weren't there, they're in the Museum of London, on London Wall, so I ran over and checked, and there indeed was my scorpion. But get this—there are *two* scorpions in the carving. There's also a kind of frieze around the edge that shows all the zodiac signs, including Scorpio."

He stopped, aware they were watching him quizzically, each detective taking mean-spirited delight in trying to guess Mallard's first comment (apart from Effie, who felt strangely sorry for the young man). But Mallard didn't speak. He simply picked up the white index card and pitched it across the table toward his nephew. Oliver looked at the blue-ink symbol without touching the card.

"Ah," he said humbly. "May I ask where?"

"The American Embassy," replied Mallard. "Show him." He sat down while the detective ran the videotape again. Oliver watched in silence.

"That happened about an hour and a half ago," Mallard told him. "We had to clean the site up quickly for diplomatic reasons. The tape comes from the embassy's security system. None of us can explain why the killer chose that particular location." Mallard's helpless gesture took in the whole room. He motioned Oliver to take a seat. "Go over what we know," he instructed Effie.

"The Scorpio's name was Vanessa Parmenter," she stated. "She was a travel agent from Kingston, unmarried, twenty-six years old. Her flat-mate says she had a telephone call a day or two ago telling her that a long-lost uncle had died in the United States and left her some money, and that she'd have to go to the embassy to prove her identity. We found a letter in her handbag, dated yesterday, asking her to come to a meeting at about eleven o'clock. It said she was to wait outside the embassy and someone would contact her."

"The bastard certainly contacted her," Mallard cut in angrily. "With a poisoned dart in the posterior. Sergeant Welkin has already made the 'sting in the tail' comment, Oliver, so don't bother. We think that's the Scorpio connection in terms of how she was killed. But we don't know why the embassy or Grosvenor Square was selected as the location. Can you think of any connection with scorpions?"

Oliver shook his head without speaking.

"Anybody?"

The room was silent.

"Damn it!" The superintendent took off his glasses and twirled them in his fingers. "This is exactly what I was afraid of when Gordon Paper turned out to have the wrong birthday. Now we've lost the connection between the location and the zodiac sign, too. We're right back where we started."

He wiped a hand over his face, as if he were trying to smooth the deep wrinkles.

"When was Vanessa Parmenter's birthday?" Oliver asked cautiously. Mallard looked to Effie.

"I don't know, Chief. I thought we'd dropped that line."

"Find out," said Mallard brusquely. He put his glasses on again and sat forward. "According to the typical profile, a serial killer doesn't know his victims and doesn't want to. They have an impersonal, symbolic meaning for him that gets spoiled if he makes contact with their humanity. We thought that symbolic meaning was the birth signs. But since we've lost that, let's see if there's something else, something we haven't spotted yet. I want you to split into five teams, take a separate murder victim and find out all you can. If there is any overlap, any connection, any consistency that we've missed, I want to discover it, either in the murderer's M.O. or in the victims' lives. Gather everything—family, work, education, personal habits, shoe sizes, favorite color. And see if there's any connection with the armed forces. Stick it all in the computer and look for linkages, anything they may have in common, no matter how obscure. Any questions?"

There were no questions.

"Then that's it. Meet back here at six o'clock. Oh, somebody tell the press office to cancel the scorpion stories."

"Actually, I do have one question," said Oliver, after the detectives filed out of the room. Mallard and Effie had stayed behind. "Can I buy you two lunch before I go back to work? I'm starving."

That Susie Beamish loved food was evident from the several shelves of cookbooks in her bedroom and from the obscenities that Oliver and Geoffrey could hear every morning through the door of their shared bathroom, when her bare feet made contact with the rusting scale. But that Susie

121

couldn't actually cook partly explained the failure of every one of her theme restaurants, beginning with a bistro called Très Tables, where she had tried to duplicate the taste of airline food (and succeeded only too well).

After this initial disaster, she had started a restaurant featuring English gourmet cooking called Not as Bad as You Think, moved on to a brasserie serving appetizers and desserts only (No Entree), and even opened a snack bar on Baker Street that offered food mentioned in the Sherlock Holmes stories (Alimentary, My Dear Watson). But these and several other novelty restaurants had all met their various Waterloos, including an ice cream parlor at Waterloo called Ticket 'N' Lick It.

Susie's latest bid for another fifteen minutes' fame was in Pimlico, close enough to New Scotland Yard for Oliver to suggest it as a place for lunch. (He never went so far as to "recommend" Susie's establishments, even though her loyal assistant chefs had become quite adept at keeping her out of the kitchen.) Mallard agreed, mainly because Susie adored him, and her attention would be a welcome distraction from his stalled case.

"Uncle Tim!" she had cried boisterously, catching sight of him across the sparsely patronized restaurant. "Welcome to Raisin D'Etre!" She ran over and hugged Mallard with unrestrained affection. A gentleman to the end, he tried to ignore the fleshy contours pressing against his jacket and patted her lightly on the shoulder blades in return.

Susie was Oliver's age—the four who lived in Edwardes Square had all been friends at university. She possessed remarkably coal-black hair and huge, chocolate-colored eyes, in a face that was otherwise totally Anglo-Saxon and fixed in a permanent beam of delight. When he first met her, Oliver had fallen deeply in unrequited love for a week, but cured himself by admitting that if Susie and he had ever become an item, her unfailing energy and optimism would have driven him to strangle her within another week.

"Hello, Ollie," she exclaimed, skipping the hug, to Oliver's relief. "Haven't seen you in the bathroom recently. Is it you who's been using my depilatory?"

"Probably Geoffrey."

"Can't be. Geoff hasn't passed puberty yet. Who is this lovely lady?" Susie asked, turning her attention to Effie.

"This is Detective Sergeant Strongitharm," Mallard told her, knowing that Oliver would botch the introduction. He always seemed to lisp Effie's name when it was attached to her rank.

"Oh, you're the famous Effie," cried Susie cheerfully. "Ollie was talking about you. So was Ben. And so was Geoff, incidentally. You've made quite an impression on our little group. Ah, Ollie, I see what you mean about her hair."

"Three for lunch, please, Susie," said Oliver hurriedly.

"Four, actually," said Mallard. "There's still one to come."

"Whom did you invite?" asked Oliver, after Susie had shown them to a table in front of the window and brought a complimentary carafe of lemon-colored wine. He was sitting next to Effie, who was unconsciously patting her springy hair.

"Someone who can give us some technical advice," Mallard answered vaguely as he studied the menu. "What the hell is all this stuff?"

"It's Susie's latest theme restaurant, Raisin D'Etre," Oliver informed him. "Everything has raisins or sultanas in it. So you can start with a Waldorf salad or a fruit compote, then go on to an English-style curry, and finish with bread-and-butter pudding."

"Why do the English insist on throwing fruit into Indian food?" Effie commented scornfully.

123

"Oliver, you go ahead and order if you're in a hurry to get back to work," Mallard said, before Oliver had time to follow up on Effie's comment.

"There's no rush," he replied. "Mr. Woodcock said I can take as much time as I like. I think he's pleased to see me busy, after two years of staring into space."

"Why do you need to work as anybody's assistant, Oliver?" Effie asked, a little disdainfully. "I've never read any of your books about Finchley the ferret—"

"Finsbury."

"Finsbury, sorry—but I understand they're very popular. Can't you be a full-time writer?"

"I doubt that I can concentrate long enough to be a full-time anything," said Oliver, pleased enough with Effie's interest in him to overlook the criticism. Could she have been rehearsing the phrase "My boyfriend, Oliver, is a . . ." and decided that "writer" was a better conclusion than "underemployed dogsbody"?

"I still work for Woodcock and Oakhampton to pay the rent," he continued. "My recent income from Tadpole Tomes has been frozen, because I'm being sued by the artist who drew Finsbury."

"You're being sued by Amelia Flewhardly?" cried Mallard in surprise. "I thought her only goal in life was to climb into a bottle of sloe gin every other day." He turned to Effie to explain. "Amelia is an eighty-year-old dypso water-colorist from Frinton, who worships Oliver. We're not sure, however, that she realizes his stories about talking animals are fictitious."

"I'm not being sued by Amelia," Oliver interrupted. "The poor dear was in for her annual detox when Finsbury first appeared. So the job of illustrating that particular Railway Mice story—copying Amelia's style—was farmed out to some callow art student who doesn't know her Hals from her El

Greco. This girl believes the world owes her a living and she intends to get it by the American method: substituting litigation for talent. She's now claiming global rights to Finsbury's visual form, which includes any income from future illustrated books, film and television rights, and merchandising. So while the lawyers are getting rich, Tadpole Tomes for Tiny Tots is legally barred from paying me anything for the Finsbury books."

"Hoist with your own pet," murmured Mallard, not unkindly, as he rattled the menu.

"Your guest is here, Uncle Tim." Susie bounced suddenly into view, leading a tall, thin, middle-aged man wearing khaki slacks, a loose, lavender silk shirt, and despite the heat, a long multicolored cotton scarf, which hung around his neck in a deep loop. His remarkably long gray hair was cut in a way that caused a floppy forelock to cascade over his left eye and cheek.

"Timothy, my esteemed friend," the man boomed, tossing his head to throw the hair out of his eyes. He extended a hand dramatically. "How's the world of slaughter?"

"Unrelenting, thank you, Miles," Mallard replied, standing swiftly. "Let me introduce you. My assistant, Detective Sergeant Effie Strongitharm, my nephew Oliver Swithin— this is my old friend Miles Lipsbury-Pinfold."

"Charmed, my dears," said Lipsbury-Pinfold, with considerable gallantry. "Effie, your hair is a phenomenon, never change it." He sat down next to Mallard. "Those cretins who pay my salary have given me an afternoon deadline, so I must drink my lunch quickly before ancient clerks with scourges come to whip me back to the word processor."

He paused to sip the wine Mallard had poured for him, made an elaborate moue, then drained the glass. Susie reappeared with a notepad and took their orders, which for Lipsbury-Pinfold was another carafe of wine.

125

"Oliver, you and Miles have something in common," said Mallard genially, playing host. "You are both better known to the world by your pen names."

"Ah, a fellow scrivener," said Lipsbury-Pinfold, tossing his fringe aside again and looking intently at Oliver as if for the first time. Oliver was always reserved when meeting new people and particularly intimidated by anyone with the sense of presence that he lacked. He described himself as shy, which he felt had an endearing quality. Mallard, who had a marked intolerance of weaknesses masquerading as lovable quirks of character, preferred the term "socially inept" and always winced inwardly when forced to introduce his nephew. He winced now at Oliver's vacant expression, but Miles Lipsbury-Pinfold was up to the situation.

"Let's have a pact, dear boy," he said, dropping his voice to conspiratorial levels. "I'll reveal mine, if you reveal yours. Pseudonym, I mean." He let a close-lipped smile sidle up his cheeks, and his eyebrows flicked themselves twice.

"Well, I write under the name O. C. Blithely," Oliver mumbled. The other man gasped loudly.

"Fornicate with a feathered friend!" cried Lipsbury-Pinfold. "You are the creator of the sublime Finsbury! I have read them all. Sir, you are the prince of our profession." He winked and lifted his glass in salute.

"Thank you," said Oliver modestly. "And how would we know you?"

For some reason, Mallard tensed. Lipsbury-Pinfold put down his drink slowly and sighed, pushing himself back from the table.

"I, too, have an androgynous alter ego, Oliver. If your intellect ever slums its way through the *London Daily Mercury*, then you will find me next to a singularly distasteful comic strip called 'Attila the Nun.' I compose the horoscope. I am Beverly of the Stars."

As his eyes lowered in mock humility, causing the lock of hair to mask his face again, Oliver glared at Mallard across the table. The superintendent spoke quickly.

"Miles, as I told you on the phone, we're dealing with a very challenging case. We have a serial killer who uses the zodiac as a theme. Now this is apparently quite common in the United States—New York had its own Zodiac Killer a few years ago. But in those cases, the timings of the murders or attacks could be related to aspects of the sidereal calendar. Our man is different. He seems more interested in the mythology of the zodiac than its astrological significance. But today, he's shifted his pattern, and we were wondering if we've missed something. What can you tell us about the sign of Scorpio?"

"Scorpio," the astrologer mused. "The sign of the scorpion, which should be fairly obvious even to someone with the mentality of my devoted readers. There was rather a lot about the vile creatures in this morning's edition." He poured himself another drink while he rattled off the information. "Let's see, Scorpio covers the period of late October to late November. A water sign, governed by Pluto. Said to have a strong influence over the genitals and the anus. If you believe in the foolishness of associating personality with birth sign, you'll find your Johnny Scorpio is a secretive and self-protective cove, tenacious, unchanging, capable of great aggressiveness, intuitive, and prone to perfectionism. But then, aren't we all. Scorpios make good friends and passionate lovers, although they are inclined to violence. Death is not alien to the Scorpio—in fact, now I think of it, they make good serial killers. And detectives, incidentally. Is this what you're looking for?"

"We're really looking for some association between scorpions and the American Embassy in Grosvenor Square,"

Mallard said as the food arrived, distributed by a laconic waiter wearing gumshoes, who spoke no English.

"Let me think about it," said Lipsbury-Pinfold. "But I pontificate better on an empty bladder, so while you're tucking into this appetizing but depressingly solid fare, I'll see a man about a man. Excuse me."

He got up from the table and enquired noisily about the location of the toilet.

"I don't believe this," exclaimed Oliver, after he'd watched the astrologer's lithe frame disappear through a curtain of plastic strips.

"Now, Oliver, I've known Miles a long time and I want you to give him a chance," said Mallard. "He writes for the *Mercury* because it pays his bills. But he's also an expert on the serious side of astrology."

"Serious side?" echoed Oliver, dropping his fork on the table, and not just because he had tasted the chicken curry. "There is no serious side as far as I'm concerned. I hate all superstition, and it appalls me most of all when a society gives it tacit approval, such as daily horoscopes. Sometimes I think we should just hand civilization back to the witch doctors."

"I agree with Oliver," said Effie, to his surprise.

Mallard, disemboweling a pumpernickel-raisin roll, was staring at them in exasperation. "And do you two bright young things think you're telling your old Uncle Tim something he doesn't know?" he snapped. "Shiver my timbers, I'm desperate. We seem to have lost two threads in the killer's pattern. We've no idea where he's going to strike tomorrow, or who his victim will be. I'll take anything I can get to stop him, and if that means picking the brain of Beverly of the Stars over a lunch of rabbit droppings, then I'll do it."

Lipsbury-Pinfold reappeared at the table, belatedly checking his zip, and took his seat again, accidentally knocking Mallard's sleeve into his veal Marengo (with raisins).

"So, Oliver, my dear friend," he continued with a genial grin. "What next for the famous Finsbury? Something truly debauched, I trust. I fancy an ecclesiastical setting. Finsbury making off with the restoration fund, questionable goings-on with choirboys, nude scenes under the rood-screen. That should keep the kiddies from playing up in Sunday School."

"Actually, Mr. Lipsbury-Pinfold, I was thinking of the perils of believing in horoscopes," Oliver began. Mallard tried to kick him under the table but caught Effie's ankle instead. "I'm intrigued that you used the word 'foolishness' to describe your work."

"Of course it's foolishness," replied the astrologer, slinging an arm over the back of his chair. "Making a daily prediction that's supposed to affect one twelfth of the population. It's poppycock. 'The excellent foppery of the world,' as the Bard put it."

"So how on earth can you justify your daily horoscopes?"

"Entertainment, sir. Pure entertainment."

"But your readers don't think it's entertainment. They run their lives by it."

"And so what if they do?" asked Lipsbury-Pinfold artlessly. "I never give them bad advice. To say, for example, 'You should take care in money matters' or 'Think carefully before confronting a coworker' can't hurt, surely? Even true astrology, based on an individual's horoscope, is descriptive, not predictive. It detects influences and tendencies, not future events. As Thomas Aquinas said, 'the stars dispose, but they do not determine.' "

"So you're still saying our lives can be influenced by the movement of planets and stars millions of miles away?" asked Oliver intently, through a mouthful of currants.

Lipsbury-Pinfold drained his fourth glass and poured another, with a surreptitious glance at his wristwatch.

"There's clearly no fooling you, you're your uncle's

nephew," he said generously. "The signs of the zodiac aren't really up there, as you know. They're just the way we choose to group the dim twinkles of stars that are unimaginable distances from us and from each other. All that apparent heavenly movement is an indication of our own motions on this traveling planet. So I merely use the celestial clock face to track earthly influences and rhythms that I believe affect mood and personality, just as you use the sun's arc in the sky to measure days and seasons."

"But then why make so much of the signs of the zodiac?" Oliver asked as the astrologer sipped more wine. "Why, for example, do you say Leos are kingly, Virgos gentle, Libras fair-minded?"

"You did say you don't believe in blanket personality types," Effie chimed in.

"I don't," replied Lipsbury-Pinfold, stroking the gray fringe from his face again. "But I also said the horoscope is descriptive, not prescriptive. You shouldn't assume, my dears, that the sign was named first and the personality force-fit after. What if it was the other way round? An ancient astronomer is staring at the patch of sky though which the sun rose on the king's birthday, and behold—he finds he can join up the dots and make out a lion, the king of beasts. Very flattering for his majesty, when the stargazer might just as easily have descried a toad. It's not so easy the other way round. Take your Scorpio. It was the Greeks who cut the sky into a twelve-piece pie, making the heavenly Scorpion one of the pieces, which they inherited from the Chaldeans, who called it Gir. Remarkably, people born in the Scorpio slice were found to be secretive, defensive, and aggressive, just like a real scorpion. However, the scorpion is a stubbornly disgusting beast, as we know from this morning's newspapers, and so astrologers had to concoct a second image in order to squeeze out some more appealing traits. Thus Scorpio is the only zodiac sign to be represented by two creatures. By the way, Tim, do I detect the hand of Scotland Yard behind the capital's current scorpion scare?"

Mallard smiled inscrutably. "So what's Scorpio's other image?" he asked.

"An eagle. That way, the eagle-eyed king of the birds can offer intuition and perfectionism to round out the scorpion's limited personality. Hello, did I say something?"

Effie had reacted suddenly, causing a mouthful of cheap wine to take a detour into her lungs. But Oliver, patting her severely on the back, asked the question that she couldn't articulate.

"Did you say an eagle?"

"Oh, yes," said Lipsbury-Pinfold happily. "In antiquity, the symbol of the eagle was always associated with Scorpio. I forgot to mention it earlier. I say, does that help?"

As Effie Strongitharm undressed that evening in her Richmond flat, she wanted to think about the zodiac murderer, but she couldn't get her mind off Oliver. Before this case, she had met him on only a few occasions, when Tim Mallard's wife, Oliver's Aunt Phoebe, had invited them to the same lunches or parties. And she had once sat next to him for an hour and a half waiting for Tim's appearance as a singing Richard the Third in the Theydon Bois Thespian's annual Shakespearian pantomime (*All's Will That Ends Will*), the first time they had realized "A horse, a horse, my kingdom for a horse!" fits the music of "Tonight" from *West Side Story*. But during those brief encounters, Oliver had struck her as standoffish and vague. Effie was envious of Tim's unswerving trust in his nephew, who failed to understand that most murders were not solved with the mind alone, but with the active support of the detective's ear, the pathologist's microscope, and feet that weren't afraid to cover the same ground over and over again.

And yet, since Oliver had appeared at Kew on Tuesday night, in the company of Ben Motley, she had been forced to reconsider. First, there was his invulnerability to the Look, after that embarrassing but—in retrospect—comical misunderstanding of Ben's photographic intentions. Then there was his admitted success at fathoming the patterns laid down by the zodiac murderer, justifying Tim's faith. This was, after all, the one case in a thousand where the young man's flypaper mind could actually help the Yard, although even he hadn't known the odd astrological fact that explained Vanessa Parmenter's sudden death below the outstretched wings of the largest eagle in London. And finally, there was the growing realization that Oliver's apparent aloofness was actually a rather endearing bashfulness, made worse by his obvious attraction to her.

Effie had come to accept she was attractive from the constant attention she received. But she resisted seeing the attractiveness for herself, often scraping back her rebellious hair and gazing at her features in the bathroom mirror with contempt. She did so now, as she stepped out of her shower, and once again felt like chanting the famous title card from the silent version of *The Phantom of the Opera*—"Feast your eyes, gloat your soul, on my accursed ugliness!" Her odd-shaped nose, with nostrils that were too small and thin, her wide, flat cheeks, her tiny mouth, the lines that swept down from her inner eyes, the mole beside her chin (which she wouldn't dignify by dubbing it a beauty spot). Her scrutiny was too deep to appreciate the harmony and proportion of her features—which the Greeks knew to be the true secret of beauty—a gestalt that made Ben Motley want her as the Queen of Heaven in his first tableau.

Oddly, she saw that harmony when she studied Oliver's face. His slightly receding chin, for example, would be ugly on a face that was otherwise rugged and sharply defined, such as Ben's; but it complemented Oliver's innocent, toothy smile, his pale, untidy hair, and the gentle, blue eyes—the same color as her own, she'd noticed—that seemed misleadingly foolish behind his round glasses. He looked like a not-too-overgrown schoolboy. But even if he was well under six feet, at least he was taller than Effie. She was pleased about this.

She wasn't falling in love with him, of course, or anything stupid like that, she told herself, sliding a cotton nightdress over her naked body and climbing into bed. (How could she ever love someone who had the bad judgment to be attracted to her?) It was true that she responded rather well to the idea of a friendship with Oliver, more than with any other man she had encountered in the three years since becoming a detective had devoured her private life. But she was certain she had no romantic interest in the hapless writer of children's books.

She turned off the light and lay awake, thinking of Oliver.

Underwood Tooth was not surprised when he woke up in the London Library at three o'clock on Saturday morning with his head resting on—or more accurately, in—a dusty first edition of *Sartor Resartus*. In the fierce heat, he often fell asleep in stuffy public buildings, only to regain consciousness hours later, when the lights had been extinguished by guards or janitors who had simply overlooked his unconscious form.

For Underwood Tooth was the world's greatest expert on being ignored. In his sixty-six years, he had been ignored by everyone. Waiters, shop assistants, cab drivers, ticket collectors, hotel receptionists—they all looked through Under-wood as if he were transparent, a fleeting retinal sensation that hadn't the energy to stroll along the optic nerve and rattle the door handle of the cortex. Most of his conversations had begun with the phrase "Sorry, I didn't see you there," uttered by strangers who had backed into him in elevators or let shop doors swing into his face. Computers found his name and address as hard to hold as a greased eel. He never received any junk mail.

As a result of his chronic anonymity, he had learned from necessity how to find his way out of dozens of locked shops, museums, and libraries in the middle of the night, invisible to infrared beams and motion detectors, and rarely setting off the alarms. Mulling over these experiences once, during a five-hour sojourn in his doctor's waiting room (he eventually felt better and went home without hearing his name called), it occurred to him that he might make a good burglar. But he feared that, like Midas, his personal touch would spread like chocolate in a child's hand, besmirching anything that came into his possession. Stolen money would never talk for Underwood Tooth; it would catch laryngitis from his fingers. So he decided instead to apply for several positions as a private investigator. He received no replies.

Yesterday evening, he realized, the librarians must have collected the books from the table on which he was slumped and gone home for the weekend without spotting him nose deep—literally—in Thomas Carlyle, the Library's founder. Fortunately, this had happened three times before, and by now he could easily thread his way through the building and into St. James's Square without leaving a trace. He half considered taking the ten books he had come to borrow that afternoon, but he had no idea how to check them out. It hardly mattered, since the Library's system invariably failed to register his loans, but Underwood believed in doing the right thing.

He drifted through the Victorian house like a benign ghost, unlocked the front door, and stepped out sleepily into the warm night air. The moon was bright, making the leaves on the square's trees sparkle like flakes of silver on an old photographic plate. Underwood took a couple of deep breaths, started cautiously down the steps, and walked head-first into the sandbag.

Abrupt collisions were not a new sensation. He often struck his head when automatic doors refused to open for him. So his first reaction was more puzzlement than pain. What was a large sack doing, seemingly hovering in the air in front of the Library entrance? Was it something from another world, another dimension? It would be a supreme irony if, of all people, alien life forms in a burlap spacecraft were trying to contact *him*.

Underwood looked up, and realized that the heavy sack was not defying gravity but hanging from an unlit streeplamp, which sprouted from the pavement beside the Library railings. And the sack was not alone. A second bag, black this time, also dangled from the lamppost, attached to the first by a length of rope. The rope had been slung over a decorative metal bar, which seemed to serve no function except to remind people that London was once illuminated by gaslight. The two bags swayed together slightly, like . . . well, the first simile that struck Underwood caused him to blush.

The second bag, hidden behind the first. Was it a bag? He touched it. It swung into view and stared at him.

A man! Gawd bleedin' blind O'Reilly, a hanged man!

Underwood started, as if death were contagious. He fell back onto his haunches, reaching for the railings for support. Fear struck him instantly, not for his own safety, but for his effectiveness. He prayed quickly that the man was dead, because the last time he had dialed 999 for an ambulance, he had been put on hold for thirty minutes.

He looked up. The hanging man was dead, no doubt about it. Those staring eyes had not blinked for a long time. Underwood stood up stiffly, ignoring his thudding heart, and looked more closely at the corpse. The man was about his age, the face hard, cold, and frozen in the moonlight, the one patch of white on the dark-clothed corpse.

One? No, now that he looked, there were two. On the dead man's chest, a light square. Underwood stared more intently. It was a card, pinned to the man's black shirt with a safety pin. And there seemed to be some writing on it. He knew he should leave it alone, don't touch anything, fetch the police. But maybe it had some important information, some way of identifying the dead man, something that could bring a policeman hurrying more quickly if Underwood succeeded in getting his attention.

He reached up and unclipped the pin, lifting the card curiously to his eyes. But it wasn't writing. It wasn't anything. Just a couple of parallel lines in what seemed like blue ink. One line was straight, the other had a bump in the middle. Disappointed, Underwood slipped it into his jacket pocket as he scurried away into the night.

Seven

OLIVER WAS SITTING BEHIND a table at the back of the crowded bookstore cursing Geoffrey under his breath for being late. Then he rapidly adopted a beatific smile as a woman dressed in riding gear approached his table, clutching a miniature version of herself by the hand.

"How do you do, Mr. Blithely," she said crisply. "My name's Mandy Brudenell and this is my daughter, Courtney."

"Hello, Courtney, have you just had a riding lesson?" asked Oliver. The child simpered unpleasantly.

"Oh, yes," she cried, "I got up to a canter today. I'm the only one in my class who can do that."

"Well done," Oliver said heartily. "Did you get a nice horse this morning?"

The girl looked at her mother with a puzzled expression.

"Courtney has her own pony, of course," explained Mrs. Brudenell.

"I'm the only one in my class to have one," Courtney said proudly. "It drives the others *crazy*. Especially Penelope. She's my best friend, but I won't let her ride Finsbury."

"Finsbury?" Oliver echoed.

"Courtney insisted on naming her pony after your creation," Mrs. Brudenell informed him fulsomely. "We love your work. You know, I often tell Courtney stories of my own, and several friends have told me I should write them down."

"Well, why not," Oliver suggested politely.

"I'm so glad you agree," she said. "So you'll read my manuscript? I have it here. I thought we could use some of Courtney's own pictures as illustrations."

The third author in half an hour. The manager of the bookstore, a sullen woman with untidy hair and glasses that were too large for her face, failed to come to his rescue yet again. Where the hell was Geoffrey? He was supposed to head these people off.

"I'm sorry," he stammered, "I get so many requests. . . . Make it a personal rule not to . . ."

"I see," said the woman, with sudden disdain. "Then perhaps you could give me the name of your editor?"

Oliver hastily supplied the name of his ex-girlfriend at Tadpole Tomes for Tiny Tots. Serve her right.

"I can say I'm writing with your recommendation," Mrs. Brudenell informed him as she briskly jotted the information into a small pocket diary. Meanwhile, Courtney passed him a copy of the latest Railway Mice book to sign.

"I'm the first one in my class to have this one," she claimed.

Oliver opened the book to the title page and mutely scribbled "To Courtney, best wishes, O. C. Blithely." He felt odd, adding curlicues and paraphs to individualize a signature that was not his own. Then he added in crude block letters, "P.S. LET PENELOPE RIDE YOUR BLOODY PONY, SIGNED FINSBURY THE FERRET."

"How charming," muttered Mrs. Brudenell, glaring at the inscription. She snapped the book shut and led the child away.

"Can I go back to calling Snaffles by his real name now, Mummy?" Courtney was saying as they went out of the shop and into the maze of paved passageways that ran between the High Street and Richmond Green. Geoffrey, who was struggling through the entrance with a huge plastic sack, held the door open for them. The noise level inside the store was suddenly augmented by the shouts of a pack of animal rights protestors outside.

"Fair deals for ferrets!"

"Weasels are winners!"

"They're not all Finsburys!"

The door swung shut. Geoffrey eyed the long line of children and parents waiting restively for their thirty seconds with Oliver and smiled.

"Not a bad house," he said as came over to the table, dragging the sack behind him.

"Where have you been?"

"Sorry, I had to park miles away, and this bag was heavy. Besides, there's cricket on the Green—Richmond police versus a team of gay dermatologists—so I watched for a few minutes. Local newspapers been here yet?"

"What's in the bag?" Oliver asked impatiently. He loved cricket and didn't want to hear that he was missing a late-season match. Geoffrey tapped the side of his avian nose and grinned in a way that made Oliver want to pinch him. He took a yellow carton out of the sack and from this, he removed a plush, beige object with stumpy legs and a long tail. It looked like an ectomorphic Persian cat.

"Meet Finsbury—the cuddly toy!" Geoffrey crowed. "Only eighteen pounds, ninety-five pee."

"Oh, no."

Oliver stared in horror at the furry doll, which Geoffrey had put on the table in front of him. It stared back with eyes that were the color of bubblegum.

"You haven't seen the best bit," Geoffrey said. He reached underneath the toy and flipped a switch, hidden in the creature's fur. The ferret whirred and started to flail its front legs, causing it to move awkwardly across the tabletop toward Oliver. He watched aghast as the toy reached his arm, nosed his wrist once, and stopped. Then with a sudden metallic yelp, it darted forward and caught the edge of his hand in its mechanical jaws. Oliver yelled and leaped back, but the ferret came with him, teeth gripping a fold of his skin.

"There's a button above his eyes," Geoffrey told him. "Press it and he'll let go, just like a real ferret." But the toy dropped off Oliver's hand anyway, taking several blond hairs with it.

"You're insane!" Oliver hissed, nursing his pinched skin. "You can't possibly give this to children!"

"It's not for children," Geoffrey replied insouciantly as he picked up the toy from the floor. "Well, not for children under five, anyway—there's a label on the boxes, so we're covered legally. We're really trying to cater to the adult market, who make up forty-eight percent of the Finsbury readership. Hence our advertising slogan—'Put a Ferret down Your Trousers.' "

Oliver wanted to tell Geoffrey exactly where to put the toy ferret, and the public relations officer's trousers were only the first stop on the journey, but the next pair of customers had stepped up to the table—a boy of about ten with moussed hair, dressed entirely in blue denim and a woman wearing, explicably, sunglasses, and inexplicably, a fur coat.

"And what's your name?" Oliver asked.

"Tristram," said the boy. He eyed Oliver suspiciously. "I thought you were going to be a woman."

"I get that a lot."

"I'm not surprised, sailor."

"Is this your mother?" asked Oliver, trying to mask his growing irritation. Tristram gave the woman a swift glance, as if noticing her for the first time.

"Do me a favor, John! No, this is my old man's secretary, if you get my drift. She's just collected me from my acting class. Call her Sharon."

"Pleased to meet you, Sharon," said Oliver.

"Likewise, I'm sure," said the woman, with a brief curtsy. Tristram raised his eyes theatrically to heaven.

"Oh, the things you see when you don't have a gun," he sighed.

"Hello, little boy," said Geoffrey, stepping over with a boxed toy while Oliver signed Tristram's book. "How would you like to buy your very own Finsbury the Ferret? You can put it down your trousers."

"Last person who said that to me is doing fifteen years in Parkhurst," said Tristram. "How—"

"Much is it?" Geoffrey interrupted, undaunted. "Only eighteen pounds and ninety-five pee. Batteries are included."

Tristram considered the toy. "Okay, shorthouse, I'll buy it," he said. "Pay the man, Sharon."

"You can pay at the cash register," said Geoffrey to the woman, who bobbed again. "Now, let me show you how it works."

"Oh, Geoffrey," said Oliver smoothly, "I'm sure a clever young gentleman like Tristram is quite capable of figuring that out for himself."

"Yes, but—"

"Yeah, I never bother with the instructions," boasted Tristram. "I'll soon find out what this thing can do."

"I certainly hope so," murmured Oliver.

The shop door was flung open suddenly, to the cheers of the demonstrators outside. A burly young woman bustled in, marched to the center of the shop and, without a pause, started to address the waiting customers through a small megaphone.

"Do not be fooled by Finsbury," she announced metallically, as she wrestled with something in a raffia bag, slung around her neck. "The ferret is only doing what comes naturally. I ask you, is this the face of a villain?"

With a sweeping gesture, she plucked a thin, struggling creature from the bag and held it up in front of the children's eyes. The manager, who was striding toward the demonstrator, stopped short. Oliver could tell from his limited research that the animal was a cross between a domesticated ferret and its wild counterpart. It had a brown body, but its appealing face was white, apart from a domino mask of darker brown fur across its sparkling eyes. The children, seeing something furry with a face like an anorexic panda, let out a chorus of "Ahhhh!"

"I don't allow dogs in here, and I certainly won't allow that badger!" cried the manager. She started to push firmly against the animal rights activist. The other shop assistants began to help their boss, trying to keep out of range of the dangling and confused ferret. With a final cry of "Release all your companion animals!" the demonstrator was hustled through the door. Through the window, Oliver watched as she stumbled into Sharon, who had exited a few seconds earlier. The two women glared at each other, and then several demonstrators converged on the secretary and sprayed red paint on her fur coat. Sharon squealed, but Tristram was too busy laughing to help her. A whistle was blown, and several cricket-playing policemen, waiting for their turn on the Green, swooped on the belligerent demonstrators.

The staff of the bookstore turned back from the door and tried to calm the line of overexcited Finsbury fans. Their parents checked their watches and shot despairing glances at Oliver. Meanwhile, a grubby-looking man with a warty nose, who had been hovering by the Beatrix Potter display, pushed into the line and approached the table.

"Are those effigies of Finsbury the Ferret for sale?" he asked throatily. Geoffrey beamed. "You bet," he replied. "How many would you like?"

"None," said the man, passing Geoffrey a piece of paper.

"What's this?" asked Geoffrey as he took the paper. "If you want an autograph, I'm not the author."

"No need. That's a summons. My client is the original illustrator of Finsbury the Ferret, and she claims all rights to income from the sale of any reproduction, two- or three-dimensional. We thought you'd try something like this. She's suing Tadpole Tomes for Tiny Tots and the agency of Hoo, Watt & Eidenau for five million pounds."

Geoffrey moaned and fell into an empty chair as heavily as his small frame would allow.

"Am I being sued, too?" asked Oliver anxiously.

"No, Mr. Blithely. You're off the hook."

Oliver relaxed. "Is that because your client recognizes my rights as the original author of the character?"

"No, sir. She just knows you don't have any money. Good morning." He made his way out of the shop, and was instantly felled by a cricket bat.

"I'm ruined!" whined Geoffrey. "They'll blame me! Why didn't I keep my mouth shut?"

"Oh, Geoffrey, look on the bright side," Oliver said with detached amusement, patting his friend on the shoulder. "They can only fire you once."

"Not at Hoo, Watt & Eidenau," Geoffrey groaned. "All three partners get to fire you, one at a time. Mr. Hoo is the worst. I only hope he's on first." He slumped forward, clutching his head in his hands.

"Can we get on, Mr. Blithely?" the manager pleaded. Oliver signaled his readiness for the next group, but as he did so, he felt something brush his ankle and looked down. A pair of quizzical black eyes stared up at him. The ferret! The demonstrator must have let it go in the confusion. Front paws on his foot, it was sniffing his trouser turn-ups, as if contemplating an ascent into the darkness above. Oliver quickly grabbed the creature and dropped it into the bag of soft toys, just as another mother and her daughter came up to the table. He knew the ferret would relish the darkness and relative peace between the boxes, where it wouldn't be tempted by the proximity of small fingers.

"Hello, I'm Tully Mandivel, and this is Gretchen," said the woman, who was toting a camcorder.

"Hello, Gretchen," said Oliver as cheerfully as possible. The little girl, who was probably six years old, stared at him owlishly.

"Gretchen, aren't you going to say hello?" prompted the woman, training the camera on her daughter.

Gretchen inserted a crooked finger into her mouth, but still made no noise.

"Darling, you're being very rude. Do you know who this is?"

Her blue eyes fixed on Oliver, the child shook her head slowly in reply to her mother's question.

"This is O. C. Blithely," Mrs. Mandivel told her. "This is

the gentleman who makes up the stories about Finsbury the Ferret," the woman went on.

Gretchen's blue eyes widened even further. She gradually opened her mouth as far as possible, extracted her finger, and screamed at Oliver at the top of her lungs.

It was five minutes before anything approaching order was restored to the line of children, who, like molecules, seemed to take up more space when they were agitated. Through it all, Geoffrey was alternately reading the summons and quietly keening his predictions of what was going to happen to him on Monday morning, what kitchen equipment it was going to be done with, and in what postal district each of his body parts was to turn up. Oliver, wishing he had decided to write employee policy manuals instead of children's books, didn't raise his eyes when the next figure arrived at his table.

"To whom shall I sign it," he asked wearily.

"How about, 'To Effie, from Finchley'?"

He looked up and gulped. She was here. She was beautiful. And, good heavens, she was smiling at him.

"Never a dull moment around the Swithin household," Effie commented. Oliver swallowed and tried to make his tongue coordinate with his lips.

"Hello, Effie. Is this official business?" he managed to utter.

"Your Uncle Tim sent me to pick you up. I notice some of the walls are still standing, so I imagine you're not quite finished yet."

"I'm supposed to be here until twelve," he said.

"Good, I can watch the cricket while I'm waiting," Effie replied.

A girl who likes cricket *and* Indian food *and* thinks horoscopes are a load of old tosh. There was nothing else for it.

The hell with the conflict of interest. Oliver gripped the edge of the table. "Will you have lunch with me?" he croaked.

She laughed, showing small, perfect white teeth. "Sure. When?"

His hands were trembling now. A glass of drinking water on the table started to rattle. "Today?" he ventured.

Effie shook her head. "Tim wants us to join him as soon as possible. Tell you what, let's have dinner on Monday evening."

"Dinner? Monday?"

"Oh, sorry, perhaps you already have a date—"

"A date?" Oliver repeated with a hysterical laugh. "Oh, no, no, no. Whatever gave you that idea? No, Monday's great." O frabjous day!

"Look, I'd better let you get back to your adoring public. But I did actually buy one of your books, just to see what the fuss was about. Will you sign it for me? It doesn't mean we're engaged, or anything."

Oliver gleefully took the book from her, uncapped his pen with a flourish, and was immediately struck with the same writer's block that hit him when handed a blank greetings card. Fortunately, Geoffrey looked up at that moment and noticed who Oliver was speaking to. He leaped to his feet.

"Hello, Effie," he said heartily, putting on a suave smile that made him look like something drawn by Mervyn Peake.

"Hello, Mr. Angelwine. It's nice to see you up on your feet again," she said with a grin, remembering their last encounter. She returned her attention to Oliver. "I'll pick you and the book up in about an hour. Write something nice."

Geoffrey nudged Oliver conspiratorially, as she walked away from the table. "I think I'm in with a chance here," he whispered. "Watch this. Girls love stuffed animals."

He picked up the bag of soft toys, oblivious to the stare of disbelief that his friend had turned upon him.

"Effie," Geoffrey called, fumbling inside the bag. "If you'd like to wait a moment, I have a gift for you. Courtesy of Tadpole Tomes for Tiny Tots." His fingers closed around an object. "Hello," he muttered to Oliver, who was already too late to warn him, "there's something furry moving about in here. I must have left one of them switched on."

One of Mallard's mental games on long surveillances—and he had been parked in front of the Magpie and Stump on Old Bailey since six o'clock that morning—was to make a list of all the people who would be his victims if he were personally allowed to "punish the wrongdoer," words he could at present read on the Central Criminal Court's facade if he leaned far enough out of the car. Because of his general good nature, the list was usually very short. Today, however, his boredom had led him to fill the cerebral equivalent of three foolscap pages, getting to "all half-educated cultural snobs who mindlessly prefer the worst of Mozart to the best of Haydn" and "all self-regarding cretins who makes jokes about your name as if you've been too dim to notice up to that point in your life that you're named after a duck" before Effie's Renault pulled up behind him on the deserted street.

"Did you stop for lunch?" he asked accusingly as Oliver and Effie climbed into the back of his Rover.

"No, we had to rush Geoffrey Angelwine to the local hospital for stitches and a tetanus shot," Effie said. "Anything going on here?"

"See for yourself," said Mallard irritably, indicating the street outside. There was no traffic on Old Bailey, and very few pedestrians. From where they were stationed, where the street fanned out in front of the Court building, they could see cars and an occasional truck rumbling along Newgate

Street toward the Holborn Viaduct. Even St. Bartholomew's hospital, across the intersection, was quiet.

"The Courts are closed, although we've got men inside, of course," the superintendent continued. "There are a couple on the rooftops with binoculars, too. If the Libra location is the Scales of Justice, we'll get him. If not, it's on to Virgo, although I still don't know how you can kill someone with a virgin. But talking of virgins, why did Geoffrey Angelwine need stitches?"

They told him about the ferret and the book signing, which improved his mood somewhat. In fact, he laughed for the first time that day. "What did you do with the animal?" he asked, when they had finished.

"It's in a cat carrier in Effie's car," Oliver said.

"You kept it?"

Oliver nodded. "Those animal rights people didn't seem to care much for it, so I'll take it to the RSPCA tomorrow. It's quite a personable beast—very well domesticated."

"When it's not savaging the Angelwine digits," said his uncle with a chuckle.

"Geoffrey frightened it. He tried to switch it off."

Mallard laughed again, turning in his seat to look out of the open car window, but he stopped abruptly when he found himself facing Detective Sergeant Moldwarp's sorrowful features. Moldwarp was used to the reaction.

"Chief, I just got a call from the Yard," Moldwarp keened. "We think our man may have struck again."

"Where?" Mallard was immediately serious.

"St. James Square. Outside the London Library."

"How long ago?"

"At about three o'clock this morning."

"And we're only just hearing about it!" exclaimed Mallard. "Are we certain it's the zodiac murderer?"

"It's him," said Effie emphatically.

"How can you be so sure?" Mallard asked. "What's the London Library got to do with scales and balances? Does it have a collection, maybe?"

"No, it's simpler than that," she said, with a regretful smile. "It's so simple we just didn't think of it. Chief, Oliver—what are the first five letters of 'Library'?"

The two men spoke the word together.

"Archibald Brock," Mallard announced. "Retired railway guard from Isleworth. Moved to Folkestone, Kent a year or so ago. Summoned to London by a telephone call yesterday. Took a room at the St. James's Hotel, a letter was dropped off at the concierge's desk at about nine o'clock last night. The letter was the same style as the others, this time arranging a meeting in front of the hotel at ten. A porter saw him go out, after which his whereabouts were unknown until he fetched up dead in front of the London Library at three o'clock this morning, suspended from a lamppost. His body weight was balanced by a large sandbag, which gives us the other Libra connection. Found by a Library patron who'd been trapped in the building." Mallard ruffled the pages of his notebook. "Sorry," he remarked to Oliver, "I didn't make a note of this individual's name. Anyway, the discoverer of the body also picked up the zodiac murderer's calling card, which is why it didn't get reported to us sooner."

Mallard tossed the notebook onto the coffee table, lay back in the armchair, and stretched his long limbs. "So our man's getting more punctual. What can we expect tomorrow? A death at 12:01 A.M. precisely?" He checked his watch with a yawn. "If so, we've got one hour."

A fish-faced waiter in elaborate, eighteenth-century livery drifted into their corner of the members' lounge, the largest public room in the Sanders Club. He put their two empty brandy glasses on a salver.

"For the member, an invitation from the club to refill his glass," he intoned solemnly. Oliver smiled.

"From the club, an invitation for the member to refill his glass," he replied, knowing the drill. "No thanks."

The fish-waiter bowed deeply and swiveled toward Mallard.

"For the member's guest, an invitation from the club to refill his glass," he announced. Mallard looked at Oliver with mild panic in his eyes.

"He won't either," Oliver said. The waiter bowed again.

"Cocoa and tarts will be available at midnight," he gurgled and began to turn away. Then he seemed to think of something.

"Would the member's other guest like some warm milk?" he asked. Oliver looked down into the clear-lidded cat carrier beside his chair. The ferret was asleep.

"No thank you. And please don't feel you have to stay up for us."

The waiter smiled in a piscine manner. "Kind of you, sir. But I shall sit here till tomorrow." He oozed away.

"This place is weird," muttered Mallard, with a haunted glance around the room, but the oak-paneled walls, Chinese rugs, and comfortable leather chairs were standard for the clubs in the area. Only the framed drawings—Shepherd, Rackham, Millar, Van Beek, Charles Robinson, all original—hinted at the purpose of the club.

When the Sanders Club was founded, there had been plans to decorate the rooms in ways that celebrated children's literature, but it had been impossible to reconcile the members' desires. The austere public school look of the Jennings and Greyfriars enthusiasts couldn't be squared with the lush foliage demanded by fans of *The Secret Garden*. And the nautical accents of Hornblower and *Swallows and Amazons* couldn't accommodate the chocolate and peach color scheme suggested by Roald Dahl enthusiasts. Instead of decor, therefore, the club chose to celebrate its members' calling through rituals and celebrations, such as the annual Snark Hunt and the Easter weekend Pooh-sticks tournament between Tower Bridge and the Thames Barrier. And there were theme nights. Tonight, being the first Saturday in the month, it was Alice night, which Oliver always relished. But he avoided the bimonthly *Tom Brown's Schooldays* evenings— some of the staff, equipped with canes, took their roles a little too seriously.

His inability to stop the litany of murders was taking its toll on Mallard. It wouldn't have surprised Oliver to learn that as well as dealing with the death of Archie Brock, his uncle had also been defending his handling of the case to his superiors. And yet, after sending Effie home for a good night's sleep, Mallard still chose to join Oliver for a drink at the club before heading home to Theydon Bois and Phoebe, in search of one more insight that could put an end to the zodiac murderer's run.

"The computer turned up absolutely nothing," Mallard reported wearily. "The victims never worked together, didn't go the same schools, didn't belong to the same clubs, didn't correspond with each other . . ."

"Four of the victims lived in London," Oliver suggested.

"The murders took place in London!" Mallard cried disparagingly. "That means four times out of six, the murderer chose victims who were only a bus ride from their place of execution. Big fornicating deal! And even that can't account for Gordon Paper, who lived all his life in Yorkshire, or Archie Brock, who was summoned up from Kent."

"But like Nettie Clapper, Archie Brock *used* to live in west London," Oliver persisted. He sensed Mallard's despondency and he knew the only way to combat it was to pepper him with fresh ideas. "If you go back a couple of years, you had the Pisces living in Barnes, the Aquarius in Brentford, the Capricorn in Richmond, the Scorpio in Kingston, and the Libra in Isleworth. Five out of the six victims were living within a few miles of each other, all close to the Thames."

"And so what?" Mallard sighed. He took off his spectacles and twirled them around his hand. "Suppose the murderer's motivation is to bump off anyone who rubbed him up the wrong way—Vanessa Parmenter bungled his travel arrangements, Mark Sandys-Penza failed to sell his maisonette, Harry refused to buy a poppy from him on Remembrance Day. Or he may have chosen his victims for convenience. You want a Pisces to come alone to Trafalgar Square at six in the morning and not put up too much of a fight? Who better than an aging writer who's been up half the night drinking at a club round the corner? A needy, working-class lady from the suburbs is exactly the Aquarius who'd want to be met at the tube station, because she's unsure of her way around the unfamiliar streets of Belgravia. A shady Capricorn estate agent from Richmond won't think twice before meeting his mythical client in the anonymous surroundings of Kew Gardens, a mile or two down the road. I need something more predictive."

Oliver glanced down again. The ferret was awake and was nuzzling the inside of the box. He lifted the animal into his lap and gently scratched the back of its head. It seemed to like the attention and settled itself comfortably.

"How does your convenience theory account for Gordon Paper?" he asked.

"It takes some bottle to entice a rural Yorkshire recluse with travel sickness into Piccadilly Circus at lunchtime," Mallard replied with a shrug. "Maybe the killer wanted to show us how manipulative he can be."

"But was that worth losing a thread of his pattern, the birth signs of his victims?" Oliver persisted.

Mallard smiled bitterly. "I have a surprise for you, Ollie. You asked the right question yesterday. Vanessa Parmenter *was* a Scorpio. And Archie Brock *was* a Libra. Gordon Paper was an odd man out. That means tomorrow's victim will probably be a Virgo, after all. Unfortunately, the restoration of the complete pattern doesn't bring us any closer to stopping these murders." He broke off, remembering uncomfortably that he had heard the same words from the lips of the Assistant Commissioner only two hours earlier.

Oliver was silent.

"I'm sorry, Ollie," Mallard continued. "I know a connection between the victims would help us pinpoint the Virgo. But the computer confirms it: The victims had nothing in common. We have to fall back on the evidence we've already collected."

"Nothing in common," Oliver repeated thoughtfully.

Then he started suddenly. The ferret looked up with a hurt expression on its face. "Then that's where we're going wrong!" Oliver exclaimed. "The computer is looking for things that the victims have in common. What we should be looking for is differences!"

He hastily dropped the animal back into its carrier and turned to Mallard with excitement.

"Uncle Tim, you're telling me that the victims have a sequential string of birth signs, right? But would your computer have even spotted that?"

"I don't . . ."

"No! Because it's looking for similarities. It would only have gone beep or ding or twang if they'd all had the *same* birth sign!"

"Go on," said Mallard cautiously.

"If five of the six victims had all been brain surgeons, for

153

example, your precious computer would have blown a gasket," Oliver continued. "But if they'd been, respectively, a tinker, a tailor, a soldier, a sailor, and a rich man, the computer would have ignored it. Because there's no similarity between those professions. It takes a *human* mind to see the pattern!"

"So our victims may have nothing in common as a group, but they could still be part of a sequence?"

"Yes!" Oliver cried. "Individually, they may each epitomize some element in another pattern, in addition to their zodiac signs. If there is a hidden pattern, and we can find it, we may finally get ahead of the killer."

"But as Effie keeps telling us, the odds against our finding any other connection are astronomical. Or astrological."

"That's when we assumed the killer was trying to find a pattern that would match twelve victims he'd already chosen. It's easier the other way round—choosing victims to match a pattern. Even two patterns. You just need a tinker who's also a Pisces, a tailor who's an Aquarius, a Capricorn soldier, a Sagittarius sailor . . ."

"But what is there to suggest a hidden connection?"

"It's the way the killer thinks," Oliver claimed earnestly. "It's all a game to him. He's gone out of his way to signal the zodiac—calling cards, birthdays, locations, methods of killing. That was for novices. Finding the elusive second thread, if it exists, is for experts at the game. What can we lose by trying it?"

It was the challenge Mallard needed. He sat up straight and ran his hands through his milky hair. "Then if we want to save the Virgo, we've got less than an hour to find this other pattern. *If* there is one." He put his glasses on. "So get fish-face to bring me a coffee."

Oliver beckoned the fish-waiter, who was floating near the door.

154

"Have some wine," the waiter said as he approached, making an encouraging gesture toward the table between the two men.

"I don't see any wine," Mallard muttered distractedly.

"There isn't any!" exclaimed the waiter, triumphantly completing the syllogism.

"A pot of coffee and a pot of tea, please," said Oliver quickly, noticing the look on Mallard's face.

"There's cocoa at midnight, sir," the waiter reminded him. "And tarts."

"Coffee, tea, now."

"Okay, what alternatives spring to mind?" asked Mallard after the waiter had drifted moodily away.

Oliver picked up his uncle's notebook and turned to a fresh page. Then he wrote the list of the victims and their professions.

Pisces:	Harry Random, writer
Aquarius:	Nettie Clapper, part-time home help
Capricorn:	Mark Sandys-Penza, estate agent
Sagittarius:	Gordon Paper, research chemist
Scorpio:	Vanessa Parmenter, travel agent
Libra:	Archibald Brock, retired railway guard

"Well, we don't actually have a tinker or a tailor," Mallard commented. "Neither do we have a butcher, a baker, and a candlestick-maker."

"Random, Clapper, Sandys-Penza. Paper, Parmenter, Brock," Oliver intoned. "Doesn't make sense. Doesn't even scan. How about first names? Harry, Nettie, Mark, Gordon, Vanessa, Archie. Not biblical names. Are these the names of characters in a play or a novel?"

"Maybe there's an additional link between the names and the birth sign. Sir Harry Random was a Pisces—fish swim at random. Nettie Clapper, the Aquarian—a net can be associated with water bearers. No, it doesn't work, does it? I suppose it would help if we knew what Nettie was short for."

"Henrietta, probably. Or Antoinette."

"And Harry's short for Henry. Any connection with kings and queens?"

"I don't think there's ever been a King Gordon," said Oliver. "And Harry Random's name was short for Hargreaves, not Henry." He glanced at a framed picture above his uncle's head, an original sketch by Henry Holiday. "How about characters in *The Hunting of the Snark?*"

"Remind me."

"The Bellman, the Boots, the Bonnet-maker, the Barrister, the Broker, the Billiard-maker, the Banker, the Beaver, the Baker, and the Butcher."

"That's only ten. Does it fit?"

The fish-waiter arrived with the tray, but they ignored him. Mallard was alert now, revitalized by the chance to save a life from his adversary. Oliver found he could still enjoy the exercise as an intriguing abstraction, grappling with the mind and intentions of the killer. It was like doing crossword puzzles, which he'd often claimed were harder to solve than to set because the setter already knew the answers. But Mallard was in deeper, and could place no distance between his actions and the expected death, almost as if he were trying to save his own life by solving the conundrum. Oliver knew there was a perverse temptation to admire the killer, almost to will him to kill again for the entertainment value of the next death. But he knew that Mallard never fell into the trap, and would be overjoyed if the Murder Squad became superfluous to the nation's needs. The potential second thread had become a lifeline that he grasped joyfully, hauling himself back to full vigilance.

As they pitched ideas and patterns between them—is there a connection with the twelve apostles? the ten commandments? Wren's churches? Pooh's companions? Shakespeare's plays? the Labors of Hercules? the "Carry On" films?—Oliver prayed his idea would yet bear fruit, and that Mallard would not be tossed back into impotence, exhaustion, failure. But as midnight approached, the second thread stayed hidden.

"I still say the places they lived are our best leads," Mallard snapped impatiently as another of Oliver's patterns failed to work—that each victim shared the same initials as successive stations on the Piccadilly Line. He drained his cup of the last cold splash of coffee. "Except for Gordon Paper we have five people who once—and not too long ago—lived no more than five miles from each other."

"And except for Gordon Paper, we have a perfect match of birth sign to site of death," Oliver reminded him.

"The phrase 'except for Gordon Paper' seems to come up a lot," Mallard commented. "Would this be easier if we left him out and tried to find a connection that works for the others?"

There was a sudden, breathy, one-note fanfare, which caused them both to jump.

"Dear God, what on earth is that?" Mallard exclaimed, looking in the direction of the noise. By the door to the lounge, the fish-waiter was tucking a long trumpet under his arm. Then he came to attention.

"The trial's beginning! The trial's beginning!" he called in a loud voice and disappeared.

"That means the cocoa and jam tarts are being served in the next room," Oliver told him. "You know, it's a reference to the Knave of Hearts's trial in *Alice's Adventures in Wonderland*. The tarts were the evidence."

"It also means it's midnight," said Mallard resignedly, getting stiffly to his feet. He began to look fatigued again. "Virgo day has begun. I'll run you and your little friend home."

Oliver leaned over the arm of his chair to see if the ferret had fallen asleep again. The creature wasn't visible, so he lifted the case onto his lap, opening the clear plastic lid. But the box was empty. He must have forgotten to secure the catches, and the inquisitive animal had pried its way out while the two men were preoccupied. Oliver leaped to his feet and searched frantically under the cushions on his chair.

"Need some loose change for the bus?" Mallard inquired languidly. "I said I'd drive you."

"The ferret's escaped. What should I do?"

"I thought you were the expert on ferrets. Where would it have gone?"

Oliver tried to remember his research. "They like to burrow into cushions and upholstery."

"So would I right now," Mallard commented with a yawn. "I suggest we shut all the doors between here and the outside world, and then search each room very carefully until we find it. It can't have got far."

Oliver led the way out of the members' lounge, scanning the floor nervously for a flash of light brown fur, and they closed the double doors behind them. The waiter was nowhere to be seen, and the club seemed to be deserted. Oliver was about to turn the catch on the front door, when it swung open abruptly into his face, and a tall man in disheveled evening dress pranced into the lobby. He was clutching a balloon.

"Nobody around?" he asked vaguely, with a broad, tipsy smile. Then he caught sight of Oliver behind the door, and his smile vanished. "Oh, it's you, Swithin. Is it some sort of family curse that causes you to haunt this lobby?"

"Good evening, Mr. Scroop," said Oliver politely. "Celebrating something?"

"Sold another book, actually. Who's this?" Scroop attempted to focus his gaze on Mallard. Oliver knew his manners.

"Uncle Tim, this is one of our members, Mr. Scroop. He writes books about footballs that are really UFOs. Mr. Scroop, this is my uncle, Detective Superintendent Mallard of New Scotland Yard."

"Pull the other one," said Scroop, spinning away unsteadily from Mallard's proffered hand. "I know you, Swithin, you're as full of tricks as your benighted Finsbury. This gentleman is probably a cab driver. Well, I'm not falling for it," he declared loudly, stumbling again. "I'm going to the members' lounge. Send the whisky in with a decanter of waiter."

"I wouldn't do that," called Oliver as Scroop lurched away.

"And why not?"

"Well, the truth is, I've lost my ferret in there."

Scroop froze. He turned slowly, rocking from side to side on rigid legs, and faced Oliver.

"Nice try, Swithin," he hissed. "But you don't catch me that weasily."

He started to fall backward, recovered, and let the momentum propel him toward the lounge doors. Oliver started to follow.

"Wait," snapped Mallard abruptly.

"Oh, but I have to—"

"Wait!"

Mallard was motionless in the center of the lobby, his hands on his hips. He seemed to have grown taller.

"The trial's beginning!" he shouted triumphantly. "Oliver, what do we need at a trial?"

"Apart from jam tarts? Well, as Lewis Carroll said, 'Such

a trial, dear sir, with no jury or judge would be wasting our br—' "

Oliver stopped. He knew what his uncle had just thought of. "A jury?" he offered cautiously.

Mallard nodded slowly. "A jury. Twelve people, drawn from the same geographic area, who have nothing in common with one another. Twelve people, upon whom somebody may want to take revenge." He ran over to the porter's desk and lifted the telephone. "We must find the last time each of these people performed jury duty," he continued breathlessly. "It's Sunday morning, so it'll be a while before we can get into the court records. But we can see if any of the surviving relatives can remember."

"No need."

Mallard looked up.

"*I* can remember," Oliver told him, grinning broadly. "Sir Harry Random was on a jury a little more than two years ago. At the Old Bailey."

"That's perfect!" Mallard exclaimed. "Two years ago, all of the victims, bar Paper, lived in the same catchment area. I'll get Moldwarp to rouse the Central Criminal Court record keepers and we'll get our hands on a list of jurors. Oh, Ollie, I'm praying there are some familiar names on that list. Why didn't this occur to us earlier?"

"Because we stopped thinking about geography when Yorkshireman Gordon Paper joined the list of victims," Oliver reminded him. "And because a jury would take us back to choosing the pattern to match the victim. Twelve jurors, each with a different birth sign—Effie would tell us the odds are against it."

"I know, but it's the best lead we have. And we already know that it fits Sir Harry."

A sudden screech of terror echoed down the corridor from the members' lounge.

"Ah, Mr. Scroop's found my ferret," said Oliver brightly, while his uncle waited impatiently for his call to be answered. "You know the last time I was here, I was in the lobby with Dworkin . . ."

He broke off, and a look of horror crossed his face.

"Dworkin," he said, clutching Mallard's arm.

"What do you mean, 'dworking'?" his uncle replied crossly. "I'm not dworking. I've never dworked. I wouldn't know how to dwork."

"No, no, Dworkin's our day porter here at the club. He got his job through Harry. Well, that's how they met—they were on jury duty together."

"Then for God's sake see if you can contact him!" Mallard urged, glancing at his wristwatch. "If Dworkin is a Virgo, his life's already in danger."

Oliver scurried away to the club office to find Dworkin's telephone number.

"Although," Mallard added reflectively, alone in the lobby, "I still can't fathom how anybody can be killed with a virgin."

Eight

ACROSS THE STREET, THE clock in St. Mary's church tower chimed midnight. Dworkin had been in bed for two hours, but he still lay awake, counting the strikes, deliberately skipping from seven to nine. Ten . . . eleven . . . twelve . . . thirteen! It jarred pleasurably. He liked to create the unusual in his mind, such as losing count of the stairs in the dark for the thrill of feeling his foot sink through that last invisible step. It made up for the too-predictable reality of his quotidian life.

Now the bell died away, and silence fell outside. But inside, in the darkness of his bedroom, Dworkin became aware again of his body's chorus: the tide of blood pumping in his ears, the liquid fauxbourdon from his lungs with every breath, the distant grumbling that refused to subside, although he had eaten the salmon paste sandwich three hours ago. There was a time—how long now?—when his digestion was silent, when he didn't wheeze, when he woke up in the morning and his chin and pillow were still dry. For years, he had deprecated the signs of his own aging that he would have found distasteful in others—a forgotten blob of shaving soap behind the ear, an occasional unzipped fly. Now, in these insomniac hours, Dworkin almost believed he could hear himself growing older, the crackle of brittle skin settling into wrinkles, the draining of pigment from his hair, and the steady pitter-patter of a day's loss of brain cells, cascading like invisible dandruff onto his shoulders.

What was that? His stomach again? No, the noise was outside himself. A cat, probably, nosing around the dustbins. His hearing was less acute, too. He didn't want to be old. Those gossipy fools at the Sanders Club were wrong when they said he was too fond of children. He wanted to *be* a child, to relive the childhood he'd failed to appreciate the first time, because . . .

There again! No doubt this time. Somebody is downstairs, moving slowly, quietly. Call the police? The only telephone is downstairs. All right, a surprise attack.

Dworkin threw back the covers and noiselessly eased himself onto the floor, sliding his feet into the waiting leather slippers. He slept naked, but his thin silk kimono was within reach. Knotting the sash, he crept out of the bedroom and down the stairs, straining his ears. There was nobody in the hallway, but the door to his living room was open. He was sure he had closed it before going to bed. He reached the bottom of the stairs and felt in the umbrella stand for the shillelagh his brother had brought him during an unscheduled stopover at Shannon airport, couldn't find it, chose a tightly rolled umbrella instead, holding it ferrule-first, like a fencing foil. Then he slid into the living room, reaching for the light switch.

"Don't move," he yelled as the room was suddenly bathed in a weak, yellowish light. He squinted and stared. Nothing was out of place in the room. Except for the little girl in the plain blue dress, sitting on the settee, who stared back at him with frightened, green eyes. She drew her knees up to her chin.

"Who are you?" he yelped.

The girl didn't speak. Dworkin lowered the umbrella, aware that she posed no threat and, more important, that he looked ridiculous.

His first impression, that she was about twelve or thirteen, had been wrong. Her figure had the slim lankiness of that age, but from her features, he could see now that she was in her late teens, if not early twenties. The sense of childishness was real, however: She wore no makeup on her pretty, freckled face and her long, auburn hair was parted simply in the middle of her head. She continued to watch him timidly.

"What are you doing here?" he demanded.

The girl lowered her legs primly and placed her hands in her lap.

"You don't know who I am, do you?" she asked meekly.

"No. I don't believe I've seen you before."

"You have, you know," the girl said, but not as an accusation. "I've lived around the corner for ten years. Since I was nine years old."

"I'm sorry, I don't remember," said Dworkin, suddenly conscious of his naked, blue-veined legs below the kimono. He dropped the umbrella onto a chair.

"Well, I don't go out much. My mother's very strict. If she knew I was here now, she'd kill me."

She tugged her dress tightly along her thighs.

"Anyway, I've decided that I have to find my own way," she continued, a new resolve in her voice. "But I know so

164

very little about the world, and I'm afraid of being an easy target for men of low morals. I'm still a . . . well, you know."

"Yes, I see," mumbled Dworkin, aware that his heart was pounding. The girl looked directly at him and mustered a tentative smile.

"You've always seemed a very kind man, sir. So I've plucked up all my courage and come here tonight to ask you a big favor."

"And that is?" Dworkin's mouth was dry.

She stood up. "Please, Mr. Dworkin, would you make me a real woman?"

"Oh, my goodness gracious," he stammered, taking a step backward and dropping into an armchair. The girl stood in silence for a moment. Then she sighed.

"Would this help you decide?" she asked. She hoisted her dress from the waist until the blue material hung in folds around her shoulders, revealing slender legs. Slipping her arms out of the dress's sleeves, she pulled it over her head and discarded it. The long red hair floated down again.

Dworkin stared at the girl's thin, pallid body, noticing the small breasts and unblemished skin. "Are you sure you're nineteen?" he asked huskily.

"Nearly twenty," she replied.

"I'm old enough to be your father," he mused. Then he smiled. "But not your grandfather. Let's go upstairs."

Later, as Dworkin lay on the bed, there were new sounds—his faster heartbeat, his shallow, rasping breathing, and the girl's steadier respiration. He reached for the alarm clock on his bedside locker. As he did, she stirred and looked at him with a predatory expression.

"That was wonderful," she whispered, kissing the loose skin on his throat. "Let's do it again." Her lips slid to his wrinkled chest, teeth pulling playfully at the few white hairs.

"No, my child," he said with an indulgent smile and a

165

comforting pat on her perfect bottom, "we should rest a while. A man needs to get his . . . breath back."

She threw her body over his beneath the sheets as if he hadn't spoken, hugging him tightly and pressing her taut belly into the folds of damp flesh around his waist. Was the rhythmic thumping in his head getting louder?

"Look, I really can't right away," he gasped, trying now to push her away, but his arms were drained of strength. "You see, I have a heart condition. I have to be careful."

Still, she didn't hear. How could she over the screaming of blood. It was deafening him. And that ringing in the head.

"Come on, old man," she snarled. "Now!"

She was suddenly heavy on his chest. Or was the weight some other pain? The ringing was louder, regular, insistent.

"I can't breathe," he wheezed. "Please . . ." But it was too late. The girl's contorted, rapacious face began to fade from view, her cries dying away, until all that was left was the piercing ringing, ringing, in his ears.

The ringing . . .

Dworkin shook himself fully awake and gazed blearily at the alarm clock, but it wasn't guilty of the noise. Quarter past midnight! Whoever was telephoning at this hour had better have a good reason for interrupting his regular Sunday night fantasy about the girl who lived across the street. Now he'd have to start all over again, and he wasn't sure he could recreate the mood. He stumbled from his bed, put his woolen dressing gown on over his pajamas, searched unsuccessfully for his slippers, and staggered grumpily down the stairs. He really should get an upstairs extension.

"Yes?" he snapped into the telephone.

"Mr. Dworkin?"

"Yes. Who's this?"

"This is Oliver Swithin, from the Sanders . . ."

"Oh, Mr. Swithin." Dworkin knew that deference was

166

never off-duty in his job. "How nice of you to call. What can I do for you, sir?"

"I have to ask you a question, very urgently. It could be a matter of life and death."

"Please go on."

"What sign are you?"

"I beg your pardon?"

"What's sign of the zodiac were you born under?"

That was it. Swithin had lost his marbles. Dworkin always thought the young man was one dormouse short of a tea party, and the behavior with the wastepaper last week had only fueled this suspicion. But to wake people up in the middle of the night with some nonsensical question about signs of the zodiac! There could only be one solution: not being Californian (which might also have excused the time of the call), Swithin had to be insane. Dworkin knew exactly what to do: humor him, then telephone the authorities. Wasn't his uncle some kind of bigwig at Scotland Yard?

"I'm Taurus, sir, the sign of the bull. My old father used to say I was born under the Bull and the Bull was rather surprised about it. Thank you for asking."

A sigh of relief came down the phone line.

"Then let me ask you something else. You were on a jury a couple of years ago, at the Old Bailey."

Juries now. Swithin had really gone over the edge. Not healthy for a young man to think about ferrets all day long. "Yes, sir. That's where I first met your late friend, Sir Harry. It was through him that I got my job at the Sanders."

"Can you remember anybody else on the jury?"

"Oh, sir, it was two years ago, and we didn't deliberate very long, as I recall. Let me see." Dworkin subsided onto the stairs, trying to remember. "Most of the talking was done by Sir Harry and another man, who was some kind of estate agent."

167

"If I say some of the names, will that help?"

"You could try."

"Nettie Clapper."

"Clapper? Doesn't ring a bell . . ."

"Some might say otherwise," murmured Oliver. "Mark Sandys-Penza."

"It sounds very familiar, but I couldn't be sure."

"Gordon Paper."

"No, I don't think so."

"Vanessa Parmenter."

"Yes!" Dworkin exclaimed. "Ah now, I definitely remember her. Young thing, isn't she? Probably in her twenties but looked younger. Blond hair. Lived in Kingston."

Bingo. Oliver was silent for a moment. "I think that's her," he said quietly. "Any others?"

"I don't know. Oh, wait, there was this old fellow who kept us in stitches. Worked on the railways. What was his name? Arnie something."

"Archie?"

"That's it, Archie. Archie . . . Brock!"

"Any more?"

A pause. "No, sir, not that I can bring to mind right now."

"Thank you, Mr. Dworkin, and please keep thinking. If you remember any other names, call me at the club. Don't go back to bed. The police will call on you shortly and ask you to go with them. There's nothing to worry about. Good night."

Paranoid, thought Dworkin as he put the receiver down. Poor Mr. Swithin, thinks he's in some Kafka story. Ah well, time enough to call the funny farm in the morning. Vanessa Parmenter, eh? He'd forgotten about her. Now what if *she* were to turn up in his sitting room in the middle of the night . . .

* * *

Oliver ran from the club manager's office, where he had been using the telephone, and found his uncle in the lobby. Mallard was still speaking to Detective Sergeant Moldwarp at the Yard. The waiter, who had bound Scroop's bleeding finger, put him into a taxi, and scooped the ferret back into its box, was sitting on a bench, watching the activity with his mouth open a little and his eyes open a lot.

"That's it!" Oliver shouted. Mallard covered the mouthpiece.

"What?"

"Dworkin remembered two of the victims. It's definitely that jury."

Mallard closed his eyes and seemed to say a short prayer.

"What sign was Dworkin?" he asked.

"He's Taurus."

"Then he's safe for now. I'll get one of my lads to pick him up and take him somewhere safe. Did he give us any new names?"

"No."

"Hell's teeth. So we still don't know who the Virgin is." He returned to the telephone. "I don't care what time it is, Sergeant, I need those records. Even if we have to wake up the Lord Chancellor. We must find out who was on that jury. Yes, it's definite now. Good, call me back."

Mallard hung up the phone. "Bloody red tape," he muttered. "I may have to go over to the Yard and add my own weight to the proceedings. I wish Effie were there—she has ways of getting things done that even I can't fathom."

"Shall I call her?" asked Oliver, hopefully. He was prepared to risk her sleepy irritation for the privilege of being the first voice she'd hear on waking. Maybe it wouldn't be the only time. He wanted to find out what had she thought of the inscription he had eventually written in the Finsbury

169

book and mutely handed over when she returned from the hospital with Geoffrey: "To Effie, best wishes, Oliver (O. C. Blithely)." Could she read between the lines?

"No, let her sleep." Mallard noticed the waiter, who had been attempting to follow the conversation without success. The Lord Chancellor was a virgin? "How about a couple of brandies?" Mallard asked genially.

"I shall sit here, on and off, for days and days," the waiter intoned, and began whistling. Then he noticed Mallard's expression, and slipped away quickly.

"Brandy, uncle?" asked Oliver. "Not champagne?"

"No celebrations yet," Mallard replied seriously. "We've only scotched the snake. We haven't saved the life of Virgo, assuming there is one, and we certainly haven't identified the murderer."

"Given that the victims were on a jury," Oliver mused, "it does rather suggest a motive—some connection with the case they were trying, a disgruntled convict, perhaps. The whole zodiac thing could have been a smoke screen to get us looking in the wrong direction."

"As soon as we get the court records, we'll be able to draw up a list of suspects. Right now, I want to get what remains of that jury into protective custody as soon as I can. Do you have Dworkin's address? Ollie?"

But Oliver wasn't listening. His features had assumed a configuration rather similar to those of the recently departed waiter, like a startled haddock.

"I think I may be able to get the names of the jurors more quickly," he said slowly.

"How?"

"Harry Random kept notes on everything that happened to him during his life. He had the most extensive personal filing system—I know, I was looking through it earlier this week. I'm sure I saw a file marked 'jury duty.' It would be like him to have recorded everyone's name, age, appearance—who knows, even their birth signs!"

Mallard produced his wallet and plucked out five twenty-pound notes. "Look, I have to go the Yard. Take a cab and get out to Barnes as quickly as you can. And you'd better hope the newly domesticated Lorina hasn't thrown away those files. I'll send over a car to bring you back. Call me as soon as you get the names."

Half an hour later, Oliver was hammering on the door of the Random home in Barnes. After a long wait, a window opened above the front door. Oliver could just make out the silhouette of a head.

"Who is it?" called a woman's voice sternly.

"Lorina? It's me, Oliver."

"Oliver?" There was a pause, then a chuckle. "This is so sudden. Are we eloping?"

"Look, I'm sorry to disturb you so late," he hissed, "but I need to see your father's files. Very urgently."

"Well, you certainly know how to sweep a girl off her feet, my Romeo," Lorina said. "I'll be right down."

A minute later, a light came on in the entrance hall and Lorina opened the front door, clutching Satan, the cat, like a baby. She was wearing an oversize white T-shirt, which had fallen down over one shoulder, and apparently little else. Dworkin would have approved. Oliver, who didn't need to be, was reminded anyway of how much he had always liked her shoulders. And her feet.

"I'm very sorry, Lorina," he said again, stepping across the threshold without waiting for an invitation. "It's very important." He set down the ferret's traveling case.

"Last time you brought roses," she said ruefully as he ran past her and headed for Sir Harry's study. She closed the front door and followed.

"So what's so urgent?" she asked, yawning. He was crouched over the filing cabinet that he knew contained Random's personal files. The light was harsh to her sleepy eyes.

"We need this information to stop Harry's murderer from killing again," he told her.

"Murderer?" she faltered. She dropped the cat and sat down on an upright chair. "Daddy was murdered?"

Oliver spun around, clutching the desk to keep his balance. "Oh my dear Lord," he moaned softly, seeing her dark eyes fill with tears. "You didn't know, did you? I completely forgot."

"You said it was an accident," she reminded him, clasping her hands in her lap and lowering her head. A tear splashed onto her wrist.

"The police thought it *was* an accident then," he said, choosing to conceal his own opinions at the time. He scuttled across the floor on his knees, causing Satan to leap aside, and without seeking permission, slid his arms around her waist. Lorina fell into the embrace, resting her cheek on the top of his head. "But now we know it's murder," Oliver continued quietly, his face pressed against her sternum. "Your father was killed because he was on a jury. Back at the Old Bailey about two years ago. He's not the only victim."

She cried for about half a minute without moving. Then she sniffed loudly and pulled herself away. "I'm okay," she said, wiping her eyes with the neckline of the T-shirt. "Thanks for the hug, Ollie. It was nice."

"Is Ambrose staying here? He should hear this, too."

"He didn't want to stay in Daddy's house. He'll be back for the funeral on Monday. I suppose I should have guessed Daddy's death was more than an accident, what with that gloomy Scotland Yard detective showing up during the week, asking all kinds of questions about Daddy's life."

172

"I should have told you. I'm very sorry." Oliver admitted. "But there were reasons why we didn't want the public to know about the murders."

"We?" she queried.

"I'm helping Uncle Tim. That's why I'm here." He glanced nervously at the files, as if they might have evaporated while he was comforting her. "Are you sure you're okay? I really need to find this information. It could save somebody's life."

She nodded, sniffing again and looking around the room in vain for a box of tissues. Oliver scurried back to the cabinet and pulled out a buff file from the hanger marked "jury duty." He dropped it onto the desk and switched on the table lamp, throwing himself onto Harry's upholstered work chair. Lorina stood up and came over, resting a hand lightly on his shoulder. Satan mewed softly, but was ignored.

"You're very clever to be assisting Scotland Yard," she whispered, watching him flick through the pages of notes in her father's handwriting. He was concentrating so intently on the words in front of him that he didn't notice her finger idly twisting the strands of fair hair that fell over his collar.

"Ollie, we had some nice times together, didn't we?" she asked.

"Oh, sure. Ah, here it is. A list of his fellow jurors. I was certain Harry's obsession with details wouldn't let me down."

Lorina perched on the desk, very close to the papers, twisting her neck and pretending to read the scrawled notes with him. She sat on her hands, keeping her knees slightly bent, as if aware that even the best-toned thigh doesn't look its best when pressed down on a flat surface.

"I forget how good-looking you are, in your own way," she continued idly, perhaps aware she didn't have his full attention. "You still think I'm attractive don't you, Ollie?"

"More than ever," he said distractedly, his gallantry on

173

autopilot. Lorina smiled and placed her feet on the edge of his chair, burrowing her toes under his leg. He reached suddenly for the telephone on the desk and pressed the number of Mallard's private line at Scotland Yard. Mallard answered immediately.

"I've got the list," Oliver said excitedly.

"Does Harry have a fax machine?"

Oliver covered the mouthpiece and turned to Lorina. "Do you have a fax?" he asked. She shook her head and slid off the desk, which briefly caused her loose T-shirt to ride up to her hips. Oliver didn't notice.

"No, I'll have to read you the names," he said to Mallard. "Here they are, with some other information from Harry's notes to help you pinpoint the right people. Nettie Clapper, Vanessa Parmenter we know about. Agnes Day, old age pensioner from Hounslow. Ingmar Twist, accountant, lived in Chiswick. Mark Sandys-Penza we have already. Boy, Harry didn't like him."

"Get on with it."

"Sorry. Edmund Tradescant, marketing executive from Twickenham. Archibald Brock, we have. Spiller Bude, unemployed, South Ealing. Arthur Dworkin, unemployed— well, he was then. Rogers Fossick, sales assistant, Kingston. And Concepta Carter-Wallace, housewife, also from Chiswick."

"That's only eleven."

"Harry was the twelfth."

"No Gordon Paper?"

"No Gordon Paper," Oliver confirmed. "You were right to treat him as an aberration."

"So ignoring Paper, five jurors are dead. We know about Dworkin. That leaves us six to find—Agnes Day, Ingmar Twist, Edmund Tradescant, Spiller Bude, Rogers Fossick, and Concepta Carter-Wallace."

174

"Correct."

"Why does Edmund Tradescant sound familiar? Never mind. We'll track them down. I wonder which is the Virgo. I don't suppose Harry noted their birth signs as well, did he?"

"No such luck."

"Ah, well. Okay, bundle up that file and give it to Sergeant Welkin when he turns up. He'll drive you home then bring it on to me."

"Don't you want me to come back with Welkin?"

"No, get some sleep. We have to make sure the rest of the jury is protected. I'll call you later. By the way, who was on trial?"

Oliver lifted the exploring cat off the file and consulted the notes again.

"It was a man called Angus Burbage."

"Really?" Mallard whistled. "That's a famous one. He was convicted for trying to blow up a police station. Well, Burbage is certainly a likely candidate for the murderer, although I would have thought twelve simultaneous letter bombs would be more in his line. Why the zodiac stuff?"

"Style? Gamesmanship?" Oliver suggested. "But wouldn't Burbage still be in prison after only two years?"

"I'll find out. Although you'd be amazed at what you can arrange while you're doing time. Good night."

Oliver hung up and turned to Lorina, who was leaning against the doorjamb, absentmindedly biting the ends of her fingers. She had turned off the room's main light.

"Thanks, Lorina. And sorry again."

She waved the apology away as if it were no more than an impertinent gnat. "I remember the Angus Burbage case," she said. "I suppose you'll be looking at it again."

"I don't know. Now we've sorted out the puzzle, I don't expect to be involved as much."

Lorina threw her head back and stared at the ceiling. In

the shaded light of the table lamp, she looked cornered, vulnerable. "Daddy and I used to have tremendous rows about Angus Burbage. He thought Burbage should be shot, I thought he was a freedom fighter for the oppressed. That was in my militant period."

"I recall your opinions vividly."

"Nobody has to know, do they? I mean, it won't come up again?" she asked anxiously.

"Why should it?"

"No reason. I was rather immature in those days, and I don't want to be reminded, what with my job and everything."

Oliver stood up and gathered the papers, without looking at her. It was true that, during their college romance, Lorina's only diplomatic skill had been a useful ability to disguise herself as an unmade bed. "I didn't think you were immature," he said kindly. "You were strongly committed to a political viewpoint, and I admired that. However, I happened not to agree with you. I didn't agree with Harry, either."

"Are you leaving?" Lorina asked, after a pause. She had moved into the room again.

"There's a rather forbidding policeman, who always reminds me of my great-uncle Henry, about to arrive to pick up these papers. I hope that's all right with you, I should have asked."

"Of course. But then what are you going to do?"

"I'm going home to get some sleep. It's been a very long day for me and the ferret."

They were standing shoulder to shoulder at the desk, neither looking at the other. He could smell the cream she had used on her face earlier that evening, feel the warmth of her arm through his shirt.

"You could stay," she said quietly.

Oliver tapped the stack of papers noisily on the desktop

to straighten them. "That's kind of you, but I don't want to trouble you to make up the guest room," he said brightly. "It won't take me long to get home this time of night. Not with a policeman driving."

Lorina nodded. The guest room was not what she had meant. Oliver knew it, too, but he had learned that feigned misunderstanding, while initially cruel, is often the cleanest way out of an awkward situation. The only casualty was Lorina's opinion of his perceptiveness, never high anyway.

They both heard the car pull up outside. Oliver was at the front door before Sergeant Welkin could use the knocker. He handed Welkin the file, recovered the ferret, kissed Lorina demurely on the cheek, and was gone.

"Mr. Fingerhood—not even my husband has seen me naked. In fact, and I say this as a matter of pride, *I* have never seen myself naked."

One of the advantages of lying in a closed coffin, thought Mallard, is that you don't have to risk injury by suppressing the overwhelming urge to laugh at your fellow actors—although he also admitted that bursting a blood vessel on cue in this production might be rewarded with a round of applause or, God forbid, another hug from his current director, Humfrey Fingerhood.

"But Mrs. Codling, I wouldn't ask you to do it if it wasn't artistically valid," Humfrey's voice pleaded. "This . . . is Shakespeare!"

Another advantage of lying in a closed coffin is that you have an opportunity to think. It was rather peaceful, in fact, after the harried days of the zodiac murders (that had now become the "Burbage Jury Murders"). Mallard hoped he would not have to make his entrance too soon.

"There will be people in the audience who know me," boomed Mrs. Codling. "I think I speak for Mrs. Godditz and

177

Miss Birdee when I say that we have little desire to parade in our birthday suits in front of members of the Theydon Bois Rotary Club."

All the surviving jury members had been successfully located and given police protection. For some reason, finding Angus Burbage in the prison system was more of a challenge, but Effie was on the case, and Mallard felt entitled to a few hours of free time. So after Sunday lunch with the patient Phoebe, he had managed to avoid missing his third *Macbeth* rehearsal in a row and was waiting placidly for the climax of the scene where Macbeth visits the witches in their lair, transformed in Humfrey's production into the catacombs of a Transylvanian castle. As the ghost of Banquo, blood-baltered according to the text, Mallard was to explode from the plywood casket soaked in gore. Humfrey had even suggested Mallard use scuba equipment until the moment of his appearance, so the coffin could be filled to the brim with red dye, but he had been persuaded—as much by the theater's cleaning staff as by the actors—that a simple makeup job would be effective enough.

Humfrey also felt it appropriate for the witches to become so sexually aroused at this point that they rip their shrouds off and fling themselves rapaciously upon Macbeth, fangs bared and everything else besides. Humfrey's last six productions had all involved nudity, including an all-male *Arsenic and Old Lace* for the Young Vic.

"I want a scene the likes of which Theydon Bois has never seen," he had declared. Eyeing the three ample, middle-aged ladies cast as the witches, the other actors at tonight's rehearsal were sure he'd achieve his ambition. Because the casting had taken place before Humfrey arrived, the witches had been selected for their general repulsiveness, not for their seductive qualities.

"Oh, Mrs. Codling," Humfrey was now exclaiming. "Who is the master—the text or ourselves? No, it doesn't say 'they take their clothes off' in so many words. But true art lies between the words, between the lines. When I read the Scottish play, I hear a voice in my head crying 'Nudity, Humfrey, nudity.' I humbly bring you that voice, Mrs. Codling. Do you hear it, too?"

"Oh, very well. But can we turn the heat up first?"

Angus Burbage, Mallard recalled in the dark, had caused mild flurries in the headlines at the time of his arrest and trial. His son Cliff, an habitual petty criminal in his twenties, had been arrested for a minor theft that, for once, he may not have committed. The young man had been released, considerably the worse for wear for his time in custody. Angus stormed down to the police station, but was met with a wall of indifference in the face of his complaints. If Cliff wasn't guilty of this one, the local inspector had more or less implied, then he was guilty of at least a dozen others that hadn't been reported, and so he deserved all he got. Angus's reply had been a homemade bomb, left brazenly in the main reception area of the police station two days later. Fortunately, it had not exploded, but that did not prevent a conviction at his later trial, despite the support of several notable civil rights activists. He was sentenced to . . . how many years? The trial was nearly three years ago, surely he wouldn't be out of prison already? Is that why he was so hard to find, or was it just the sluggish service Mallard had come to expect on an English Sunday?

"I suppose you want me to take my vest off, too?"

"Everything off, Mrs. Godditz. As nature intended. Follow my example."

But if Angus Burbage was out of jail and taking revenge on those who convicted him, why should he risk early detection for the sake of engaging the authorities in an enigmatic and flamboyant series of murders? Was it a case of gamesmanship, as Ollie had suggested? A chance for personal aggrandizement through outwitting the police, his original bugbears after all? Perhaps Angus took more satisfaction from dumping six unsolved murders into Scotland Yard's lap rather than completing a dozen ritual executions of his peers. The risk of that analysis, of course, is the possibility that he might start again, a new pattern, a new game, a new group of victims. Mallard made a mental note to offer protection to the court officials at Burbage's trial and to the police officers who had appeared as prosecution witnesses.

"I must admit, Mr. Fingerhood . . ."

"We're naked, Mrs. Codling, you can call me Humfrey."

"Humfrey, then. I must admit there is a certain devil-may-care feeling of freedom that I have never experienced before. I just hope I don't run into the vicar."

How had Burbage identified the members of the jury? If Mallard searched, would there be evidence of tampering with the records? Burbage's son, Cliff, was no stranger to breaking and entering. Or were court records on computer these days, accessible to a skilled and purposeful hacker? What else would Burbage need to know? Their current addresses—easy, the telephone book, or for those who had moved, some gentle inquiries. Something about the victim's lives, to find out what would entice them to meetings with people they didn't know. Harry Random's life was an open book, he was even listed in *Who's Who*. Contact with the victim always began with a telephone call. Did the killer fish for more information then, following up on the merest hints until he was able to offer the appropriate inducement? How much would Nettie Clapper or Vanessa Parmenter give away about their hopes and dreams to a strange male voice? And one other essential piece of information: their birthdays. Where did Burbage get that? He had to know all the jurors' birthdays before he could determine whether the zodiac pattern would draw in a string of them. Was that available from the public records office? Can you find out birthdays from the main files or do you have to order up birth certificates?

"Tim."

Or would the murderer have been more brazen, calling each person, perhaps several weeks earlier? "I'm calling on behalf of Tasty Crispy Wheaty breakfast cereal, and if it's your birthday today, you could win five thousand pounds." Who could resist supplying the missing information: "No, it's not my birthday today, my birthday's in October. The sixth."

"Tim!"

And what other information had been gleaned but discarded in the search for a red herring pattern?

"Tim, come out!"

Stan, the interior decorator playing Macbeth, was shouting. Damn, Mallard must have missed his cue. It was hard to hear inside the box. Well, let's make up for that. Even without the costume and makeup, he could give them a revenant Banquo to remember.

He snatched off his glasses, slipped them into his shirt pocket, and flung the lid aside with all the strength he could manage from his horizontal position. The plywood lid frisbeed across the stage, knocking over a freestanding flat that represented a gothic arch. Mallard grasped the sides of the coffin and hauled himself to his feet, thrusting his arms ahead of him and extending his fingers as if he were a dwarf playing the piano. He stepped down nimbly from the plinth and stalked the blurry white figure ahead of him, which he assumed was Macbeth—Stan was still wearing his painter's overalls. Remembering he would be fitted with fangs and a

181

blood capsule, he bared his teeth and opened his eyes wide, allowing a demonic hiss to leave his throat. In two or three stiff-legged strides, he was in front of the dim, retreating figure, reaching out with the menacing hands until his fingers closed on . . . flesh?

"Actually, Tim, we just wanted to tell you that you have a phone call." Stan's voice, which did not come from the individual in his hands, dissolved in giggles. Mallard quickly put on his glasses to see whom he had accosted. To his credit, the stark-naked Humfrey was equally embarrassed. "I would never ask my cast to do something I wouldn't do," he explained weakly, while Mallard mentally clocked up the number of offenses with which he could charge the director, starting with indecent exposure and including conspiracy to commit a lapse of taste. He hurried away to the theater manager's office.

"How's the rehearsal?" It was Effie's voice, familiar, comforting.

"I just accidentally groped a naked man," Mallard sighed.

"Don't you hate it when that happens?" she remarked.

"Where are you calling from?"

"The Yard. Phoebe gave me your number. We've just found Angus Burbage. I thought you'd want to know as soon as possible."

"Where is he?"

"Kensal Green."

"Do you mean the prison, Wormwood Scrubs?"

"I mean the cemetery. He's dead."

"What?"

"Died in the Scrubs about six weeks ago. Of liver cancer. I'll assume the name of the condition is an unfortunate coincidence."

Mallard thought for a moment. "Then it's not him," he

said carefully. "But it could be someone who blamed the system for his death in captivity. If Burbage died six weeks ago, it might take this long for his avenger to plan, research, and execute the murders. Let's continue to pursue this."

"Okay. So is he good-looking, this new boyfriend of yours?"

"I didn't have my glasses on," Mallard explained.

"They all look better that way. See you in the morning."

Back in the auditorium, Humfrey had dressed, but the three witches were still enjoying their unencumbered freedom and had now taken to prancing around the stage, striking elaborate poses last seen during a pre-war visit from the *Ballet Russe*. The other members of the cast were slumped in the first row of seats, watching with a mixture of horror and amusement.

"I feel so open, so liberated!" cried Mrs. Codling, pirouetting like a gelatin spinning top. "Oh, thank you, Mr. Fingerhood, thank you. Wheee!"

"Very good, ladies," called Humfrey, clapping his hands. "You can get dressed now."

But the witches continued to cavort upon the stage. Each had shed forty to fifty years of British lower-middle class repression and prudishness with their nether-garments. It was as if the unfamiliar nudity could finally expiate a lifetime of changing into swimming costumes on chilly English beaches beneath purpose-made, neck-to-foot sacks, donning winceyette nightgowns over their underwear to hide their bodies from their uninterested husbands, and even—in Mrs. Codling's case—covering the mirror with a towel before taking a bath.

"I am fire," cried Mrs. Godditz, writhing in one place. "I am flame. See me burn, feel my heat!"

"I am water, I am a river," sang Miss Birdee, the largest of the three matronly nymphs, flinging herself onto the floor and undulating without difficulty.

"I am a gazelle," shouted Mrs. Codling, crossing the apron in a series of fleshly, floor-shuddering leaps. "I am lithe and beautiful. Watch me skip and jump."

"I think we'll end the rehearsal here for tonight," Humfrey muttered sheepishly to the other stupefied actors. "Nice stalking, by the way, Tim," he added to Mallard, while the three ladies joined hands and began to circle joyously in the middle of the stage. "I don't suppose you'd care to join me for a cappuccino afterwards?"

"I think not," growled Mallard, finding the lower register of his voice. "My wife is expecting me."

"Their husbands are expecting them tonight, too," Humfrey replied nervously, with a nod toward the corybantic trio. "Frankly, Tim, I'm worried for my safety."

"Don't be. By tomorrow morning, those men will either be very grateful to you, or . . ."

"Or?"

"Or they'll be dead from exhaustion," Mallard said with a chuckle.

Nine

OLIVER HATED TO BE asked what he did for living, and not merely because he was embarrassed about being the pseudo-nymous creator of Finsbury the Ferret. He was nervous, too, when conversation turned to his job as the general factotum (or rather, facnullum) for Woodcock and Oakhampton, Ltd., for it inevitably meant he would have explain what the firm did. And Oliver had no idea.

"I suppose you might say we're in the business of busi-ness," Mr. Woodcock had answered cagily, on the one occa-sion when Oliver had cornered him on the issue. "Yes, that's it. We're available for advice. If any potential client wants it. We . . . *consult*. Or rather, we are consult*ed*. Now how are you getting on with your stories about that toothsome Billy Field Mouse? Named after jazz great Billy Strayhorn, no doubt? No? No matter."

Oliver never did establish what sort of advice would be sought from the jolly Woodcock and his taciturn partner, and there was no clue from their surroundings. Apart from the telephone and his word processor, the office's furnishings were all old-fashioned, although they seemed to have had very little use. Certainly, there were no dents or scratches on the polished oak filing cabinets and rolltop desks—which Oliver knew to be empty. And how many offices still had inkwells and rosewood-and-brass rolling blotters, which were unstained with ink? But the mystery had one advantage: Mr. Woodcock seemed chronically guilty that he kept Oliver idle and so encouraged him to use his work time for personal matters. Oliver hardly had to breathe his apologies for disappearing from the office to be with Mallard; and if he dared think he needed permission to attend Sir Harry Random's funeral on Monday morning, Woodcock would probably have leaped from the ground-floor window with remorse.

The hot day clearly added to the grief of the numerous mourners milling around outside the Barnes parish church—including several members of the Sanders Club, "a blight of Blytons," mused Effie, watching from across the road—who appeared distinctly sticky and uncomfortable while they waited for their opportunity to speak to a dark-haired young woman in a short, black dress. Compared with his fellow writers, Effie thought Oliver looked quite presentable in a charcoal-gray Italian suit, neatly ironed white shirt, and subdued purple tie. She was almost prepared to overlook the black Reeboks and navy socks that completed Oliver's ensemble. And the battered leather satchel slung over his shoulder, which she knew always held a book and a folding umbrella.

"I suppose that's Lorina," she hazarded, as she stepped out of Mallard's Rover, where she had been waiting while her boss went to the funeral. Oliver had crossed the road to join her.

"Yes. The prize geek beside her is the abominable Ambrose, her half-brother. He and Harry didn't get along."

Oliver indicated an overweight young man, standing beside Lorina Random. He wore a brown corduroy suit and what seemed like a tea cozy on his long red hair, and he had the kind of fussy beard worn only by Baptist missionaries and beatniks in Walt Disney comedies. As they watched, Mallard emerged from the crowd and, after a perfunctory handshake with Ambrose, hugged Lorina warmly. Oliver, enjoying Effie's company, hoped his uncle would linger.

"Tim's always getting into embraces with attractive young women," Effie remarked, remembering the lunch at Raisin D'Etre. "It must be the white hair. Or maybe it's a family tradition. After all, the young ladies concerned always seem to be your old girlfriends, Ollie." There was an archness in the statement that caused an involuntary quiver to run between Oliver's elbows. But he noted that she had shortened his name for the first time.

"Susie Beamish was never my girlfriend," he said starchily, "and Lorina Random and I broke up a long time ago."

Across the street, the flower-decked hearse pulled away from the curb, and the mourners started to break into smaller groups. Lorina turned, caught sight of Oliver and gave him a broad smile. He waved distractedly.

"Who was the Virgin?" he asked quickly, before Effie could tease him about the exchange.

"Is that a question about your past dalliances?" she persisted with amusement, noticing his flinch.

"I meant, who was the Virgo. On the jury."

"There wasn't one. And there wasn't a Virgo murder yesterday."

187

"Then I suppose there wasn't a Sagittarius on the jury either, which would explain Gordon Paper," Oliver reflected. "My guess is he was chosen as a wild card, to fill up the blanks."

Effie smiled. "Actually, Ollie, there *was* a Sagittarius on the jury. And Gordon Paper was not so much a red herring as a flounder."

Oliver's jaw dropped involuntarily. "Then what *are* the birth signs of the seven surviving jurors?" he asked.

"A Sagittarius, a Cancer, three Tauruses, and two more Aquariuses. No Virgos, Leos, Geminis, or Aries."

"So all in all, not a particularly unusual distribution."

"It depends how you look at it. We couldn't believe that a randomly chosen group of twelve people would each have a different zodiac sign. But if you're genuinely selecting juries at random from the population, there are more ways for that particular distribution of birth signs to occur than any other."

"Really?"

"Oh, yes," she continued eagerly. "Its tidiness seduces us into thinking it's somehow mathematically special. But the one-member-per-sign distribution should pop up, on average, once in every eighteen thousand or so juries."

"Although you're saying it didn't pop up this time."

"No. One in eighteen thousand is rather a long shot if you've already specified which jury you want to assassinate. But if you want to kill *any* jury that has that distribution, you'll probably have several chances during a typical year. In contrast, all twelve members' being Leos, say, should occur only once in nine trillion juries. American trillion, of course."

"You like this probability stuff, don't you?" said Oliver with awe.

"I've always been good with numbers."

"Then you can work out the tip this evening."

If Superintendent Mallard had been a dog, his ears would have pricked up as he caught Oliver's last remark. Did Oliver and Effie have a dinner date? But not being alone, he was unable to pursue the issue. He had crossed the street in the company of two men, the ready-funereal Detective Sergeant Moldwarp and a clean-shaven man in his late forties, who seemed familiar to Oliver, Although he could not remember from where.

"Thanks for waiting, Oliver," said Mallard. "I thought you'd like to hear what Mr. Tradescant has to tell us."

Tradescant. Edmund Tradescant. One of the jurors, thought Oliver, a name that Mallard had recognized when it was read from Harry's files, although Oliver had not. But where had he seen him before?

"I believe you've already met my companions," Mallard said to the man. "Sergeant Strongitharm, Oliver Swithin."

"Ah yes, the psychic," said Tradescant, shaking Oliver's hand. Psychic? What was he talking about?

"We won't keep you long," Mallard continued. "I think you mentioned when we met in Piccadilly Circus that you knew Sir Hargreaves Random."

"Only slightly," Tradescant replied. "I'm delighted to have this opportunity to pay my respects, but I doubt I would have come to his funeral if you hadn't requested my presence. I suppose you will get around to telling me why I'm here and why I'm in protective custody?"

"Very soon, sir. How did you know Sir Harry?"

"We once served on a jury together. I believe I started to tell you that before, but we were interrupted."

"If I'd let you finish, we might have been at this point a lot sooner," muttered Mallard ruefully. "You said you were in Piccadilly Circus for an appointment. Can you tell us about that?"

"Well, it's rather an unusual story," Tradescant answered

genially. "I had a telephone call the night before, purportedly from a man who worked for one of our competitors in the pharmaceutical business. He wouldn't give his name, but he claimed to be dissatisfied with his employer and was looking for an offer. He wanted to bring over the formula for a new drug, as an inducement for us to hire him. Naturally, I was intrigued, although I have to say we don't do business that way."

"You have a commendable concern for ethics, sir," Effie commented. Tradescant beamed at her, as if she were a favorite daughter.

"I'm delighted you think so, Sergeant, but the truth is that we don't hire defectors for our own protection. They're notoriously untrustworthy. You should never marry a man who's cheated on his wife, even if it was with you. Next time—and nobody cheats just once—you'll be the victim. But I was curious to see who this chap was."

"So you arranged to meet in Piccadilly Circus," Mallard prompted.

"Not immediately. He sent over a letter to my office the following morning, asking for a lunchtime meeting in the Circus."

"Do you still have this letter?"

"I brought it with me," Tradescant replied, reaching into the inside pocket of his jacket. "I was wondering if there was a connection between my clandestine appointment last Thursday and your desire to see me this morning."

He produced a folded sheet of paper. Mallard took it by the corner and held it so they could all read the laser-printed words in Helvetica type:

Further to yesterday's phone conversation, please meet me in front of Lillywhite's on Piccadilly Circus this afternoon at 1:00 P.M. I'll recognize you.

"Just that? No return address?"

"Nothing. It was dropped off at the reception desk of our office on London Wall, and nobody could identify the messenger. Well, naturally, I cancelled my lunch and went off to meet the man of mystery. And then I bumped into my old colleague, Gordon Paper. My initial thought was that he had sent the letter as a joke, but I quickly realized that it hadn't been Gordon's voice on the telephone. And then he dropped dead in front of me, shot by some crazed archer on the far side of the Circus. As you can imagine, it took my appointment right out of my mind."

"And you never heard from the caller again?" Effie asked.

"Not a word. Does my presence here mean you think there really is a connection between Gordon's murder and Sir Harry's?"

"Can I ask something?" Oliver cut in. The pieces were falling into place in his mind. "Are you a Sagittarius?"

"As a matter of fact, I am," replied Tradescant, openmouthed. "Good heavens, you people really do have a sixth sense! I'm intrigued—go on, what else can you tell about me?"

"One thing, sir," said Oliver seriously. "You're a very fortunate man."

Later that morning, Mallard called Effie, Welkin, and the melancholy Moldwarp into the Scotland Yard conference room.

"Our killer makes mistakes," Mallard announced to his three colleagues. "I hate to weigh the life of one man against another, but if Gordon Paper hadn't crossed in front of Edmund Tradescant a fraction of a second after the murderer pulled the trigger, then we'd probably be well on our way to twelve murders."

"We might have spotted the jury connection, anyway," Welkin protested gruffly.

"I doubt it. If Tradescant had died instead of Paper, then the first six murders would have consistently fit the zodiac pattern, and that would have been enough to hook us completely. The killer was fortunate to have astrology as his smoke-screen—the zodiac theme has already been used by several other serial killers, especially in America, so it had an extra authenticity. Okay, we'd have been puzzled yesterday, when the victim wouldn't have been a Virgo. And we'd be scratching our heads when today's victim isn't a Leo, assuming we're even bothering to check birthdays by this point. But there'd be a Cancer for tomorrow, and a choice of three Tauruses for the next day but one, and our euphoria about being right and clever and perspicacious would surely have carried us through all the inconsistencies until the triple-decker horror-scope was complete and all twelve jurors were in their graves. No, Gordon Paper's accidental death saved seven lives."

"An expensive mistake," lamented Moldwarp.

"An ambitious kill," Effie remarked. "Maybe the murderer wasn't such a good marksman, after all? Or maybe the distance across Piccadilly Circus was simply too great for the dead-on accuracy required? Either way, Paper's mismatch kept alive Oliver's belief that something else was going on, despite the odds against it that I kept quoting."

"So the good news is, the murders have stopped," Mallard concluded, noting Effie's sudden generosity toward his nephew. "The bad news is, we still have to find the killer."

"I've been looking over the transcript of Angus Burbage's trial," Effie told them. "It was a very clear case, no question at all of guilt. Burbage's fingerprints were all over the bomb and several people, not just police officers, heard him making threats. This was an important case, because accusations of police brutality against Burbage's son, Clifford, came up in the trial, and there was a subsequent investigation of the officers involved. It didn't lead to any prosecutions, however."

"How long did Burbage get?" asked Welkin.

"Twenty years," Effie continued. "It sounds stiff, but if that bomb had gone off, a lot of people could have been killed or seriously injured. And the incident occurred in the middle of a series of IRA bomb scares, which made it worse in many people's eyes."

"Anything else we should know about from the trial?" asked Mallard.

"Angus Burbage gave an interview to 'World in Action' after his sentencing. I've cued up what I think is the crucial part."

She turned on the video player in the room—still in place from the viewing of Vanessa Parmenter's death. The monitor showed a tight close-up on the face of a middle-aged man smoking a hand-rolled cigarette. He spoke in a husky, educated voice.

"I'm not guilty. The policemen who savagely and indifferently beat my son, they're the guilty ones. I planted the bomb as an act of war—a war against an injustice. Well, what is a private citizen to do when the so-called checks and balances of democracy are all ranged against him? What is any citizen to do, to preserve the freedoms we have come to expect in this country? I committed an act of war, which is what you do when democracy fails."

He paused and sucked at the cigarette. "You could have killed innocent people," an off-screen voice gently prompted.

"In a war, civilians can be hurt," Burbage replied. "It's regrettable, but you accept that."

"Your trial is over, and you've been found guilty by a jury of your peers. Do you still say the establishment is against you?"

"Of course. The judge, the prosecutors, the jury. They're all serving a system that has proved itself fallible. Because a jury said I was guilty, it doesn't make me so."

"Legally, it does."

"I'm at war. I no longer recognize the legal system of this country."

"But the jury—they weren't part of the system. They're twelve ordinary people who heard the evidence and said your actions were not justified. What would you say to them?"

Burbage thought for a second and smiled.

"I would curse them," he said quietly.

The image faded.

"Angus Burbage is dead," Mallard pronounced. "But he left some unfinished business. So who else springs to mind as a likely suspect?"

"The son, obviously," said Welkin immediately. "He was duffed over by the cops for something he didn't do; then after all the fuss, he still wasn't vindicated by the DPP's investigation; and finally his old man spent his last days in the nick."

"I agree," said Mallard. "You and Sergeant Strongitharm bring young Cliff in for questioning. Anybody else?"

"Angus had no other family," said Effie. "Cliff is his only child, and his wife died a year ago, while he was in prison."

"Yet another reason why Cliff may be bitter—he may blame his mother's death on his father's incarceration," Moldwarp moaned knowingly, as if fulfilling a prediction he had made during some earlier jeremiad.

"We also have the possibility that Angus himself decided on revenge," said Mallard. "He may have planned the murders inside and used an agent to carry them out."

"The agent is still most likely to be Cliff," commented Welkin.

"Agreed. But Angus will have made some new friends in

the nick. Sergeant Moldwarp, check on Burbage's known associates, especially those who've been released in the last six months. Any other suggestions?"

"Someone who was frustrated on Burbage's behalf?" ventured Welkin. "Another victim of police brutality? A bleeding-heart liberal?"

Mallard screwed his face up, as if the possibility caused him minor pain. "Look into that if Cliff Burbage doesn't pan out," he conceded. "Okay, anything new from our continuing investigations? How about that crossbow?"

"Still no leads," Moldwarp complained.

"The dart gun?"

"He didn't leave it behind," Welkin reminded them. "None have been reported stolen recently. They ain't that hard to get hold of, apparently."

"The drug that was used on Mark Sandys-Penza?"

The detectives shook their heads.

"So much for the 'instruments of darkness' our man uses," Mallard grumbled. He had been waiting for an opportunity to use the expression since discovering that it originated in a speech by Banquo.

"Sir," said Effie cautiously.

"Yes, Sergeant?"

"At the risk of being labeled a pedant," she continued, not that anyone in the room would dare take such a risk, "now that we know the murderer was only pretending to be a serial killer, perhaps we should consider the possibility that he's not necessarily . . . a man?"

The sky was blue over Camberwell as Effie and Detective Sergeant Welkin made their way along the concrete walkway that gave access to the third floor flats. Down in the open area between the pre-war buildings, boys were playing soccer around the parked cars, flitting in and out of bands of sunlight. Beyond the housing estate, they could see the bright livery of a Southern Region train rattling lazily across a honey-colored viaduct. They passed the kitchen windows and the pale blue front doors of the flats, each offering a tantalizingly audible hint of life within—children laughing, loud reggae music, a couple arguing, a television playing an Australian soap opera.

Welkin rang the doorbell of the flat at the far end of the passage. On the third ring, they heard a shuffling, and the front door was opened a fraction. A young woman with dyed blond hair and a bad complexion peered through the gap.

"Yes?" she snapped.

"Wendy Burbage?" asked Welkin.

"Who wants to know?"

"Is your husband home?"

"No, he ain't. What do you want?"

"We want a word with him, love. Where can we find him?"

"How should I know? I don't arst what he does during the day."

A baby started crying inside the flat. She glanced behind her impatiently.

"Mrs. Burbage, we're sorry to trouble you," said Effie kindly. "But we need to speak to Cliff. It's very urgent."

The woman looked her up and down critically, making wet noises with her chewing gum. "Has the bastard knocked you up too then, girl?" she asked with an unpleasant smile. Her teeth were bright and flawless. "Blimey, his tastes have changed."

"Now then, you watch it," Welkin cut in sharply.

"Don't you tell me to watch it," she snapped. "I got enough to watch without you telling me to watch it. Piss off."

She tried to shut the door, but Welkin placed his shoulder against it. "What's your game?" she snapped, facing up to the big man without fear.

"We're police officers, love," he said, making no attempt to show any identification. "Detective Sergeant Welkin and Detective Sergeant Strongitharm. We want to talk to Clifford Burbage."

The woman paused, with another surreptitious glance behind her. The baby's cries died away. "What's he done this time?" she asked at last.

"Never you mind that, where can we find him?"

"I don't know. I told you. He ain't here."

"Then you won't mind if we come and see for ourselves," said Welkin, pushing harder against the door. It opened, but the woman, who seemed to be wearing only a cheap dressing gown, blocked the hallway. Welkin paused, knowing that he could not get away with any further physical force. The flat smelled of mildew and marijuana.

"Wendy," said Effie firmly. "We know somebody's in the flat. It'll save us all a lot of trouble if you just let us in."

The woman broke eye contact first, and with a sigh, stood to the side, making a sarcastic gesture of welcome.

"I knew she had company," Effie said to Welkin as they headed back to the car.

"Maybe, but unless he's been getting a lot of sun, that wasn't Cliff Burbage," Welkin replied with a grin, remembering the look on the naked Trinidadian's face as Effie swept into the bedroom. "Still, she'll think twice before she tips Cliff off that we're looking for him."

They reached the bottom of the graffiti-marked staircase. An older woman in a paisley housecoat ran up to them with a stooped scurry that seemed to imply a well-timed arrival, although they had spotted her lingering there from the walkway.

"Are you looking for Cliff Burbage?" she asked nosily. Her arms appeared to be locked in the folded position.

"If you know where we can find him, we'd appreciate it," Welkin told her without slowing down.

"You from the Social Security?"

"It's a sort of social security, yes."

The woman drew the corners of her mouth down as if extracting Welkin's admission had been a personal triumph. She walked with them.

"I thought so. I knew he was on the fiddle. And Wendy with a new babe, too. Course, that one's no better than she should be. Coh!" She jerked her chin up with the exclamation. They had reached their car, so there was a reason to stop. Welkin played with the keys, smiling at an attractive Indian woman in a colorful sari, who hurried by.

"Still, I blame Cliff," the woman continued, "he should be around for the little one. He's supposed to be unemployed, but as far as I can tell he spends all his time over at Brixton, running a fruit stall. I said to my hubby, you don't pay taxes just so he can get away with that malarkey."

"You interfering cow!" came a shout from above them. Wendy Burbage's head was poking over the third-floor parapet.

"So bloody common," remarked the older woman as she backed nervously out of the young woman's sight and hurried into a ground floor flat. The door slammed. Mrs. Burbage swore loudly and disappeared.

"Brixton, I think," said Effie.

A row of makeshift stalls had been set up beside the railway viaduct, selling fruit, vegetables, and flowers. They spotted Cliff Burbage at the fourth stall—a younger, stockier version of his late father.

"Mr. Burbage, I wonder if I could ask you a few questions," said Welkin, vaguely showing his warrant card. Effie took up position a few paces away.

Burbage, who had been packing a shopping bag with fruit for an elderly lady, paused, a honeydew melon in his hand. "What for?" he asked suspiciously.

"I'd prefer not to explain here, sir."

Burbage shrugged and made a gesture of concession, passing the carrier to his customer. Then he suddenly flung the melon as hard as possible at Welkin. The detective took it full on the side of the head and went down. Burbage kicked away one trestle of the fruit stand, causing the wooden top to drop heavily on Welkin's shin, followed by a shower of apples, oranges, and grapefruit from the open crates. He ran.

Effie instantly took off after him, hoping someone would go to Welkin's aid. Burbage reached Brixton Road first and veered left under the railway bridge. She made it to the busy road in time to see him crash into an elderly West Indian lady, bringing her down hard on the pavement and spilling her shopping into the street. He staggered, but kept his balance. Then he ran on like a juggernaut through the Monday shoppers, pushing several out of his way with his hands or a shoulder. Effie kept up the pursuit, praying Cliff wasn't carrying a shooter. She hurdled the old lady rolling in her path with a single stride, regretting the callousness of the action, but glad she had chosen to wear jeans that morning.

Effie knew better than to cry out for help. Reactions would be too slow, and shouting "Stop! Police!" was a ploy used so often by bag-snatchers that some public-spirited citizen might "have a go" by bringing her down instead. She was an easier target than the heavyset man thirty yards ahead of her, running like a charging bull across a side street and under the second railway bridge.

She was gaining as they reached Brixton Underground station. Burbage risked a glance back, saw her, and ducked into the station entrance. When she skidded round the corner after him, three seconds later, he was already out of sight. Had he shot through the arcade of shops to the left, or hurtled down the steps into the station itself? There was an indignant cry from below. It was enough.

Effie leaped down the steps, in time see Burbage vault over the ticket gate ahead and vanish down the escalators. "Police officer," she cried to nobody in particular as she followed. She jumped the barrier and landed on the other side with a jar that caused her to fall forward, scraping the palms of her hands on the floor. As she got up, she felt the sudden weakness in her left ankle, the first sign that the chase was aggravating an old injury. She shook her head violently and ran forward onto the escalator.

She tried at first to go down two steps at a time to catch up with Burbage, who was still in sight. But each leap downward sent flames of pain into her ankle. The striped metal treads strobed on her retina, making it hard to judge the distance. She gave up halfway and switched to one step at a time, which was slower. Near the end she tried sliding side-saddle down the rough moving belt that served a handrail, but the friction on her denimed bottom slowed her even more.

When she got to the lower level, she lost Burbage. Brixton was the end of the Jubilee Line, and both platforms—one on each side of the deserted antechamber—had trains with their doors open. Which would Burbage have taken? she thought as she paused, panting and sore, her skinned palms oozing blood. The first train, as indicated on the departure board, in the hope that the doors would close before she caught up with him? Or would he hide on the other stationary train, expecting her to leave with the first? Then he could double back while she was safely on her way to Stockwell. How would he play the game?

The loudspeaker suddenly hissed and delivered its genial reminder to "Mind the doors." The first train was about to depart. She ran toward it, forced to guess that Burbage was less intelligent than she was, with less time to review the choices. A second or two later, the doors slammed shut, and the silver carriages eased themselves suggestively into the tunnel ahead.

As the train's rear lights shrank into the darkness, Burbage popped his head out of the shallow alcove and peered cautiously along the now empty platform. He grinned. The policewoman had behaved as he had expected—she'd assumed he would jump on the train that was about to depart. It never occurred to her that he could jump off again at the last second and hide himself from view on the platform. It hadn't occurred to him at first, either. As it was, he had to react almost instinctively to the idea, with barely enough time to flatten himself against the tiled walls before he heard her run by.

Burbage tiptoed back toward the platform entrance and listened. Members of the public posed no threat to him, but there was always the chance that the other cop was behind, although that melon had taken him down pretty hard. (His days of putting the shot at school weren't wasted, he thought with amusement.) Apart from the constant rumble of the escalators, out of sight around the corner, there were no other noises. Still, even if the male cop couldn't follow, he might have called for reinforcements on his radio. Better move sharpish, Burbage decided, setting off quickly toward the up escalator.

The handcuffs were snapped on his wrists before he had time to register that it was Effie who had been leaning nonchalantly against the wall around the corner, waiting for him.

"How did you guess what I'd do?" he asked despondently,

after she had read him his rights. "Was it pure luck? Or did you spot my double-bluff?"

Effie grinned. "Clifford, what I spotted was your double butt. Sticking out from the alcove. You could lose a little weight, you know. Try eating more fruit."

Burbage went quietly.

"I wouldn't lie to you, Mr. Mallard. Integrity is my middle name."

"But how often do we use our middle names?" said Mallard impatiently, with an ironic glance at the computer printout of Cliff Burbage's criminal record. The two men had been sitting in the interview room for more than two hours, but so far, the thickset son of the late urban terrorist had said nothing about the murders. He didn't seem to know that any murders had even taken place. Burbage claimed to have panicked on seeing Welkin—whose tibia had snapped under the avalanche of fruit—because he was operating an illegal stall while on probation for handling stolen property. Finding himself under suspicion of a string of more serious crimes, he came clean about all his current petty larcenies, to which, Mallard reminded him, he had just added several more, including assaulting a police officer with a melon.

"Would you call that a deadly weapon, Cliff, or a blunt instrument?" Mallard asked.

"Do me a favor . . ."

"No, you do me the favors, son," Mallard riposted angrily. "You tell me what you know about the murders of Sir Hargreaves Random, Nettie Clapper, Mark Sandys-Penza, Gordon Paper, Vanessa Parmenter, and Archibald Brock, and the attempted murder of Edmund Tradescant."

Burbage looked scared. "I told you, I don't know nothing about no murders," he breathed. "I never even heard of them people, 'cept for the first. Didn't he write them snooty kids' books? You have to believe me, Mr. Mallard. I'm as honest as the day is long."

"Yes, but the days are getting shorter, aren't they?" muttered Mallard. He flipped on the VCR, which he'd wheeled down to the interview room, and froze the picture as Angus Burbage's face appeared.

"Your father knew those people," Mallard said. "He knew them very well."

"Dad's dead. He died in the nick. Didn't you know?"

"Yes, I knew. So did he plan the murders and get you to carry them out? Or was it all your idea?"

Cliff was staring at the screen. "I remember that time Dad was on the telly," he said reflectively. "I had no bleeding idea what he was talking about."

"Your dad did a lot for you," Mallard persisted. "He went to prison for you. He tried to kill people for you. Why shouldn't you kill people for him?"

The other man broke his eyes from the television and looked down at the floor. "I don't know why he did those things, Mr. Mallard," he grumbled. "I didn't ask him to. I didn't understand what it was all about at the time, and I still don't. I wish he'd left it alone. So the cops did me over—no offense, sir, but they did. That's the way it is sometimes. If you play the game, you gotta know the rules."

Not the way I play, thought Mallard, no matter how much I'm tempted, no matter how much I want to beat a confession out of this whining mouth-breather.

"He didn't understand," Burbage was saying. "He thought the world was different. Look where it got him. He never even got to see his grandchild."

Mallard turned off the monitor. "Tell me about your father," he prompted quietly.

Burbage continued to study the carpet without answering. Then he looked up at Mallard, his eyes glistening.

"Dad would have done anything for me. Just like I'd do anything for my nipper. Dad always stuck by me, never threw me out like a lot of me mates' dads did when they got into trouble. But I was too stupid to see what he was getting at. Eventually I got so far in that I dragged him down with me. He couldn't dump me, so he got to be like me. Only more so—I couldn't plant a bomb, couldn't even make a bomb." He rubbed at his eyes with the heel of one hand. "Can I have a cigarette?" he asked.

Mallard slid a packet across the table. Burbage took a cigarette and lit it, drawing the smoke deeply into his lungs. It reappeared with a long sigh.

"The irony is, Mr. Mallard, my dad risked everything and lost because he thought he saw an injustice—his son getting beaten up for a job he didn't do. But there was no injustice. I was actually guilty of that job, and the coppers knew it all along, though they couldn't prove it. I never told my dad that, not even in his last days. But I deserved what I got in that interview room."

"No, you didn't," Mallard said quietly. "Guilty or innocent, you should not have been beaten while you were in police custody. Your father was right about that."

Burbage stared at Mallard. "Don't know what planet you're living on, guv," he said wryly. A chill struck Mallard, a physical sensation in his stomach that almost threw him from the chair. The dawning realization that Cliff Burbage was telling the truth. This man was no murderer. He was the sempiternal victim.

The door opened, and Moldwarp's woeful face came into view. Mallard signaled him to wait. He scribbled the dates and times of the zodiac murders on a piece of paper and slid it toward the suspect.

"Cliff, I want you to tell me where you were at these times, starting with last Monday morning at six o'clock." Just over a week since Harry was found, reflected Mallard. It's a long time in murder, too.

In the corridor outside, Moldwarp almost sobbed out the news that a search of Cliff Burbage's flat had revealed nothing.

"He has a lock-up garage, too," sighed the lugubrious detective, as if confirming the start of Armageddon. "We found several items that we think will interest the local police—not to mention said items' original owners—but nothing to connect him to the murders."

Mallard took in the information stoically. "We can hold him for a while because of the assault on Sergeant Welkin. He also assaulted some members of the public when he was trying to get away from Sergeant Strongitharm. Who would have thought Effie would have that effect on the youth of Britain?" He watched Moldwarp carefully after this quip, because he had never seen the detective sergeant smile. He was disappointed yet again.

Back in the interview room, Cliff Burbage wanted to talk.

"I was working my stall every day last week," he said. "Oh, apart from Thursday lunchtime."

The Sagittarius. Could Cliff have been in the vicinity of a Piccadilly Circus rooftop? Or would he have an obviously concocted alibi?

"I had an appointment in Streatham," Burbage continued. "I was there from ten until about one o'clock."

"Who was this appointment with?" asked Mallard, still hoping the story could be challenged.

Burbage grinned. "My probation officer," he said.

"Effie, I believe you have a date with Oliver tonight," Mallard remarked casually, catching the policewoman at her desk as she was preparing to go off duty. Effie smiled to herself, continuing to rub Germolene onto her skinned hands.

"I said I'd have dinner with Oliver," she replied. "Is this to remind me to get your favorite nephew home by ten o'clock?"

"I don't mean to pry into your personal life, I'm sure," said Mallard stiffly, although Effie knew very well that he was lying. "But if you see Ollie, ask him to give me a call tomorrow."

"No luck with Clifford, then?" she deduced. "After all my hard work?"

"Your hard work is appreciated, as always, Sergeant Strongitharm. But I think Cliff Burbage is innocent of the zodiac murders."

"I could have told you that," she said casually, tossing the tin of antiseptic into a drawer and gathering the personal items that were scattered around her desk top.

"How, pray tell?"

"We've always agreed the killer is smart. Cliff isn't. And we've seen the killer on videotape, riding a motorbike around Grosvenor Square. As we said at the time, it could have been a man or a woman. But whatever the sex, it certainly wasn't anyone of Cliff Burbage's ample build."

"Back to square one tomorrow, then," said Mallard blandly.

Effie paused, her open handbag on her lap, and looked soberly at her boss.

"No, Superintendent Mallard. We're way past square one and don't you ever forget it! The murders ended on Saturday. The intended victims are all safe. We've solved the puzzle— now we just have to find the person who set it. And this guy makes mistakes, remember. He is not the perfect murderer. For once, *we're* in control of the game."

Mallard held her gaze, enjoying the solemnity in her ice-blue eyes, the hue of the copper sulphate solution he used to mix up with his chemistry set, fifty years ago, just because he liked the color. He'd always liked that color. Even without her dimpling smile, and with the planes of her face set harshly to emphasize that she expected him to take her seriously, Effie was lovely. And that hair! If he were unmarried and thirty years younger—it was a conjecture, not a regret, Mallard respected the difference—but if he were . . . well, he'd be Oliver. And Oliver, thank the Lord, seemed to be making progress with this remarkable woman.

"Thanks, Eff, I needed that," he said warmly. "Have fun tonight."

He chose not to tell her about the meeting he had just concluded with his superiors, and the message they delivered.

"How do I look?" Oliver asked anxiously. "Does this shirt go with this jacket?"

"It's only dinner with the girl, for goodness sake," Susie Beamish sighed over her cheeseburger. "The shirt's fine."

Ben Motley had brought in the takeaway meal from Burger King for himself, but a ravenous Susie had pounced on him and offered to swap half his food for a helping of bread-and-butter pudding. After he had accepted, she smugly revealed that the dessert was at Raisin D'Etre, and to get it, he would have to give her a lift to work.

"Although, I don't know why I'm bothering to turn up," she had sighed.

"Business is bad?" Ben asked sympathetically.

"Raisins are no longer current," she lamented.

Ben agreed to drive her to Pimlico, noting that he had to be back at the house by ten o'clock to photograph a diva, who wanted to put her Motley portrait in the programs of all the world's opera houses. Throughout the negotiations,

Oliver had bobbed in and out of the kitchen more often than a Pavarotti curtain call. He had so far asked them to check on the accuracy of his parting (moderate), the quantity of after-shave he had applied (sufficient), the visibility of an incipient pimple on his chin (below the threshold of perception), and the accuracy of his parting again (deteriorating).

"It's not as if this is your first date," said Susie through a mouthful of burger, "although it's been a while since I saw you with a woman. I was even thinking of taking pity on you myself." She chose to ignore Oliver's look of exaggerated terror, but rewarded Ben's guffaw by pouring sugar onto his french fries. He let her, knowing that passive acceptance would get her to stop sooner. Instead, he stood up, put his well-muscled arm around Oliver's shoulders, and compressed him heartily.

"You're missing the whole point, Susie," he said. "Oliver's understandably nervous because of the lady in question, the divine Effie. What I wouldn't give to be in his shoes!" He punched Oliver playfully in the upper arm and went back to the table.

"Yes, Ben, that reminds me," said Oliver humbly, rubbing his unremarkable bicep. "I want to thank you for not moving in on Effie when you had the chance. I don't think I could have taken the competition."

"What on earth do you mean?"

"Well, you have so much success with the opposite, er, sex," Oliver said, somewhat abashed. "But I notice that you left the way clear for me with Effie."

Ben smiled, even though he was eating a sugared fry. "Oliver, my interest in Effie was purely photographic. There wouldn't be any point in competing with you for her affections."

"Why not?" Oliver asked testily. "What's wrong with Effie?"

Ben looked at Susie, who looked back with a similarly puzzled expression. "Effie's potty about you," he said, with surprise. "I could tell immediately when I first saw you two together at Kew Gardens."

"She hardly spoke to me that evening."

"Exactly. A woman doesn't play that hard to get with a man unless she really wants him to notice her. So go ahead, Olls, sweep her off her feet."

"Well, she has been a lot friendlier," Oliver said thoughtfully.

"Ollie, let me assure you," said Susie, laying down her food and addressing him seriously. "Effie's got the major hots for you. The pheromones were wafting in waves the other lunchtime. We girls can always tell."

The doorbell rang. Oliver started, stared open-mouthed at each of his friends, ran a hand through his floppy hair, and darted from the kitchen.

"Think he bought it?" muttered Ben.

"Of course. We were brilliant," said Susie. "A few raised expectations, founded or otherwise, will at least get him out of the starting gate."

The kitchen door swung open again and Geoffrey Angelwine stormed into the room, flung his briefcase onto a counter, and collapsed into an empty chair. A disappointed Oliver hovered by the door.

"And on top of everything else, I forgot to take my keys this morning," Geoffrey complained.

"Have a good day at the office, dear?" asked Susie brightly. Geoffrey glared at her.

"I have had the worst day of my life, and it's all the fault of that bloody ferret," he said. "I had to explain to Mr. Hoo, Mr. Watt, *and* Mr. Eidenau that the firm and one of its major clients are being sued for five million pounds by a litigious art student. How was I to know those toy Finsburys were only for publicity purposes until the lawsuit is settled? And today, the manager of the bookshop called to complain that I released a live wolverine on her premises. I don't even know what a wolverine is."

Behind Geoffrey's back, Oliver checked his watch.

"So, did they fire you?" Susie asked gently.

"Fire me?" Geoffrey said with a bitter laugh. "No, worse. They promoted me. Apparently, it's the best publicity anyone at the firm has managed to engender for a book since Bunty Devereux mistook William S. Burroughs for the author of Tarzan."

"Then why on earth are you so—"

"Cross?" Geoffrey thrust a bandaged finger under Susie's nose. "That's why!" he cried. "My stitches have been hurting all day. I'm probably going to get rabies. And it's all Oliver's fault." He turned to look at Oliver as if noticing him for the first time. "What are you all dolled up for?" he asked.

"Oliver has a date tonight," said Susie proudly. "With—"

"Lorina Random, eh? You sly dog!"

"No," Susie persevered, "With Effie Strongitharm."

Geoffrey let out a cry and clutched his heart dramatically. The he let out another cry, because the action had caused him to squash his damaged finger. "Oh! Oh! *Et tu, Brute!* There I am, suffering for the cause of your literary success, and all the time you're running behind my back, stealing my girl!"

"*Your* girl?" they repeated in unison. The massed doubt caused Geoffrey to modify his indignation, but he remained defiant.

"Absolutely," he averred. "I rather fancy my chances with Effie. She's come to my aid twice now when I was in great distress. Times like that create a bond between a man and a woman."

"Let me see," Susie mused, "she helped you out of a pair of boots when you were scared of imaginary scorpions, and she took you to the hospital because you got a tiny bite from a very friendly ferret. Sounds like the perfect start to a beautiful romance."

"I was getting around to asking her for a date."

"And what would that take?" Susie persisted. "To get her out for a drink, you'd probably have to be savaged by a pit bull terrier first."

"Dinner and dancing would entail the loss of at least one limb to a pack of coyotes," Ben suggested.

"And I don't think you could propose marriage unless you'd been bisected by a shark."

"Laugh, I thought I'd never start," muttered Geoffrey.

"Poor Geoffrey," sighed Susie as she got up from the table. "Another evening at home, arranging your sock drawer. How are you going to do it this time, in alphabetical order of their pet names?"

"You know your problem, Susie," said Geoffrey. "You're a woman trapped in a woman's body."

"Ben, I'm going to freshen up and then we'll head off." She went out, following Oliver, who had quietly slipped away a few seconds earlier.

"Great," grumbled Geoffrey to Ben, who was idly picking up the shards of his french fries with a dampened forefinger. "You're all going off and leaving me. This is the story of my life, Ben. I have absolutely no luck with women. Do you know, I didn't undress a woman with my eyes until I was twenty-three."

"Really?" said Ben absentmindedly.

"Yes. And she was a nun. The religious guilt took away all the enjoyment. Besides she had a terrible figure, even in my imagination."

"Really?"

"Yes. And I had to give up self-abuse when I caught myself faking an orgasm."

"Really?"

"Yes. Well, not give it up exactly. Call it something different, which is the politically correct approach to personal transformation. I now refer to it as 'intracourse.' "

The doorbell rang again, and they heard Oliver's footsteps pass the kitchen door. The front door opened and closed. Geoffrey sighed.

Ten

"No."

"And it's not Ephemera?"

"No!" Effie protested, with mock indignation.

"Then I give up," said Oliver. "What is Effie short for? Effervescence? Effluvium? Effrontery?"

"I thought you'd given up," she laughed. Their conversation was interrupted by the rare appearance of their waiter, a young man with a mane of blond, curly hair that rivaled Effie's and a sculptured three-day growth of beard.

"Can I interest you in dessert?" the waiter articulated, his attention focused on his reflection in one of the large Victorian mirrors covering the distressed stucco of the restaurant. Narcissism was the principal theme of Gadzooks, the popular restaurant on Kensington High Street, which explained its enduring popularity with the young and fashionable. The lighting was bright, not just for the video cameras that threw the patrons' frequently famous faces onto large monitors dotted around the restaurant (a tip to the maître de' would secure several instant replays), but also to enable those diners who insisted on wearing sunglasses indoors to read the menus. Where many restaurants allowed palm readers to drift from table to table, Gadzooks had a psychoanalyst.

Oliver had chosen the restaurant because it was within walking distance of Edwardes Square, entailing a later promenade with Effie in the warm evening air as he escorted her back to her car—and possibly into the house. (He had not anticipated her painful ankle, and she didn't tell him about it.) Susie had helped him get a reservation at short notice, although she had complained that the tryst was not to take place at Raisin D'Etre, "where I can keep an eye on you," as she had put it.

Oliver and Effie ordered tea only, which caused the waiter to toss his head disdainfully and stalk back to a table of drunken debutantes and their escorts, who had occupied his attention for most of the evening.

"Effie is my initials," she continued. "F. E. Do you see?"

"Boy, if you use your initials, you must hate your names!"

"I do."

"So what are they? Ffrydeswyde Eulalie? Faustina Elfleda?"

She laughed again. "No, they're Frances Erica," she confessed, sipping from the single glass of wine she had conscientiously allowed herself as an off-duty policewoman who may have to drive later. She was having fun without alcohol, enjoying Oliver's attentiveness, and almost forgetting the soreness of her scraped hands.

Oliver looked puzzled. "Those are nice names," he said. "Why not use them?"

214

"My father's name is Francis Eric Strongitharm," Effie replied. "And everytime I use my full name, it reminds me that he really wanted a son instead of a daughter."

"I'm delighted he didn't get one," said Oliver gallantly. "In fact, I doubt I would be sitting here if he did."

This remark pleased Effie. She had concluded several days earlier that Oliver's immunity to the Strongitharm Look was attributable to his young man's basic innocence, and she was almost pleased that her defenses had not proved impregnable to this rare property. Perhaps there were other men she had judged too hastily in her twenty-seven years, but Oliver may have been worth waiting for.

"But you use a different name too, for your writing," she was saying. "O. C. Blithely. Where does that come from?"

"Blithely is just a made-up name that my editor thought sounded good for a children's author. She said I do everything blithely." Oliver thought back to the particular activity his ex-girlfriend had been describing and chose not to elaborate. "And O.C. are my real initials. O. C. Swithin."

"What does the C stand for?"

"Chrysostom. It's not that funny," he complained as Effie spluttered into her napkin. "It was one of Mozart's middle names."

"One of them?"

"Yes, he had three. Chrysostom Wolfgang Amadeus. His first name was really Johann. I wonder why he dropped it?"

"Well, why did you drop *your* real name?" she persisted. "If you wrote as Oliver Swithin, you wouldn't be mistaken for a woman so often."

Oliver looked soberly at the candle on their small table. "Because 'Oliver Swithin' wouldn't write second-rate rubbish about a pernicious ferret and a family of peripatetic field mice," he said.

"I read the book you signed for me."

"What did you think?" Oliver asked cautiously.

"I thought it was the best book I'd ever read . . . about a pernicious ferret and a family of peripatetic field mice," she replied, her eyes twinkling.

"A dubious achievement."

"But why resent it? Why does Oliver Swithin disparage O. C. Blithely, the hugely successful children's writer?"

"Do you like O. C. Blithely, too?" the waiter chipped in as he arrived with a tray of too many items for just two cups of tea. "I think she's marvelous. Perhaps we could discuss this over a mochaccino later, when your friend goes home. You've noticed the debt that Finsbury owes to the writings of Derrida, of course. I've been asked to deconstruct *The Railway Mice and the Bloated Stoat* for *Granta*, you know."

"The bill, please," said Oliver firmly. The waiter shrugged and walked away, leaving Oliver and Effie wondering which of them he had been talking to.

"I don't resent being a children's writer," Oliver said. "But it's not what I want to be when I grow up."

"What do you want to be?"

"I don't know. And the way things are going, I'll have my mid-life crisis before I finish my identity crisis—the psychological equivalent of going straight from puppy fat to middle-age spread. Ben Motley lives and breathes photography. No amount of commercial failure will deter Susie Beamish from opening restaurants. Geoffrey will always hate his job, but he loves his career. They know what they want. I envy them. I envy you."

"Me?" Effie exclaimed.

"Oh, yes. I love taking part in these mysteries. I've had more fun in the last week, pretending to be a detective, than I ever have tapping out the Finsbury stories. You get to do it all the time."

"I've enjoyed your company," Effie found herself saying,

causing Oliver's heart to lurch. "Oh, by the way, Tim said to call him tomorrow. There may be some more detective work for you."

Effie's weak ankle had made her reach for his arm as they left the restaurant, and Oliver had folded her hand tightly in the crook of his elbow, as if he were afraid that she might otherwise float away into the night. As they entered Edwardes Square, they were talking about the murders, but Oliver's mind was half on the future. Was this the evening to attempt a goodnight kiss, in front of his house, beside her red Renault? If on the lips, which way would her nose go, to the right, or was she a southpaw? Where could he put his hands, on her upper arms or could they grasp her shoulder blades?

"There was an unbroken string of six consecutive birth signs among the jury members," he said. "What were the chances of that?"

"Pretty high, if you don't specify which six signs or which six of the twelve jurors have to have them."

Oliver thought about this. "Even so," he objected, "I still say the murderer was rather fortunate that his particular target jury had such a sequence."

"Ollie, you're still thinking astrology first, jury second," Effie sighed. "That's because we discovered the threads in that order. But for the murderer, it was different. He already knew who he wanted to kill. He just had to find some elaborate pattern that would hide the true connection between his daily victims."

They had stopped in front of Oliver's house. The curtain at Geoffrey's bedroom window twitched.

"Well, I enjoyed our conversation, but here's my car and here's your home," Effie said, slowly searching in her handbag for her keys. Oliver swallowed.

"We could go on talking indoors," he stammered nervously. "Over another cup of tea, I mean. Or coffee—I could make coffee. If we have any . . ."

Effie looked up at him with amusement and cocked her head on one side. "You're not very good at this, are you?" she said.

"No," Oliver replied immediately with an embarrassed laugh. "Chalk it up to inexperience." He cleared his throat. "Effie, I'm having such a good time that I don't want you to go yet," he stated. "There, how was that?"

"Let me ask you something," she said, idly tossing the car keys in the air and catching them with the same hand. "When you signed that Finsbury book for me, you thought for two hours and then wrote 'To Effie, best wishes, Oliver.' And I have to say, I was severely underwhelmed. So tell me, Ms. Blithely, how are you going to sign the next one?"

He took a step toward her. "I'm not going to sign it at all," he said softly. She raised one eyebrow. "I won't need to," he continued, "because I'm going to dedicate it to you."

The smile crept across her face in slow motion. "In that case, some more tea would be very nice," she said, taking his hand despite her sore palm and leading him up the steps. But as Oliver fumbled for his keys with his free hand, the front door was abruptly opened in their faces.

"Hello, you two," said Geoffrey, too enthusiastically. "Are you both coming in? Or does Effie have to leave? It's getting really late, Effie."

"We're going to have some tea, Geoff," said Oliver firmly, using every movable feature in his face to signal outrage at his friend's intrusion.

"Oh, are you sure?" Geoffrey blabbered, glancing anxiously behind him. But Oliver pushed past him and ushered Effie into the house. Upstairs, in Ben's studio, the stereo was playing an opera aria—"Ritorna Vincitor" from *Aida*. A second voice was singing along with the recording. Geoffrey shut the door and tried to get ahead of them again. "Look, tell you what, why don't you two go off to Oliver's room and let me bring the tea to you. Wouldn't that be nice? No need to go into the kitchen or anything like that."

"That's kind of you, but I'm quite capable of making a pot of tea," said Oliver, irritated at Geoffrey's behavior. Did he think this was going to make a difference with Effie? And what was this nonsense about not going into the kitchen? There could be nothing in there that Geoffrey didn't want him and Effie to see, Oliver thought, stubbornly opening the door, apart from . . .

"Lorina!" he almost shouted.

She stood up from the table, a dark vision in a black taffeta dress, gusting her expensive perfume in his direction. Unusually for her, she was wearing makeup, which gave her eyes a feline, predatory quality. Oliver froze in the doorway.

"I had to see you, Oliver," she said quickly, the words coming in a rush. "Ever since Saturday, I've been thinking about you. It's not every day you find an old boyfriend on your doorstep, begging to come into your home in the middle of the night, but I wanted you to know how much I appreciated what you did for me that night—you were so kind, so gentle, so loving."

Lorina broke off, catching sight of Effie watching the scene over Oliver's shoulder. Geoffrey had slunk away.

"Oh, I'm sorry," Lorina said contritely, "I didn't realize you had a guest."

Oliver stood aside mutely and let the women gaze at one another. He knew he should attempt an introduction, but in his confusion, he suspected that he would stumble over Effie's name. Lorina covered his hesitation, striding across the kitchen with an outstretched hand.

"My name is Lorina Random," she announced kindly. "Oliver and I are old friends."

Effie shook Lorina's hand, clearly recognizing the woman she had first seen that morning. "My condolences on the loss of your father," she said coolly. "I'm Effie Strongitharm."

"A new friend of Oliver's, perhaps? I don't recall his ever mentioning you," Lorina said, with polite curiosity. Oliver fought to find his voice.

"That's because I've hardly seen you in recent years," he said purposefully.

"Apart from Saturday night," Effie muttered. Lorina smiled self-consciously.

"I do apologize for turning up unannounced," she said. "It's not like Oliver to be out this late, and when Geoffrey said you were expected back soon, I rather bullied him into letting me wait. But I've said what I came to say. Oliver was very kind to me the other evening, and I wanted to tell him how much I appreciated it, for old time's sake. Now I must go."

"Oh, there's no need to rush," said Effie sharply. "Stay and have some tea with Oliver, he was just about to make some. Unfortunately, I have to leave."

She was at the front door before Oliver caught up with her. The *soprano lirico spinto* upstairs was into a cadenza comprising a series of sustained high Cs, although the recording had stopped. "Please don't go," he entreated, gently holding Effie's arm. "There's been a terrible misunderstanding."

The singing stopped. Effie stopped and turned slowly. Her eyes were wet. This hurt more than her skinned hands.

"I believe the cliche now is to say 'there certainly has, and I'm guilty of it,'" Effie said in a controlled voice. "I'm sorry—you have every right to have a girlfriend, of course, but I wish you hadn't lied to me this morning, when you said you broke up with Lorina a long time ago. Thank you for dinner, Oliver. Good-bye."

He dropped his arm, knowing he could not find the words to convince her that she was wrong. He was still staring at the back of the door when he heard her car start and head noisily out of the square.

"I'm sorry, Ollie, I can't stay for tea," said Lorina, coming up behind him. She kissed him briskly on the cheek, leaving a pink lip-print. "But now we're alone, I also wanted to say I may have implied a few things in the middle of the night that I'd prefer we forgot about in the cold light of dawn. You behaved like a perfect gentleman, as always. Did your friend leave already?"

"Yes. She left."

"You should try a little harder next time, she's very attractive," Lorina said with a sly grin. "No wonder you didn't want to go to bed with plain old me. Ah, well, must rush, I have a late date with a minister. Political, not religious. *Ciao*, sweetcakes."

And she was gone.

Music began again in the upstairs flat, "Vesti la giubba" from I *Pagliacci*.

" 'On with the Motley,' " Geoffrey translated ironically. He was sitting at the top of the stairs, his chin on his knees, barely visible in the gloom. "Music to get dressed to. A tenor aria, so Ben's client must have finished."

Oliver turned the latch on the front door, walked slowly to the staircase, and leaned heavily on the banister. "How's your finger, Geoff?" he asked eventually.

"A lot better, thanks."

Oliver sighed. "I appreciate your trying to head me off."

Geoffrey shrugged away the acknowledgment. "Want a drink?" he asked.

"No, I'm going to bed," said Oliver wearily. "Good night."

Sleep was slow to arrive and brought dreams. In the last before waking, Oliver was trying to count the number of people sitting at a dinner table in a large, dark, Victorian
greenhouse. He knew there should be twelve, but each time
he counted, he could never get higher than six, although
out of the corner of his eye, all the seats seemed to be taken.
He tried again, recognizing some of the people—Geoffrey
was there, Lorina, Sir Harry—but their names were not on
the manifest that he found himself clutching. Effie was sitting at a computer a few paces away, and he pleaded with her
to help him, but she was staring adamantly at the screen.
When he turned back, the greenhouse was gone, and he was
in a prison cell, like the one in Bow Street, while his uncle
watched him from the doorway.

Oliver came to sudden consciousness in his bedroom,
but the blurry image of Mallard did not vanish. He shook his
head vigorously. Yes, still the Mallard.

"Good morning, dear nephew," said the superintendent
breezily.

Oliver's curtains failed to meet in the middle, and from
where he lay in his bed, he could see watery sunlight falling
into the wilderness of the back garden.

"What time is it?" he asked, lifting himself stiffly onto his
elbows.

"Half past six," said Mallard. "I wanted to catch you before you went to work." He flipped on the light, causing
Oliver to groan and dive under the bed covers.

Mallard stared at the room. His nephew had mastered
the subtle distinction between hygiene and discipline; the
bedroom was both impeccably clean and hopelessly untidy.
Not that Oliver was disorganized; the room was a palimpsest,
where a distinct underlying order struggled to show through
the randomness on the surface. Inside his wardrobe, the

clean clothes were folded or hung neatly, although a batch of freshly laundered shirts lay over a chair, still waiting to be put away from the previous Friday; his personal files within the desk drawer were as clearly labeled as Sir Harry Random's, but Oliver had let the unsorted papers build up on the desktop for several weeks; and while his extensive bookshelves were rigidly categorized (by color—Oliver believed that you always remembered the color of a book jacket even when you forgot the name of its author), there were telltale gaps, and several piles of books were stacked on the mismatched items of furniture in the room. He had, however, cleared the floor and the bed of debris, his one concession to the possibility of a visit from Effie the previous evening. This allowed Mallard, a rare visitor, an unobstructed path to the window. He threw back the curtains and pushed the sash all the way up.

"What do you want?" moaned Oliver, his voice muffled by blankets.

"Two things," said Mallard, lifting a large map of London from the room's only armchair and seating himself. Oliver had marked the victims' homes on the maps, to see if they formed any geometric patterns. "First, what on earth did you do to Effie last night? I got a very distressed telephone call at about eleven o'clock. Phoebe and I were already in bed. She called you a philanderer and a Lothario."

Oliver flung back the bedclothes and sat up. "Aunt Phoebe called me that?" he asked, rubbing his eyes. "Then I guess I'm out of the will."

Mallard tutted impatiently. "Effie called you that, as you can well imagine. She wanted me to cause you physical and psychological damage, as only an uncle can. But I come in peace. What happened?"

Oliver gloomily outlined the events of the previous evening, causing Mallard to replace his expression of avuncular concern with one of enjoyment, and finally to break into sustained and uncontrollable laughter.

"And I thought Geoffrey Angelwine and the ferret was the funniest thing I'd heard in days," he said when he had recovered his breath, wiping his eyes on a large cambric handkerchief. "But you beat it, Ollie. I mean, I'm worried that there aren't enough girls in your life, and suddenly they come pouring out of the woodwork. My nephew, the Casanova."

Oliver glared at him humorlessly from the bed. "Thank you for your concern," he muttered. "Making Effie unhappy is the last thing I wanted to do."

"No, no, my dear lad—making Effie unhappy is the second to last thing. Making Effie *angry* is the last thing you should want to do. She came top of her class in karate."

"I'll remember that."

"All right, don't worry," Mallard continued, as his amusement died down. "I'll tell Effie that I asked you to go to Lorina's house on Saturday night. And that Welkin picked you up more or less immediately, before you had time for any rumpy-pumpy. But after that, you're on your own."

"You implied that there was some other reason for your intolerably early visit?" Oliver said with as much dignity as a young man in yellow pajamas could muster. He groped for his glasses on the bedside table. Mallard stood up slowly and moved to the window, watching the sparrows playing in the dry earth outside.

"I spoke to my superiors yesterday afternoon," he said eventually. "They don't think I've made enough progress. So I'm going to be replaced on the case. Today's my last day."

"You cracked the case—" Oliver began, but Mallard's abruptly raised finger silenced him. The superintendent breathed deeply.

"They're right, of course," he continued reasonably, still with his back to his nephew. "The trail's gone cold with the

Burbages. Now we're down to guessing who may have been politically motivated to kill the Burbage jury. Perhaps another mind will find something I missed."

How like Mallard to deal with Effie's distress before revealing his own agony, Oliver thought. He knew that Mallard had never been taken off a case in his entire career.

"But what could we possibly have missed?" Oliver asked, trying to share the responsibility. He climbed out of bed and put on his toweling bathrobe.

"I *must* have missed something, clearly. After all, the killer makes mistakes. But if he's that clumsy, that stupid, why haven't I caught him?"

"It was his marksmanship that failed in Piccadilly Circus, not his intelligence," Oliver replied steadily.

Mallard turned around. The white hair that fell over his forehead, the straggling white moustache, and gold-rimmed glasses often obscured his facial expressions, and Oliver could not be sure if his uncle was challenged or defeated by his superiors' ultimatum.

"Oliver, I appreciate your trying to bolster my sagging spirits," he said, with a smile. "You always have so much enthusiasm for the game, when your old Uncle Tim just gets rather tired of it all. But remember what Doctor Johnson said: 'When a man knows he is to be hanged in a fortnight, it concentrates his mind wonderfully.' You see, I've been thinking. I've been trying to think like the murderer. And I think that with the twelve signs of the zodiac and the twelve good men and true on the jury, there are far too many twelves in this puzzle. So I've decided to ignore them both."

Oliver sat down abruptly on the bed, bouncing several times, and clutched his head.

"Let me understand this," he whimpered. "You're saying that the daily schedule of the murders, the locations, the methods of death, the victims' birth signs, their jury duty—

none of these matter? That there's yet another connection still to be discovered?"

Mallard chuckled wickedly. "No. No more connections. No connection at all. That's the point. But if I'm right, we've only got a day to prove it."

A few minutes later, Susie Beamish, who had just arrived home, was cheerfully preparing scrambled eggs, a task that was barely within the limits of her culinary skills. "I add chives," she reported ominously. Mallard managed to warn her not to ask Oliver about the previous evening's date with Effie, before his nephew appeared in the doorway, dragging a sweatshirt over his tousled fair hair.

"Here's what struck me last night," said Mallard, taking a gulp of tea. "Suppose you're the killer. You want to kill twelve people who have a specific connection—they served on a jury. So you look for an alternative pattern such as the signs of the zodiac, which you emphasize very strongly in your murders, in the hope that it will hide the original connection. Okay so far?"

"Crystal clear," Susie brayed from the stove, scraping at the contents of the frying pan with a level of energy that could only mean the eggs had stuck to the bottom. Oliver merely nodded.

"Now let me ask you this," Mallard continued slowly. "There are twelve signs of the zodiac. And there are twelve members of a jury. But if you *really* wanted to disguise the jury connection, why would you choose an alternative pattern with the same magic number, especially when it failed to work for more than six of the intended victims? Why not a set of six or seven . . . or ten, such as Lewis Carroll's Snark-hunters?"

"So you're saying that the killer *wanted* us to find the jury," said Oliver.

"Yes."

"Because he wanted us to believe that the deaths had something to do with the Burbage trial?"

"Yes."

"But now you're saying that the jury isn't the real reason why these people are being killed, no more than their birth signs?"

"It doesn't look like it."

"Yet there's no additional connection to be found among the victims?"

"No. A third thread would be almost impossible."

Oliver sat back in his chair and stared at his uncle. "Then I don't get it," he said helplessly. "The only possible explanation takes us back to the mischievous serial killer playing Consequences—that it's a game for its own sake."

"Of course that's not the only explanation, silly!" exclaimed Susie, bustling over to the table with two plates, each bearing several steaming yellow pellets with green flecks and brown stripes. She placed them smugly in front of the two men. "Oliver, it's perfectly obvious what Uncle Tim's getting at. Ever since you spotted your precious patterns, you've been looking for reasons why a *group* of people had to die. Apart from the first one or two victims, you haven't looked at any of them as individual cases. Sorry about the eggs, darlings, they caught a bit."

Mallard stared at the food, wondering how he could avoid eating it under the watchful eye of its perpetrator. Oliver, better prepared for Susie's cooking, absentmindedly smothered the scrambled eggs in tomato ketchup. At that moment, Geoffrey Angelwine walked into the kitchen. Mallard and Susie greeted him, but Oliver was still thinking about Susie's outburst. Eventually, he spoke:

"The murderer wants to kill only one person. But he hides his real victim somewhere within an elaborately contrived sequence of deaths. Two sequences, in fact. And we spend so much time looking for the key to these sequences that we totally ignore any individual motivation."

"That's it," said Mallard and Susie simultaneously. She waved Geoffrey to help himself to the rest of the scrambled eggs.

"So when, for example, poor old Archie Brock turns up in St. James's Square," Oliver continued, "we were conditioned by that stage to say 'Oops, another one for the zodiac murderer.' We never bothered to ask if he might have any personal enemies down in Kent who wanted to kill him."

"It would seem so," grunted Mallard through a mouthful of egg, which was strangely crunchy. He reached quickly for his tea again.

"And so it didn't matter that the murderer could only manage six murders out of a potential twelve," cried Oliver, as Geoffrey joined them at the table. "As long as the intended victim was one of the six, he didn't actually *need* to go any further. It all fits! Very good, Susie!"

Susie covered her flush of pleasure by taking her plate to the sink. While her back was turned, Oliver grabbed his uncle's plate and with a wink, scraped the offensive eggs onto Geoffrey's, who immediately ate them. Oliver threw Mallard a slice of dry toast in compensation.

"So who's the murderer?" Susie asked as she returned.

"Someone who had a personal motive to kill one of the six victims, evidently," said Oliver.

"I think we can narrow it even further," Mallard claimed, munching contentedly on the toast. "Until we spotted the zodiac pattern, we were looking at each victim rather searchingly. We had quite a few suspects for Mark Sandys-Penza, the Richmond estate agent, for instance—his wife, his secretary's boyfriend, his business partner, several competitors. But the murderer would want to avoid that kind of scrutiny.

Now, I don't think he'd have expected us to tumble to the zodiac connection until the fourth murder. So I think we can ignore murders one, two, and three."

"But the fourth one was Sagittarius, the mistake," said Oliver.

"That doesn't matter, we know the *intended* Sagittarius victim was Edmund Tradescant. Is there anyone who might want to kill him? We never actually asked."

"I can't believe Tradescant's the ultimate target," Oliver commented. "Imagine it from the murderer's perspective—you spend weeks researching your victim, you discover one pattern to distract the police from your actual motivation, you discover another pattern to distract them from the first pattern, you gather the equipment you need, you set up a set of meetings, you execute one, two, three bizarre murders, and after that, when your true target is finally in your crossbow sights, you miss! I think the last thing you'd do is blandly go ahead with the next two murders, while Edmund Tradescant walks free."

"So that leaves us five and six—Vanessa Parmenter and Archie Brock," Mallard commented.

"Would it be the last one in the series?" Susie asked. "Isn't that too obvious? The killer achieves his aim, so he stops. Wouldn't he do at least one more?"

"That's what I thought," said Mallard, throwing his napkin onto the table. "So today—my last day on the case—I'm going to look for someone who wanted to kill Vanessa Parmenter, the travel agent from Kingston." He got up from the table, kissed Susie warmly on the cheek, and headed for the door. Oliver followed, draining his tea mug. Susie started to gather their dirty plates, with a resentful glare at the ketchup skidmarks on Oliver's.

"Hold it!" cried Geoffrey suddenly. He remained in his

seat, arms folded, as if seeking a parent's approval for good behavior. "I've been thinking."

"And I thought it was an air lock in the pipes," said Susie.

"What is it, Geoffrey?" asked Mallard with interest. Although he often felt that the young man's belt didn't go through all the loops, he also respected his intellect.

"This is nothing personal, you understand," Geoffrey continued doggedly, "but every time you've come up with some solution to these crimes, you've found the murderer one jump ahead of you. What if he's still playing with you? You're looking for the true target among his six victims. You just rejected five of them, on very logical grounds. But what if that's what the murderer wanted you to do?"

"Go on," said Mallard thoughtfully.

"You rejected victim number six, because he was the last in the series, and too obvious. But you may have tumbled to the jury connection sooner than the murderer expected. Might he not have been planning a number seven and a number eight? If so, number six wouldn't have been last."

"Well, Archie Brock was the last in the unbroken sequence of zodiac signs, but we'll check on him, too."

"That's not all. Oliver said number four couldn't be the 'real' victim, because the murderer continued to kill after hitting the wrong man. But what else could he have done? Surely the killer's best bet would be to push on with the murders as planned until you spotted the jury connection. Then he'd seem to have a reason for coming back and killing Tradescant."

"Edmund Tradescant is back in the picture," said Mallard. "Any more?"

" 'Fraid so," said Geoffrey apologetically. "Your zodiac murders took place on a daily basis. One, two, three days—that's not too long for a murderer to cover up his or her guilt until the police stop looking for personal motives and start hunting for a mythical serial killer. If I remember rightly, you didn't really think Sir Harry Random's death *was* a murder until after you'd already reached victim number three. You never even started to wonder if Ambrose or Lorina or anybody else had a motive to kill him. You only arrested Oliver."

"So you're saying Uncle Tim should investigate *all* the victims individually?" asked Susie. Geoffrey nodded glumly, causing Oliver to slam his fist unexpectedly against the wall where he was standing.

"Damn it, Geoffrey, don't you understand?" he shouted. "We don't have time to widen up the field again! Uncle Tim has to find this killer today!"

"It's okay, Oliver," Mallard cut in softly, resting a hand on his nephew's shoulder. "Geoffrey's been very helpful. Very helpful indeed."

"But you don't have time, Uncle!" Oliver wailed. "Not to go through all of them. Not by the end of the day."

"I'm not going to go through all of them. I don't need to. I believe I still know where to look."

"Despite what Geoffrey said?" asked Susie.

"Because of something Geoffrey said," Mallard replied steadily, with a warm smile that somehow failed to convince them that he was content with the idea. "But I need a little time to think about it."

"Would you like me to come with you today?" Oliver offered.

"No, no, you go to work this morning—we've used enough of your time for this case. I'll call you later if I get anywhere."

"Will you let us all know?" Susie inquired insistently.

"If I make an arrest this afternoon," Mallard said, "you can all be there."

Eleven

AT TEN O'CLOCK THAT Tuesday morning, an elderly man cautiously read the name of Woodcock and Oakhampton, stenciled on the reeded glass of their office door. Then he pushed the door open and crept inside, in time to see Oliver, who had been halfheartedly composing a letter of explanation to Effie, crumple several pages of laser-printed text in disgust and hurl them unsuccessfully toward the wire wastepaper basket.

The man cleared his throat. "Mr. Woodcock, perhaps?" he enquired. Oliver assumed the best greeting face he could manage, although his mind was filled with thoughts of Mallard and Lorina and, above all, Effie.

"These are indeed the office of Woodcock and Oakhampton," he rattled off distractedly. "How can I help you, sir?"

The man seemed perplexed. He was short and slight, and wearing all three pieces of an ill-fitting blue serge suit, which was at least one piece too many for the outside temperature. His oversize tie-knot was almost as wide as his neck.

"Well, I suppose I'd like to see either Mr. Woodcock or Mr. Oakhampton, if that's at all possible," he said timidly.

It was possible, because it was one of the days when both partners had turned up at Cromwell Road. However, Oliver had strict instructions to protect his employers from any caller who wasn't a potential client. It had not been a challenge to maintain a flawless record.

"Do you have an appointment?" Oliver asked casually, pretending to call up a calendar on his computer screen, although he actually flipped to his shopping list for the weekend.

"No," said the man. "I really called on the off-chance, Mr. . . . ?"

"Swithin," said Oliver reluctantly, already seeing it on a promotional ball-point pen or key ring or whatever personalized premium the man might use to support his sales pitch. "Mr. Woodcock and Mr. Oakhampton are both very busy today, sir, but if you'd care to leave a brochure describing your services, I'm sure we'll get back to you if we're interested."

He flashed the man a tight smile and deleted "condoms" from his shopping list to suggest the encounter was over. The little man hesitated and then cleared his throat.

"I'm not sure you quite understood me, Mr. Swithin," he quavered. "I'm not selling anything. I'm enquiring about engaging the firm's services."

Oliver's fingers slipped off the keyboard and landed in his lap. He stared at the visitor.

"You're a client?" he gasped.

"Er, possibly."

Oliver had rehearsed the drill hypothetically on numerous occasions—usher the man unctuously into Mr. Woodcock's office and then prepare coffee using the silver service that had been gathering dust in a creaky filing cabinet. But this curiosity was too great.

"What do you think we can do for you?" he asked, hoping for an answer to the mystery of Woodcock and Oakhampton's brand of business consulting. The man seemed taken aback.

"I was hoping you could tell me," he confessed. "You see, I'm thinking of starting a business. I want to manufacture Trilons."

"I beg your pardon?"

"Trilons. Ladies' panty hose with three legs."

"Not too many ladies have three legs."

"No, no, Mr. Swithin. They're to be worn by ladies with two legs, of course. You see, with a standard pair of hose, if a lady gets a run in one leg, the pair must be thrown away. With Trilons, she always has a spare leg to stand on. In, I mean. There are three different ways that two real legs can occupy three panty hose legs, you know."

Effie would have known that, Oliver reflected, and the thought caused a physical sensation in his stomach. Should he telephone her?

"Anyway," the man continued, "I was passing your building, musing on this, and your brass plaque was so encouraging that I called to see if you could offer me some assistance."

Oliver blinked. "Have a seat," he said, indicating a maroon chesterfield near the door. He hurried to Mr. Woodcock's door and tapped on the panel. Woodcock listened to him in amazement, threw down his *Independent* crossword puzzle, and bolted for the door.

The visitor was quickly conducted into Mr. Oakhampton's office and the door was firmly closed behind them. For five minutes, there was silence. Then Oliver heard a long bray of hysterical laughter. His first thought was that the little man had undergone a transformation into a murderous maniac, plucking a meat cleaver from the ample folds of his waistcoat; then it dawned on him that the sound was the unfamiliar voice of Mr. Oakhampton, expressing glee.

The door opened again and the visitor came out, mopping his face with a red handkerchief. He looked at Oliver strangely and then dashed out of the offices. Next came Mr. Woodcock, oddly downcast, followed by the lean form of his partner, who was grinning broadly. Woodcock plucked his wallet from the depths of his trouser pocket, drew out a banknote, and passed it to Oakhampton. Then he went into his office and slammed the door behind him.

"A fine day, Mr. Swithin," Oakhampton called cheerfully. Oliver, amazed that his employer knew his name, nodded pleasantly.

"A client at last, Mr. Oakhampton," he replied. Oakhampton winked.

" 'At last' is correct," he said. "He's the last client in every sense." He chuckled to himself.

Oliver seized the opportunity. "Mr. Oakhampton, what do we actually do here? I mean, specifically."

"We do nothing."

"I know, but what are we supposed to do?"

"Nothing."

Oakhampton sat on Oliver's desk and twirled the rotary stand designed to hold ink stamps. "Let me explain," he said affably. "Woodcock and I have known each other all our lives. We're rather well off and since we have a lot of time on our hands, we make the occasional wager. Well, we were discussing the merits of advertising one day, and I bet him that if we set up a company with a totally nondescriptive name, rented a set of offices, hired a staff, put ourselves into the telephone book, but undertook no publicity whatsoever, then sooner or later, someone would march in and try to engage our services. And so, we created Woodcock and Oakhampton, Ltd. to find out. You've just seen our first real client, which means I won the bet."

"How much did you win?" Oliver asked in amazement.

"Ten pounds," Oakhampton replied proudly. He hauled himself to his feet and jerked a thumb in the direction of his partner's office. "Woodcock's taken it bad. He rather enjoyed his time as a company director. Better leave him alone for a while."

"When did you make this particular bet?"

Oakhampton thrust his hands into his pockets. "I think it was 1968," he said. "May have been '69. Ah, well, fun while it lasted."

He headed into his own office and closed the door. Then he opened it again and put his head out.

"By the way, Swithin, you're fired," he said amicably.

Oliver found himself staring curiously at the telephone for several seconds before he realized it was ringing. He picked up the receiver as if in a trance.

"Last call for the train to Woodcock and Oakhampton," he intoned.

"Oliver? It's your uncle. Can you get some time off work after all?"

Oliver shook himself into a higher level of awareness.

"As much as I want, apparently," he said.

"Good. I want you to join me. I know who the murderer is."

Big Ben was striking five o'clock when Oliver scooted across Trafalgar Square. For the first time in weeks, the square was not bathed in brilliant sunshine at this hour, and its monuments and bollards cast only dim shadows. During the last hour, the cloud coverage had thickened ominously, and waves were slopping over the fountain's rim. There were few pedestrians on the square apart from the group clustered around Mallard.

"Sorry I'm late," Oliver gasped. He surveyed the group. Some he expected to see—his uncle, Detective Sergeant Moldwarp, Detective Sergeant Welkin on crutches. Effie was there, but she did not look at him. Susie Beamish, Geoffrey Angelwine, Ben Motley—well, Mallard had promised they could be present for the grand unveiling. But Lorina, too, presumably still unaware of the heartache she had caused him? And Ambrose Random, looking ridiculous in a caftan. My goodness, Constable Urchin has made a reappearance. And Dworkin. And there was Edmund Tradescant again. But who was that hefty type handcuffed to Moldwarp?

"You'll be late for your own funeral," said Mallard humorlessly. He, too, was dodging Oliver's gaze. "I think the one person you don't know is Clifford Burbage, there in the bracelets," he added. Oliver nodded amiably, but Burbage seemed preoccupied with avoiding Welkin's continual glare.

"Thank you all for coming," the superintendent announced. "However, I have to say that one of you is going to regret accepting my invitation. Before we leave this place, I plan to arrest the zodiac murderer, as we persist in calling him."

He allowed the group time to react. "Him?" echoed Ambrose over the general murmurs of surprise.

"We've been using 'him' as shorthand. I'll keep that up for now, but we'll soon see if the male truly embraces the female."

Mallard began to wander through the small audience. "Untangling this case has been like peeling back the layers of an onion," he said. "We think Sir Harry Random's death in this fountain is an accident, but it isn't. We think Nettie

237

Clapper's murder is an isolated mugging, but it isn't. Then we think we have a serial killer using the signs of the zodiac, but there's more. We find a jury, but maybe that's not the solution either. Now we're looking at the murders individually, but we have no clue where to start. Oh, we're dealing with a very clever murderer here."

He paused, allowing his gaze to sweep across all their faces. Then he slowly stretched an arm toward Edmund Tradescant.

"But the fact that Mr. Tradescant is still with us is living proof that the murderer, while clever, is not perfect," Mallard continued. "And I've come to realize that the shooting of Gordon Paper in Piccadilly Circus was by no means the murderer's only mistake. Let's see some more evidence of his failings."

He walked to the fountain and pointed at a statue that rose from the water—an open-mouthed merman, clutching two dolphins, with water streaming from their mouths into the overflowing basin.

"Sir Harry Random died here, near that waterspout. When we looked for a connection to Harry's birth sign, Pisces, we found it in those fish."

Ambrose Random snorted suddenly.

"Fish?" he echoed, in a voice that, in one syllable, moved from baritone to falsetto and back again.

Mallard turned to him. "Something wrong, Mr. Random?" he asked innocently.

"Anyone with an atom of intelligence can tell you that a dolphin is not a fish."

"He probably thinks it's a bird," Oliver whispered to Ben.

"A dolphin is a mammal," Ambrose announced smugly, looking around for approval.

"So you're saying this statue is not the most accurate representation of Pisces?" Mallard asked. "I agree. If anything, it works better as Aquarius, the Water-bearer. But the Aquarius death happened the next day at Sloane Square station, near the duct that carries the River Westbourne across the railway line. This second murder was flawless. The only trouble is, poor Nettie Clapper, the Aquarian victim, wasn't really an Aquarius. Like Oliver, she was born in the blurry boundary between two birth-signs known as a cusp. But most newspaper and magazine horoscopes would put her birthday, January 20, in Capricorn. On that day in 1932, when she was born, the sun was definitely in Capricorn. So why select Nettie for the Aquarius death, when there were two other jury members available who were decidedly Aquarian? I suggest the answer is carelessness."

He took a folded sheet of paper from his pocket. "Let's move on to death number three. This is the letter that was sent to the Capricorn, Mark Sandys-Penza. It invites him to a meeting at the 'Tropical House' in Kew Gardens. We rather slavishly picked up the killer's terminology, thinking the name 'Tropical' was our link to the birth sign, as in the Tropic of Capricorn. But I checked this afternoon with the Royal Botanic Gardens. There's no such place as the Tropical House. It's actually called the 'Temperate House.' "

Mallard paused, but there were no comments from the group. All except one, they were mentally willing him to continue, to present the solution to the mystery.

"Death number four was the biggest mistake of all, which we've already acknowledged: The murderer killed the wrong man. Death number five, in contrast, was immaculate—although our genius had to dredge up an ancient connection between Scorpio and an eagle to make it work. There are scorpion images in London, as Oliver himself discovered.

"And victim number six, the Libra, was found outside a library. A nice verbal link, which Sergeant Strongitharm spotted first. Except the word 'library' takes its root from the

239

Latin word *liber,* meaning a book, while *libra* is a different Latin word, meaning a balance. The similarity between these two words is a phonetic coincidence. You can trace them all the way back to their Indo-European roots, and you won't find any connection."

"Would you really count that as an error?" asked Lorina.

Mallard paused, looking at her carefully. "There are two or three big mistakes, there are perhaps insignificant lapses. My point is that our killer is not as clever as we thought he was. In fact, I could argue that every single murder was flawed in one way or another. Rather a second-rate job."

"This is getting too complicated for me, Uncle Tim," Susie complained, "and poor Geoffrey's little brain is getting decidedly fuzzy." Geoffrey scowled at her.

"Bear with me, Susie, I'm nearly finished," Mallard said. "We come now to the biggest lapse of all—biggest, because it affected all the murders. The killer was working the wrong way through the zodiac, *backwards* not forwards. That remains a conundrum. After all, there was a continuous sequence of six birth signs among the jury members—Libra to Pisces. Why go backwards? Oliver's explanation, which we were quick to accept, was that Pisces is traditionally the last sign of the astrological year. But what if there's another explanation? What if the killer had no choice over his first victim? It had to be Sir Harry Random, here in Trafalgar Square."

"Ah, then the late Squire Random was the reason for all this, and the other five died to draw attention away from his murder!" cried Ambrose. "How deliciously intriguing!" Oliver glanced unavoidably toward Lorina, who remained impassive.

Mallard smiled for the first time. "I'm not looking for your father's murderer, Mr. Random. I'm about to arrest the person who killed those other five people."

240

"You mean there were two murderers?" Ben blurted out.

"Two murderers?" Susie repeated. "I can't take this."

"No," Mallard stated emphatically. "I'm not looking for Sir Harry's murderer, because there's no such person. Sir Harry Random wasn't murdered. His death was an accident, as the police believed in the first place."

With a cry, Lorina tottered. Ben swiftly caught her and, with Effie's help, lowered her to the ground. Ambrose ignored his sister's reaction.

"She'll be okay," said Effie, cradling Lorina's head in her lap. Mallard responded by strolling over to Geoffrey and laying a hand on his shoulder. Geoffrey gulped apprehensively.

"This morning, Geoffrey Angelwine gave me food for thought," the superintendent continued, unavoidably remembering the other food he had been given for breakfast. "He said that every time we come up with one solution, the murderer is another jump ahead. Another layer deeper into the onion, if you like. It's like a game, played out between the murderer and the police. And I think Geoffrey's hit on the real reason for these killings." He let go of Geoffrey, who gratefully dropped back a couple of steps.

"This whole thing has been no more than a giant puzzle!" Mallard proclaimed. "It's a game played across London, just like Oliver's hide-and-seek Snark Hunt, with real people—real human lives—as the expendable pieces. There is no hidden motive for any one of these murders. There is no zodiac serial killer, no Cliff Burbage taking revenge on the jury that convicted his father, no hidden malcontent whose target is Sir Harry Random, or Nettie Clapper, or Mark Sandys-Penza, or Mr. Tradescant here, or Mr. Dworkin, if he'd got that far, or the other jury members. These suspects, these victims—actual or potential—have all been pawns in the murderer's game. The true targets for these vile crimes are still alive, standing here—the police investigators who joined in that game!"

"But who would want to do that?" squealed Susie.

"Who?" cried Mallard incredulously. "Isn't it obvious? There's only one person who had the opportunity and God help me, I gave it to him."

"Oliver," breathed Effie.

"Oliver," Mallard confirmed, pointing at his nephew, "by all that's damnable."

Nobody seemed to move, but Oliver suddenly found himself standing alone, almost in the center of the group. He brushed his hair from his eyes.

"This is, of course, ridiculous," he mumbled. "Uncle Tim—this is me, your nephew Ollie. I'm not a murderer. I've been helping you *catch* the murderer. I'm on your side."

Mallard continued to stare at him, without speaking further. Oliver looked down at Effie, who still held Lorina in her lap. Two pairs of eyes, ice-blue and coffee-brown, gazed back. "Effie, you got the wrong end of the stick the other night, Lorina will tell you! Say you don't believe it!"

Mallard spoke before Effie could answer. "At six o'clock in the morning, eight days ago, Sir Harry Random left the Sanders Club and went out for some air, perhaps to clear his head before going home. After five minutes, Sir Harry found himself in the middle of a deserted Trafalgar Square. We'll never quite know what happened, but he was old and he'd been drinking and I think the temptation to climb onto the rim of this fountain was irresistible, as it is to a child. He lost his balance and fell, striking his head on the stonework, and then rolled into the basin. Any trace of blood or hair on the stone was soon washed away by the overflowing water. It was an accident, a sad, regrettable accident, just as we thought initially."

"No!" cried Oliver, "I discovered the letter in the lobby

of the club, arranging the meeting. And there was the symbol for Pisces drawn on his dress shirt!"

"Oliver found Sir Harry a few minutes later," Mallard continued stubbornly, "but he was too late to save him. Oliver was distraught, angry, maybe even slightly guilty for having been asleep while Sir Harry stepped out alone. In those frantic moments, maybe it was understandable that Oliver couldn't accept the banality of his mentor's death by drowning, and that by imagining it as a murder, he was somehow giving Sir Harry more dignity. And then a policeman turned up—Constable Urchin here, who quite rightly refused to believe in a murder for which there was no evidence.

"This annoyed Oliver. He wanted to give Urchin something to think about. He'd had cause to remember Sir Harry's birthday, the twenty-ninth of February. He knew this made Harry a Pisces. He noticed the dolphins on the nearby statue—not fish, but close enough. In Oliver's mind, it all came together, and in a fit of wilfulness, while Urchin's back was turned, he opened Harry's jacket and scrawled the Pisces symbol on his wet shirtfront."

"And I just happened to have a blue marker pen on me?" said Oliver sarcastically.

"No. No marker pen was found on you when you were arrested, nor at the crime scene, nor in the fountain."

"Then I couldn't have drawn it, could I?" Oliver cried in exasperated tones. "The symbol must have been there *before* Harry was thrown into the fountain."

"The police didn't retain Sir Harry's shirt," Mallard remarked. "So we assumed the blue symbol on Harry's starched shirtfront was drawn by the same marker pen used for the later zodiac symbols. But maybe it wasn't."

Welkin handed him a small valise, from which Mallard took a white garment. Then he fished in his pocket for something else.

"This is a starched evening shirt like Sir Harry's," he said. He held up a small blue cube. "And this is a piece of billiard chalk, used for marking the end of cues. Watch."

Mallard dunked the shirt in the fountain, wrung it out, and spread it flat on the ground. With the chalk, he scrawled the double-ended fork that represented Pisces. It left a dull blue stain on the white fabric.

"But I didn't have any chalk either!" Oliver insisted.

"Not when you were arrested. You'd already thrown it into the fountain, where it floated with the rest of the debris until it broke up. But you had blue chalk when you left the Sanders Club. It was part of your equipment as one of the characters in Lewis Carroll's *Hunting of the Snark*. Harry had needle and thread in his lapel because he was the Bonnet-maker. And Oliver, you had chalk because you were the Billiard-marker!"

Mallard plunged the shirt into the fountain again and shook it underwater. When he took it out, the blue mark was almost gone.

"As you can see, for the sign to show up, it had to be drawn *after* Sir Harry's body had been taken from the fountain. Oliver was the only person who had the opportunity to do this."

"What about the letter that was sent to Harry?" Oliver said fiercely. "You saw that!"

"Nobody saw that letter in Sir Harry's possession. Not the club's night porter, nor the fellow Snark-hunters. You may have recovered it from the club lobby a day or so later, under Mr. Dworkin's eyes, but that's because you printed it and planted it there yourself after Sir Harry was dead."

"Why? Why would I do all this?"

Mallard passed the wet shirt back to Welkin and rested on the edge of the fountain, staring at his nephew. The others might as well be invisible, a silent audience to a two-character play, the watchers of a film that was unreeling to its climax.

"Here's what I think happened, Oliver. By now, you've inwardly accepted that Harry died accidentally. But it annoys you that Constable Urchin failed to believe you, or that despite your fabricated evidence, the CID don't believe you, and nor do I when I turn up unexpectedly at Bow Street. You wonder what it would take to make us accept your story, even though it isn't actually true. And what it would take, you decide, is more murders.

"What if Sir Harry's Pisces death were only the first of a series? Wouldn't that be fun—to devise a sequence of deaths combining zodiac signs and your detailed knowledge of London? How and where would Aries die? And Taurus? And all the others, one a month, or one a week, or hardest of all, one a day, in strict order. Then in Sir Harry's study, you notice that he kept files on everything, including the names of a jury he once served on. Twelve jurors, twelve signs of the zodiac. Could that add another level of complexity to your puzzle?

"It obsesses you. Back home on that Monday afternoon, a clever series of telephone calls tracks down the jury members and elicits their birthdays. And lo and behold, you can get a sequence of five more consecutive zodiac signs, stretching away from Sir Harry—Aquarius, Capricorn, Sagittarius, Scorpio, and Libra. You have to go backwards through the year, not forwards, but still . . . How easy would it be, you wonder, to get Aquarian Nettie Clapper up to Sloane Square, to die near the River Westbourne, her skull smashed with a length of lead pipe? You call again, this time pretending to be a solicitor with good news of a bequest. She takes the bait. There isn't much time, so you drive out to Harold Wood that night and drop off a letter, arranging a meeting early the following morning."

"This is all so farfetched," Oliver complained, with a mute appeal to the watchers. But each face was expressionless. Mallard lowered his voice, like a priest reaching the holiest point in the liturgy. His eyes never left Oliver's scowling face.

"On that Tuesday morning, you turned up at Sloane Square, only one stop from South Kensington, where you work. Until then, I think you just wanted to test the extent of your ingenuity, to see if you could make the pattern work. But when it did, when poor Nettie Clapper stood before you expectantly, you couldn't resist. It's no longer about the indignation of not being believed. It's about power, the power of mischief, the power of the puzzler. One swing of that pipe into an old woman's face and the game would begin—the race to get through your sequence of five daily murders before Scotland Yard could solve the mystery. You couldn't resist. And may God damn you, you succeeded!"

"I was helping you!" Oliver shouted tearfully. "I was the one *solving* the mystery, not creating it."

Mallard advanced a step toward his nephew, which emphasized his greater height. "We didn't get to Gemini, the Twins. But you could be their symbol, Oliver—so arrogant that you even challenged your own intellect to a duel. Could you, the killer who already knows the solution to the puzzle, get to the end of the sequence before you, the stand-in detective, found the answer?" He thrust a pointing finger behind him. "The dolphin statue as a fish. The wrong name for the Kew Gardens greenhouse. You were very quick to spot those erroneous connections."

"I know a dolphin's not a fish," Oliver growled. "And the murderer's letter spoke of the 'Tropical House.' Just because I try to follow his thinking, that doesn't turn me into him! I was with you! I was on your team!"

246

"You weren't with us when any of the murders took place. You don't have a single alibi!"

"Effie! Tell him he's wrong!" Oliver pleaded.

Effie continued to watch him coldly, stroking Lorina's head. "It's you, Oliver," she said viciously. "You knew you only had to dangle the suspicion of a pattern in front of the police and, superstitious creatures that we are, we would go hunting mythical serial killers. And all the time, it was your smug, dirty secret that at the core of this mystery was a mean-ingless accident—Sir Harry Random's random death!"

"But it was a second-rate job, Oliver," snarled Mallard. "Too many mistakes. You even killed the wrong person. Even now, even with five murders behind you, you're still second rate."

Oliver's abrupt scream of animal rage froze them. Almost in slow-motion, they saw his hand go into his satchel and pull out the omnipresent folding umbrella. He began to flail it crazily above his head, as if swatting invisible demons. It was a ludicrous, pathetic sight.

"Take him down!" Mallard commanded, concerned for the civilians. The detectives responded, the others backed away quickly. But Effie, on her knees, was encumbered by Lo-rina, and Moldwarp was chained to Burbage. The limping Welkin was the first to reach Oliver, and was quickly felled when the young man struck him on the head and kicked a crutch away. Urchin came up from behind, but Oliver reeled on him angrily and threw him with brutal strength toward Moldwarp and Burbage. All three men tumbled to the ground.

For an instant, Mallard and Oliver faced each other, al-most motionless. Then there were two gleams of silver metal: one from the police whistle that Mallard placed in his mouth, ready to summon other detectives from the north side of the Square; the other from the blade that Oliver pulled from the umbrella's shaft, glittering through the air in front of his uncle.

A fine red mist sprayed from the whistle, but no sound. Instead, Mallard's breath seemed to hiss wetly from the jagged new mouth that had opened across the folds of his throat. Blood cascaded onto his collar. He dropped.

Oliver was gone, lost among the cars and buses around the square, before Mallard hit the ground. Speckles of rain began to appear on the dusty pavement.

Twelve

THE VOLUME WAS HIGH on the CD player, perhaps to keep the quieter moments of the string quartet audible through the occasional thunderclap. But there was still only one point in the last movement when the music grew loud enough to mask the cautious opening of the first-floor French window and the sudden hiss of rain, falling in the Twickenham street outside. Surprisingly, the action did not trip the burglar alarm of the smart, eighteenth-century house in Montpelier Row, and the window was closed again before the quartet's chiming garlands subsided, and the four instruments returned to the steady, tolling pace of the passacaglia, its theme inspired by Venetian church bells.

In the room, the simple E major melody comforted the ear with its insistent tonality, drawing the listener on to that shattering, consoling, searching final chord of Britten's final quartet. Not the expected E major, foretold for so long, but a bare triad of C sharp minor for the upper instruments, while the cello descends to the modal D natural that had haunted the movement. Critics question its meaning. Is it death? When he wrote the movement in Venice, Britten was certainly under the sentence of death, delivered by his failing heart, and the quartet quotes from the composer's last opera, *Death in Venice*, including Aschenbach's distraught confession of his impossible love for the passing boy, Tadzio. But death did not come for Britten for a year, and in Aldeburgh, not Venice.

The compact disc stopped, and a very wet Oliver Swithin was forced to choke back a gobbet of illogical outrage that he and the room's occupant could both take the same pleasure from such a sublime moment of music. Then Oliver stepped out from behind the long wine-colored curtains.

The man standing by the expensive stereo equipment spun around, and for a second Oliver saw terror in his eyes. He enjoyed this. With his inoffensive features and naturally bemused expression, Oliver was not used to intimidating people, although he privately admitted that an unexpected appearance looking like a drowned ferret helped. But the man facing him was too good at this. His instinctive suavity quickly returned.

"I trust you haven't returned to make good on your biggest mistake," Edmund Tradescant said, with annoying sangfroid. "It wouldn't be very tidy to slay a Sagittarius at this stage."

"I'm not here to kill you," Oliver told him. Tradescant absorbed this information with a quizzical twist of the head.

"In that case, can I offer you a drink? I was just about to top myself up before going to bed." He raised a whisky tumbler and rattled the ice cubes.

Oliver demurred, but watched Tradescant closely as he

turned his back and fiddled with decanters and glasses on the cocktail cabinet. Was he contemplating hurling the ice tongs at the intruder or smashing his whisky tumbler and grinding the shards into Oliver's face? But perhaps he thought twice. It was Waterford, after all.

The large room was decorated as Oliver expected. One or two of the pieces of furniture were genuine antiques; the others were period reproductions, or more comfortable modern pieces of an enduring neutrality that work in any setting—like blue denim jeans that match paint-spattered T-shirts and Hermes scarves with equal composure.

"Cheers," said Tradescant, turning around and sipping from the recharged tumbler. "So if you don't want to kill me, what *do* you want?"

"The truth about the murders."

Tradescant shrugged dismissively. "I thought your actions this afternoon were tantamount to a confession. Is there a word for murdering your own uncle? 'Avunculicide' or something?"

"He is dead?"

"No doubt about that from where I was standing. I think that brings your tally to seven."

"I did not commit the zodiac murders," said Oliver emphatically.

"Then you have a peculiar way of protesting your innocence."

Without asking, Oliver fell into the armchair that Tradescant had just vacated, with his back to the door, and ran his fingers through his fine, damp hair. Tradescant didn't move, but stood nursing his glass. Oliver had noted that he was too wise to play the outraged householder, leaping for the telephone or his burglar alarm's panic button. "He wants to hear what I know," he thought.

"Uncle Tim made me angry," Oliver said wearily, as if he

251

were finally speaking words that he had been rehearsing silently for several hours. "He said the one thing he knows I hate to hear—that I'm 'second rate.' I *know* I'm second rate, for God's sake: I live with that self-reproach every day. I'm a second-rate writer, who can't do better than stupid stories for children. I'm a second-rate lover, who finally meets the perfect woman and doesn't bring himself to act because of some prosaic ethical code. Now, I'm supposed to be a second-rate murderer, too, who can't even fool himself. When Uncle Tim said those things about my being two people, one who murders and one who solves the murder, I thought for one brief second that it might be true—that there is indeed another Oliver, dancing beyond my reach. Perhaps that other Oliver finally erupted to the surface in Trafalgar Square, settling the score for twenty-five years of failing to make my mark on the world, of secretly knowing I was truly second-rate."

Tradescant stared into his drink. "In a case of multiple personality," he said, "which is what you seem to be suggesting, there's a school of thought that believes you—the sane, gentle Swithin, who wants to help the police—aren't guilty of the murders committed by the other Swithin, the gamester, the trickster."

"But neither Swithin is guilty of the zodiac murders," Oliver replied obstinately. "I was confused when Uncle Tim threw those accusations at me. Now I think I can refute them."

"You mean, you've found an alibi?"

"No. It was an odd coincidence that I wasn't with my uncle or my friends at the time of the deaths. Listen, though. Uncle Tim said I devised the murders after I was supposed to have spotted a file on jury duty in Harry's office on Monday afternoon, the day of his death. But I didn't go to Harry's home until Tuesday, and by then, the Aquarius death had already taken place!"

"Perhaps you saw the file on an earlier occasion," said Tradescant, drinking again.

"I hadn't been to Harry's house in years. And what about the morning of his death. Uncle Tim claimed I had a cube of blue billiard chalk in my pocket because I was playing the Billiard-marker in the Sanders Club's Snark Hunt. But I wasn't the Billiard-marker! I was the Banker. The other Snark-hunters will vouch for that. So will the police—I had Monopoly money in my pocket as a prop, which the police found when I was arrested."

"I doubt the police will be forthcoming with a defense, given that you've slain one of their own."

Oliver ignored the comment. "I also had a toy telescope, because Henry Holiday's illustrations for the poem show the Banker with a telescope. And anyway, a Victorian billiard-marker wouldn't carry chalk. His job wasn't to chalk the cues, it was to keep score of the game."

"A little arcane," Tradescant muttered. "Had you been playing billiards that evening?"

"No. Harry and I played poker. We didn't go into the club's billiard room."

"You could still have slipped a cube of chalk into your pocket. Not that it matters, because the police think Sir Harry was the one person you *didn't* kill."

Oliver shook his head. "I didn't kill any of them."

"Then who did?"

"You did."

Tradescant raised his eyebrows, but did not look at Oliver. "Ah, now I see why you've come here," he said. "Well, if you're going to accuse me, perhaps I may sit down. I prefer to be comfortable when I'm listening to fiction. Although I should tell you immediately, I have alibis for several of the deaths."

He sat upon a damask-covered sofa, almost underneath a shaded standard lamp, the room's only illumination. Damn him, Oliver thought, he was so bloody collected, placing his drink neatly on a coaster on the mahogany end-table. But Oliver also noted Tradescant's arm, casually draped over the back of the sofa. What was he reaching for?

"You see," said Oliver, "there's one person I can't get out of my mind."

"And that is?"

"The man we said was a mistake. Your colleague Gordon Paper, struck by a crossbow bolt aimed at you. What an astounding coincidence that he happened to walk up to you at that crucial moment."

Tradescant smiled suddenly, as if suppressing a hiccough. "They say Piccadilly Circus is the place for coincidental meetings," he remarked.

"I don't think Gordon Paper was a coincidence. Or a mistake. I think he was the point of all this. The only mistake was losing sight of him when we found out he wasn't on that jury."

"Tell me, Mr. Swithin," said Tradescant, after a pause, "since you seem rather a bright lad for your age, why on earth would I want to kill Gordon? He was the company's most valuable asset—and I'm a company man."

"It's obvious now," Oliver answered immediately. "A travel-sick recluse turns up in Piccadilly Circus. Why? We thought at first that the killer was showing us how clever, how manipulative he could be. But 'why?' was the wrong question. We should have asked 'how?' And we should have asked it even after we decided Paper was a mistake. He would need more than a couple of Dramamine to get himself down to London. There can only be one explanation: Gordon

Paper had found his permanent cure for travel-sickness. He must have told you, and you decided to kill him and take it for yourself."

He paused, expecting some comment, but Tradescant said and did nothing.

"Paper turned up unexpectedly in London a week before his death, a personal demonstration that he'd found his cure," Oliver continued, keeping an eye on the other man's nonchalant arm. "You were the first person he contacted. You told him to lie low for a few days. Perhaps you tempted him with promises of a grand unveiling to your senior management, a congratulatory *viva*, with the newly mobile Mr. Paper as a surprise guest. But the only thing you were planning was his death.

"Paper was an eccentric inventor, a man so valuable to his employer that if he were to die under mysterious circumstances, you and other colleagues would inevitably become part of the investigation. You had to find a way to kill him that would avoid any police scrutiny of his private life. An accident, perhaps, where he's one of many to die? A seemingly random act of terrorism? No, you dream up something much better: Gordon Paper will die because of an apparent mistake made by an obsessed serial killer who had very well established reasons for murdering someone else. That someone else was you, in fact. Because you speculate that the safest place for a murderer to hide is behind the mask of his own intended victim.

"You had the freedom to play with a hundred biographical details about yourself before lighting on two that could be woven together into a suitably elaborate pattern: that you'd served on a jury, which had been obliquely threatened on television; and that your birth sign was Sagittarius. You researched it quickly—it wasn't difficult, you already knew who the other jury members were and what they were like.

You executed your pattern, one by one, complete with little errors. It's quite easy for the executive of a pharmaceutical company to get his hands on some 'squidgy,' on the fast-acting poison that killed Vanessa Parmenter, on the dart gun used to deliver it. Then, when your turn came to die, you stepped out of your place in the charmed circle and threw Gordon Paper in instead, and the switch is perceived as just another of the murderer's mistakes. Even if the police had seen beyond the zodiac connection and the jury connection—and they did—you were still safe. Because any further investigation would involve looking for someone who wanted to murder you, Edmund Tradescant, not non-Sagittarian, non-jury-member Gordon Paper!"

Tradescant shuffled on the sofa, crossing one leg over another, but keeping his hand out of sight.

"You forget," he said quietly, "I was standing in front of Gordon when he was shot from behind. From a rooftop on the far side of Piccadilly Circus. How am I supposed to have accomplished that?" He thrust his visible hand into the pocket of his fawn cardigan and straightened his arm. Oliver could tell from the garment's bagginess that this was a regular habit, a rare lapse from his studied correctness. He could tell, too, that the small pocket was empty.

"You claimed he was struck by the bolt as you moved toward one another. But that wasn't what happened. You called Paper at his hotel and told him to meet you in Piccadilly Circus. You got there early and planted the crossbow on the roof, with the Sagittarius symbol taped to it. Then you came down to face Paper."

"And who killed him?"

"You did. You had the crossbow bolt in your pocket. As Paper walked up to you, you took it out, plunged it into the back of his neck, and dragged his dying body down on top of you, crying for help, as if he'd been shot from a distance."

"You're doing very well, but you still haven't told me why I should want Gordon's formula."

Oliver hesitated, wondering if he had just heard the admission he had come for. "Presumably it was worth a lot of money," he said. "Oh, there may be plenty of products that relieve motion sickness or vertigo. But a total *cure* . . . I imagine you wanted to claim that you had invented it and get all the rewards yourself."

Tradescant started to shake his head emphatically before Oliver finished speaking, before he had even had time to process the young man's language. Oliver had always hated that particular habit.

"Wrong, I'm afraid," sighed the older man, reaching languidly across his body for the glass of whisky. "You disappoint me, Swithin. Let me explain. The company might make a billion dollars from the worldwide sales of a permanent cure for acute travel sickness. But we'd lose the *ten* billion dollars we already make from those other products you mentioned, which offer only temporary relief. We couldn't allow Gordon Paper's drug to be manufactured. It would be like that legendary everlasting light bulb. And we knew it was no use buying Gordon off—he's too devoted to the purity of science. So we killed him, in a way that was guaranteed never, *never* to draw attention to his work."

" 'We'?" Oliver repeated, startled. Tradescant looked at him with exaggerated puzzlement, as if his visitor were stupid. Oliver did not feel stupid and resented it.

"Surely you don't think I could do this alone?" Tradescant asked, with scornful surprise. "I told you I had alibis. Yes, I killed Sir Harry Random, with the same lead pipe I used the next day on Nettie Clapper. I just had time to draw that symbol on his chest—with a pen, incidentally, not chalk, your late uncle was overstretching himself there—and push him into the fountain before you blundered into the square. I hid

257

behind the lions and slipped away while you were fishing his body out of the water. But it was a pretty female colleague who lured lecherous Mark Sandys-Penza to Kew Gardens, hence the importance of the breath mint. And I can't ride a motorcycle—we had an enthusiastic young management trainee shoot Vanessa Parmenter."

"Your victims were innocent people, with real lives. You speak about them as if they were characters in a book."

"Oh, don't be melodramatic, Mr. Swithin. There was nothing personal about this. I even gave you an opportunity to stop the murders after Gordon's death, by dropping a big hint about my serving on a jury with Sir Harry, but I was rather rudely cut off by that pert little policewoman, the one with all the hair. You must understand, these murders were company business, pure and simple. Decisions like that are taken at board level."

He flung his whisky into Oliver's face and lunged out of his seat.

Tradescant's hidden hand was wrapped in the flex of the standard lamp. It went out, and in the darkness Oliver heard it crash heavily into the stereo equipment. He tried to jump out of the chair, but Tradescant got to him first, pushing him back into place with strength that Oliver didn't expect. Tradescant was still dragging the lamp. As Oliver struggled to sit up, he felt the cable go across his neck. He flailed his legs, but Tradescant twisted his body aside and the impetus of the empty kick pressed Oliver back into the chair.

The cable was cutting hard into his windpipe. He tore at it helplessly, scratching at his neck to slide a finger under the taut plastic. Then he tried to dig his nails into Trades-cant's hands on either side of his throat. It suddenly occurred to Oliver that he was in pain, rather more than he had ex-pected when he first clambered up to the window. It also oc-curred to him, as he became aware that consciousness was leaving him, that the time had come to put an end to the struggle.

"Effie!" he managed to gurgle.

There was an ear-splitting scream behind them. Oliver felt the cable suddenly relax against his throat. A body shot by him in the dark, and he heard the deeply satisfying noise of a pharmaceutical executive smashing into a cocktail cabinet. The room's main light was switched on by somebody near the door. Oliver tried to shake awareness back into his head, but found he was too dizzy to stand. He watched Tradescant stagger to his feet, swinging a decanter wildly. There were two sudden, balletic blurs of blue denim, and two more lung-emptying screams.

Effie's first kick caused the decanter to fly from Tradescant's hand and shatter against the ceiling. The room rained whisky. Her second kick spun his face to the wall, his head cracking the glass in a framed architectural print. He stayed there, his hands clawing the wallpaper.

"That's my boyfriend you're strangling," she snapped and backed toward Oliver. As she looked with concern at his reddening throat, Tradescant turned again. Oliver tensed and tried to shout a warning to Effie, but Tradescant had frozen in place, staring in horror at something behind them. Then, the fear faded, and was replaced with a smile. He relaxed, shook his head, and laughed. He was still laughing when Moldwarp dragged him handcuffed from the room.

"Does it hurt?" Effie asked, touching his neck gently. Oliver winced.

"It'll be okay," he croaked. "I think I can talk."

"That's not what I asked," she replied and kissed him, pushing his glasses off his face. Then she sat in his lap, lifted his glasses onto the top of his head, and kissed him again, harder. Their noses did not bump, as Oliver had once feared, but they had already established a clockwise facial approach

259

that afternoon, in the deserted office at Scotland Yard, after Tim Mallard had told Effie the true reason for Oliver's visit to Lorina Random and had diplomatically withdrawn for a good ten minutes. Oliver, for once sensing the need for determined action, had apologized for no apparent reason and then decided to leave words alone for a while. Effie's hair felt even better than it looked, he rapidly concluded.

"For a second-rate murderer, you're a first-rate kisser," Effie whispered, brushing her lips across Oliver's bruised neck.

"Never mind the sob stuff, did you get it all?" The gruff voice came from the doorway. Effie grinned, flicked her tongue swiftly over Oliver's earlobe, and stood up.

"It's all here, Superintendent," she said, pulling a small tape recorder from her pocket and passing it to Mallard, who had walked into Oliver's field of vision. He bent over his nephew and inspected the livid marks on his neck.

"Did Tradescant do all that, or were you and Effie necking behind the curtain?" Mallard asked facetiously, although Oliver looked up and saw the anxiety in his uncle's eyes.

"I don't need any medical attention," he replied painfully, knowing he was answering an unspoken question. "Frankly, I'm amazed at Effie's accomplishments as a housebreaker. She took out the alarm and picked the window lock in about two minutes. Do all detectives make good burglars?"

Mallard laughed. "Talking of housebreakers," he said loudly, "you can come out now, Geoffrey."

The long curtains covering the window shook slightly. "Is it safe?" said a muffled voice.

"Oh, yes. Mr. Tradescant's well on his way to the Yard."

"I mean, has Ollie stopped kissing Effie? There are some sights even a public relations executive can't stomach."

Mallard strode across the room and pulled the drapes aside, revealing Geoffrey Angelwine's avian features above the collar of an oversize yellow oilskin. "Sergeant Strongitharm's still on duty," Mallard said, "so she'll have to keep her h—"

"Hormones in check?" Geoffrey concluded wickedly.

"As a matter of fact, that's exactly what I was going to say," claimed Mallard, with an admonitory glance in Effie's direction.

"Well, thanks for letting me be here, Uncle Tim," Geoffrey continued. He moved into the room, creaking with every step.

"A promise is a promise. I'm sorry I couldn't let Ben and Susie come, too, but there's only so much room in the charabanc for civilians. However, you were the one who gave us the clue we needed."

"So you said this afternoon. It was that business about the murderer playing games with the police. Only Tradescant was the player, not Ollie."

Mallard shook his head. "It wasn't that at all. We just used that to set up the false accusation of Oliver."

"Then how did I help?"

"I'll let Oliver explain, if he's up to it," said Mallard, who had noticed that his nephew had struggled to his feet and was vacantly stroking his sore neck. "I have to go and see a man about a search warrant."

As Mallard left, Geoffrey turned quizzically to Oliver.

"This morning, you reminded Uncle Tim that the police thought Sir Harry Random's death had been an accident at first," Oliver rasped. "In fact, Harry's death was never reported in the newspapers as a murder. It was a surprise to Lorina when I let it slip that night." His voice faded conveniently, and he began to cough. Effie smiled wickedly.

"Your comment jogged Tim's memory," she said, as Oliver hunted for some water among the debris of the cocktail cabinet. "When Tradescant had first tried to clue us in

261

about his connection with Sir Harry, he said that Sir Harry had 'been killed.' Now that expression applies to a murder; it applies to a car crash, where there is a clear agent of death; but it isn't used to describe a drowning accident. So we looked back at Tradescant's statement. He claimed to have heard a whizzing sound before the bolt hit Paper. But you only hear that when a bolt or an arrow goes *past* you—on the receiving end, there's little time for noise before the weapon strikes. And why would he immediately tell us that Paper had no enemies? Why should he assume that a death in a public place was a targeted act of murder, and not a random killing? Later, at Sir Harry's funeral, he speculated about the connection between the 'murders' of Gordon Paper and Harry Random. But at that point he hadn't been told why he was in protective custody, and so he still had no reason to believe Sir Harry was murdered."

Oliver returned with a glass and a crystal soda syphon.

"Uncle Tim called me this morning at about half past ten," he said. "By the time I arrived at Scotland Yard, he and Effie were looking again at Gordon Paper, and they'd concluded that Edmund Tradescant may have had a motive for killing his surprisingly mobile colleague. But we couldn't prove it. That's when I dreamed up the idea of posing as the murderer myself and staging the death of Mallard under Tradescant's nose. If we could secure a confession, then we could conclude the case before Uncle Tim's midnight deadline."

"It was essential to provide enough interested parties in Trafalgar Square so that Tradescant's presence among the witnesses would not look too pointed," said Effie as they left the room and headed down the stairs. "We also needed a lot of people to cluster round the dying superintendent, keeping Tradescant at a safe distance, in case he spotted the deception. It's a shame you had to leave, Ollie. You missed some

262

choice performances. Did you know that Cliff Burbage, who for obvious reasons hadn't been briefed, set off in hot pursuit of you, dragging a protesting Moldwarp along after him? They got as far as Charing Cross station before Moldwarp could stop him and explain."

"Susie Beamish rather overdid it, if you ask me," said Geoffrey with a sniff. "After you cut Tim's throat, she pretended to faint dead away."

"So did you," Effie murmured. "Only I don't think you were faking it."

Geoffrey avoided her eye. "Did it have to be so gory?" he asked plaintively.

"I doubt that Tim would have taken such a risk if he wasn't about to be removed from a case for the first time in his life. Even so, the opportunity to perform his Banquo death-scene in the middle of Trafalgar Square was probably what tipped the balance. He is not without his vanity. We used the makeup from his blood-soaked *Macbeth* production—a fake fold of flesh among the other, natural flaps under his chin, and a bag of blood behind it, supplemented by a couple of tubes behind the collar. All Tim has to do is jerk his head upwards and the latex ruptures across a pre-scored line. Then he goes down, pumping more blood from a bottle hidden in his pocket. If every other member of the Mallard theatrical troupe performed on cue, then Tradescant would believe the murder really happened, and that he may speak with a certain amount of license to the fugitive, Oliver Swithin."

"Which is where we came in," said Geoffrey. "Sorry about your loss, Ollie." They had reached the front door of the building, which was opened grandly for them by Constable Urchin, once he had figured out that he had to pull it rather than push it.

"My loss? You mean my voice?"

"Why would I mean that?" Geoffrey sounded mystified. "No, I mean your beloved umbrella. You must have taken it apart to make a sword-stick."

"Ollie's umbrella is safe in my desk at Scotland Yard," Effie reported. "The sword-stick umbrella was a rather unpleasant exhibit borrowed from the Yard's Black Museum. But it does remind me that you're the only one who's equipped for this weather, Geoffrey. Will you bring my car round? I'll give you both a lift home."

She tossed him the keys to her Renault, which he promptly dropped. He fished them out of a puddle, pulled a large yellow sou'wester from his pocket, and scurried away into the rain like a clockwork lemon. Effie and Oliver waited for him under the shelter of the porch.

"Will you come in for tea this time?" Oliver asked her tentatively. Effie turned to him slowly and gazed at him.

"I thought you'd never ask," she said. And as Oliver looked down into her aquamarine eyes, he was convinced they were the most erotic words he had ever heard. Did the celebrated Strongitharm Look also work in reverse? Although he needed no supernatural compulsion to kiss her again.

They stood there together, watching the rain, enjoying the unfamiliar wetness, the relief from the oppressive heat. English summer was English again. Gradually, Oliver became aware that a third person was standing beside them on the porch.

"As for you, Uncle Tim," he said pointedly, "you got a little personal in Trafalgar Square. I hope you're going to apologize for those 'second-rate' jibes."

"Don't worry," Mallard replied genially, "there was nothing second-rate about your performance tonight. If you were a member of the Theydon Bois Thespians, you'd get a standing ovation, an honor that is normally reserved for the prompter. And talking of theatrical events, isn't there something about this situation that reminds you of the beginning of *Macbeth?*"

"When shall we three meet again?" Oliver ventured. "In thunder, lightning, or . . ."

"In rain!" they all shouted. Mallard laughed and hugged the other two. Then they stepped happily together into the glistening street, soaking in the English rain.